Random Connections

A Collection of Interconnected Short Stories

By Charles W. Parkinson

PublishAmerica
Baltimore

© 2002 by Charles W. Parkinson.
All rights reserved. No part of this book may be reproduced in any form without written permission from the publishers, except by a reviewer who may quote brief passages in a review to be printed in a newspaper or magazine.

First printing

ISBN: 1-59129-700-1
PUBLISHED BY PUBLISHAMERICA BOOK PUBLISHERS
www.publishamerica.com
Baltimore

Printed in the United States of America

*To Cindy,
my wife, my love,
who has put up with my storytelling for years.*

TABLE OF CONTENTS

RANDOM CONNECTIONS	7
MURPHY'S OLD TRUCK	11
IMPACT	25
THE VOICE FROM WITHIN	33
BUGS	43
GONE FISHING	55
THE BOOK	73
ENDANGERED SPECIES	95
MAY ALL YOUR WISHES	113
THE GREEN IN THE FOREST	125
THE MOUNDS AT MIMA	139
DOUBLE, DOUBLE	167
MIRROR, MIRROR	173
THE LADY IN THE LAKE	183
THE GHOST LIGHTS	199

RANDOM CONNECTIONS

The bell on the door chimed as the two men entered the shop. Their conversation filled the empty spaces of the store. There was only one other customer in the place. He was an old man. He was sitting back in a corner booth reading a paper. He looked up as the two men came in. Marie, the girl who worked the store this time of morning, set down the tray of donuts she was carrying and headed over to the counter. The two men came over and stood there. They were having a heated discussion.

"It's all random," said the first man. "I tell you it's all just random."

"How could it be?" said the second man. "How can you think everything is just due to random chance? There has to be a reason, it all has to be connected somehow."

"May I help you?" asked Marie as she came up to the counter.

The first man looked at her. "Yeah," he said abruptly. He turned back to the other man. "It's all just random. There are no connections at all, there's no reason for anything to be connected. It just happens and that's it."

Marie interrupted the two men. "Would you gentlemen like to order anything?" she asked in a slightly perturbed tone of voice. She didn't need to have people fighting in the shop. Especially this early in the morning. It was bad for business.

The second man looked at her. "We'd like a dozen donuts and two large coffees," he replied shortly. He turned back to the first man. "That sound all right to you, Jack?"

"Yeah sure, Art, that sounds good," said the first man. "Anything will do. Why don't you make it a random selection?"

"There you go again, Jack! Quit trying to rub it in."

The men's argument was escalating as Marie watched. She was starting to feel a little uncomfortable with it. It sounded like it was almost to the point where there could be a real fight. She looked over at the old man sitting in the corner for some help. She caught his eye and he got up slowly and sauntered over toward the counter. He knew exactly what was happening.

He had been listening to the argument from the moment the men had entered the shop.

"There's nothing random about it!" said Art. His face was starting to turn red. "Nothing is random. Why that girl might stick a maple bar in your random box of donuts just because the old guy over there had ordered a maple bar earlier. That's a connection. So then your random box of donuts would not be random anymore!"

"That would never happen," said the old man as he came up behind the two men at the counter.

"What?" said Art as he turned to face the stranger. "You mean to tell me that this girl would never inadvertently stick a maple bar in a box of donuts just because she had sold you one earlier?"

"Nope," said the old man. "That would never happen. I don't care for maple bars. Actually to tell the truth I prefer crullers myself. So Marie would never sell me a maple bar. She knows I don't like them."

The old man took a sip from a styrofoam cup of coffee he had carried with him. "Which makes me think," he said. "Marie, why don't you set me up with a dozen when you're done with these fellows."

Marie felt a wave of relief rush over her just knowing that she wouldn't be left alone with these two combatants who were standing at her counter. "Certainly, Jim," she said. "A dozen crullers just as soon as I'm done with these gentlemen." She picked out a box and went over to the display with the donuts and started filling it.

"I'm Jim Murphy," said the old man as he stuck out his hand in introduction to Art.

"Art MacDonald," said the man as he took Jim's hand. "And this is my friend Jack Squire."

Jack raised his hand in a weak Boy Scout salute.

"I couldn't help but overhear your conversation," said Jim. "I'm sorry for eavesdropping, but, what I did hear kind of caught my interest, if you know what I mean. So, if you really wouldn't mind and you didn't think that I was too rude, could you fill me in about it?"

"It would be a pleasure to have somebody else's opinion," said Art. "Jack and I have been fighting about this question for the last hundred miles."

"The last hundred miles? Is that all?" said Jack as he as he picked up the coffee cups that Marie had just set on the counter. "Admit it, Art. We've been discussing this question ever since we met. And if I remember right that was at least ten years ago."

"All right," said Art. "I'll give you that. We've been deliberating this point ever since we met. And if I remember correctly that was around ten years ago."

"Well," said Jim.

"It's this," said Art. "My good friend Jack here seems to think that there's no plan to the universe. That everything just seems to happen. You know, randomly. With no rhyme or reason for it all."

"That's right," said Jack. "Just a happenstance of random events. No reason for it at all, shit just happens."

"On the other hand," said Art, "I feel that everything has a reason, a connection. One event leads to another. Cause and effect you might say."

Marie set a box of donuts on the counter. "There you are, Sir," she said, "a random selection of donuts." She pushed the box a little bit closer toward Art. "That will be six fifty."

Art reached into his pocket and took out his wallet. "I'll catch this one, Jack," he said. "You can get the next one." He laid a ten-dollar bill on the counter.

Marie opened the cash register and set his ten inside. She withdrew the change and handed it to him.

Art scooped up his change and shoved it back into his pocket.

Marie then turned back to the bins and started loading a box of crullers for Jim.

"But how can you possibly think there is any kind of a plan to all this?" said Jack as he picked up the box of donuts. "Sure, I'll concede the point that things can happen coincidentally, that some things might cause other things to happen, but, a conceived plan, a reason for it all. No way!"

Marie finished counting out the donuts for Jim and set the box on the counter. Jim took six dollars out of one of his pockets and started rummaging around in his other one for some change. "It seems to me," he said as he laid the exact amount of change on the counter, "that both of you are talking about the same thing."

"The same thing?" said Jack and Art at the same time.

"Sure," said Jim. "The same thing." He picked up the box of donuts and started for the door. "See you tomorrow," he said to Marie as he opened the door.

Art and Jim followed him out the door.

"What do you mean the same thing?" asked Jack once they were outside. "We have totally different opinions!"

"Not really," said Jim as he opened the door of his old green Dodge truck and set the box of donuts on the seat. "What I see," he said as he climbed into the truck, "is that you guys have been debating random connections."

"Random connections?" said Art.

"Random connections?" said Jack.

"Sure," said Jim. "Random connections. Something happens, just randomly. And the next thing you know something else that is related to that random act just happens. That's what I mean by a random connection. One thing leads to another in a random sort of way. Yet in the end it will all connect some how."

Jim closed the door and started the truck. He rolled down the window. "Life is just a bunch of random connections," he said out the open window. "That's all it is. That's all it can be. You guys just think about it that way and maybe you'll quit arguing about it." He put the truck into gear and backed out of the parking stall. "Just a bunch of random connections." He put the truck in first gear and started out of the parking lot.

Art and Jack watched him leave. The truck vanished down the road in a blue oil haze. When it was gone Art unlocked the doors of his car with his remote key and climbed in. "You know," he said, "that was profound."

Jack got in the passenger side with the box of donuts. He set them carefully on his lap. "You know," he said, "that old guy just might be right."

MURPHY'S OLD TRUCK

I rode to work with Jim Murphy for six months. The job was two hours out of town and we made the drive every day. We got to drive through some of the most beautiful country in the state of Washington. The highway wound around Alder Lake and over White Pass, through forest and along the rivers of the Cascade Mountains. We would turn off the main road at Morton, drive fifteen miles down a dirt road and that would get us to the parking lot for the Cowlitz Falls Hydro-Electric project. We were building a dam.

Jim drove an older green Dodge Power-Wagon. The truck had seen better days. It was a kind of moldy green in color with great big rust spots. The rust almost formed a pattern, that if you really saw it you would think it was mildly offensive. When you closed the passenger door you had to lift up on the door so it would catch the latch. On the driver's side the wing window was broken out and the armrest was gone. Driving down the road it sounded like a 42-foot Chris Craft leaving the dock and bound for parts unknown. The muffler was totally shot!

The most annoying thing about the entire truck, though, was a star in the windshield. It was right in the middle of the passenger side at eye level. The spot was about the size of a silver dollar and kind of looked like a tattoo. If it had been a tattoo it would have been put on by a master artisan. The broken spot resembled a lion done up in three colors! Each color would have been laid on exactingly and done with the most loving care. There was a clear definition in the bands of broken glass. You could see the lion's eyes looking at you from out of the fracture. You could count its teeth in the shards of the crack. You could even see the crook of his tail in the ragged edges of the chip.

It was raining like hell. Raindrops poured in the missing wing window. Water ran down the windshield and made the lion dance; just as if he had been drawn on a large, shabby man's bicep. "Hey, Woody, don't you think that a beer would go real good with this kind of weather?" Jim said as we left the parking lot of the project. "Or, maybe a good shot of sipping whiskey would be more to your liking. The liquor store is on the way through town and if you happen to have some change we could pitch together and get a pint for the trip home." I was cold and wet and a couple of shots sure sounded good. Going for my wallet I pulled out a five-dollar bill and told Jim that was wonderful idea. The truck rolled into the parking lot at the liquor store as the rain came down and the lion danced.

Jim went into the store and I sat in the truck and watched the lion watching me. The town cop came down the main road. I turned my head to watch him drive by. The rain that had been pounding on the truck just a minute before eased off. There was a Seven Eleven store next door to the liquor store. It had stopped raining and I was out of smokes. It would be a long drive back to Tacoma without a cigarette. Jim didn't smoke, but he didn't mind if I did. I got out of the truck and went into the store.

There was a sign on the door of the Seven Eleven. The sign said, "PLAY LOTTO! TODAY'S JACKPOT IS $6,000,000!!!!" I rummaged around in the store for a minute and grabbed two large cups of coffee. There's nothing better than an Irish coffee in cold weather. I stood at the counter and looked at some of the magazines. The girl behind the counter asked me, "Is that all, Sir?" I caught a glimpse of the Lotto sign and thought for a second. "No," I said. "Let me get a pack of Camels and I guess I'll take one of those lotto tickets." She rang up my coffee and smokes. Then she rang up the lotto ticket. It has to be done separately. She turned around and punched the button on the lotto machine after the sale was made. The machine made some percolating noise and then it spit out a single lotto ticket. It told her "thanks" as she passed the ticket across the counter and then I asked her for some matches. I pocketed the ticket in my shirt with the cigarettes. Picking up the coffee I pushed the door open with my butt and headed back to the truck. When I got back to the truck I saw Jim coming out of the liquor store. I set the coffee on top of the truck and tried to open the door. It was a little stuck so I jerked on the handle. The door came open all at once. The coffee cups on top of the truck jumped. I was able to reach out with my left hand and stop one of the cups from spilling. The other cup spilled down the side of the truck and across the front of my shirt! "Shit, Jim," I yelled as I pulled the scalding shirt away from my skin. "Why the hell don't you get this thing fixed?"

Jim came up to the Dodge with a brown paper bag. "I don't know, kid, I guess it kind of likes being this way. Pick up the cups, kid, and get in. It's time we started heading for home."

I was slightly mad and a little burned. Also I had a big brown coffee stain down the front of my shirt. I picked up the coffee cup from the ground and got in. The door slammed as I got in. Of course it didn't latch and I had to open the window to lift up on the damn thing to make it catch.

Murphy got in his side of the truck. I handed him the full cup of coffee. He placed the key in the ignition and started the truck up. The motor turned over making a *no-no-no* sound before it finally caught and the engine started. Jim took a sip from his coffee and put the Dodge in reverse. He backed out of the parking lot. We hit the main road and headed out of town.

Handing me the brown bag, Jim asked for a shot. "Pour some of that whiskey in your cup and add some of this here coffee. Then dump the rest of the jug into mine to make up for the coffee that isn't there." I mixed the two Irish coffees and handed Jim's back to him. We had just left town and were on the road to Elbe. "This is good stuff," Jim said. I tried some of mine and agreed with him.

I pulled my cigarettes out of my pocket and tapped them on the dashboard before opening them. I got the matches out of my pocket while I fished open the pack. "Those things will kill you if you let them," said Jim. He looked down and saw the lotto ticket lying on the floor. It must have fallen out of my pocket when I extracted my smokes.

"Hey, kid, that your ticket laying on the floor?" I looked down and there it was just lying there. I reached down to pick it up when a gust of wind came in from the missing wing window and picked up. It floated toward the gaping hole where the window should have been. I snatched it from the air before it could flutter across the truck and out the broken window. "Better hang on to that thing," Jim said. "It could be worth a lot of money."

"I know," I said. "The lotto is worth six mill this week."

Jim took a huge sip from his coffee. "I usually buy twenty dollars' worth of those things a week. You know, ten bucks for Wednesday's drawing and another ten for Saturday's."

"Well, I don't go as far as that," I said. "I'll only spend a buck, and then it has to be over three mill before I'll do that. I figure that it only takes one ticket to win and I can lose a dollar just as well as some guys can lose a hundred."

I sat back and watched the scenery pass by. It really started to rain. The windshield wipers were going full blast. There was a pinging sound that came from under the dashboard. The wiper on my side flung itself off the truck and into oblivion. "What the hell," I said. "Jim, when are you going to ever fix the crap on this truck?"

"That's the third time that wiper has gone to shit, kid. I guess I'll have to go to the wrecking yard one of these days and try to find another one."

I watched the river run down the windshield. The lion in the crack looked like he was laughing at me. "Hey, Jim," I said. "What would you do if you hit the lotto?"

"Gee, Woody," he said, "I don't really know. I would probably go out and buy a 50-foot boat or something. You know, like an old Monk. One with potential. Not one of those rotten pieces of junk you see, but a real fixer upper. A guy could take something like that up to the San Juan Islands and charter it out. Sure could do a lot of fishing that way. Just running all around those islands and having a ball. I can tell you, though, I sure wouldn't be working for a living!" He looked at me for a second and then said, "And if that ticket of yours hits, what would do with it, kid?"

"Well, Murphy, me, I'd open a bookstore. Not just any old bookstore but one that dealt in used and out-of-print books. You know, the really good ones worth big bucks. I'd set up an espresso machine in the store and sell coffee so people could have a cup while they're browsing the shelves. I'd locate the store in Gig Harbor or some little town like that, right next to a ferry slip. I think a guy could do really good that way."

The glove box popped open. When the door fell down it hit my hand spilling the rest of my hot Irish coffee in my lap! "Damn it, Jim, I'd get this stinking truck fixed up for you too!"

"That wouldn't do any good, kid," said Jim. "Ever since I bought this truck things just seem to go wrong with it. I mean it runs like a charm. Never left me in the lurch or anything, just little things seem to want to be messed up all the time. I bought it from Tacoma Dodge as a closeout model; you know, one of those trucks that was left over from the previous year. They have to clear them off the lot to make room for the new ones coming in. Well, it had a broken windshield, just like it does now." Jim motioned toward the crack on my side. "They made me a really good deal on it. I paid cash and took it home that evening."

I made arrangements with the dealer to have the windshield replaced eight times! It always seems to break in the same damn place though."

"Maybe there's something wrong with the glass they're using," I said. "You know, like a bad casting or something."

"No, Woody, to tell you the truth, I think it just likes to have a broken window. It just seems that everything on this truck is just the way it wants to be. All the little messed up bits and pieces. It took this truck years to perfect its look. I mean just look at the paint. Do you think for one minute that I would have left it that way if I could have had it fixed? Why, I've had this truck painted twice and it still looks this way!"

I had to agree with Jim that nobody in their right mind would have left a truck looking like it did. It was a muddy green with rust highlights. He told me that even when he washed it you couldn't tell the difference. It still came out looking the same muddy green that it was now.

We had just entered Spanaway. I looked at my watch and saw that it was five thirty. "Not bad time tonight," I said to Jim. He pulled off into the Safeway parking lot and let me out at my car.

"See you Monday," he said as I started to climb out of the truck.

"OK, I'll see you in the a and m," I said as I slammed my shoulder into the door to keep it from springing open.

I opened the door of my car and tossed my thermos and lunch bucket onto the back seat. I got into the car and tried to start it up. There was nothing! I tried again, there was still nothing. I got out of my car and started waving and yelling at Jim. He saw me and stopped, as he was about to leave the parking lot. He turned the truck around and slowly drove back to me.

"Hey, Jim, I seem to be having a little problem here."

He looked at me out the window of the truck and said, "Well, I guess I can give you a ride home if you need it."

"No," I said. "I think the battery is just dead. If you've got a set of jumper cables I can probably get it started."

"Nope, I don't ever carry them. Never had a need for a set of them you see."

"Well, if you can get me to a phone I can call the auto club and have them come out."

"No problem," said Jim. "Hop in." He gave me a ride to a phone booth and I called the auto club. They told me when I got hold of them that they would have somebody out there in less than an hour.

Jim hauled me back to my car. "Thanks a lot," I said as I got out.

"You want me to stick around until they get here?"

"No, I can wait. They'll be here in a little bit anyway. See you Monday."

Jim started his truck up again. The motor jumped to life and he cruised out of the parking lot.

In about forty-five minutes the tow truck showed up. The guy from the auto club asked to see my membership card. I showed it to him and he started to work. He walked to the front of the car and had me open the hood.

"Try to start it up," he said from under the hood.

I turned the key and the car started the first time. "Well, I'll be. I couldn't get this thing to even fire up the radio let alone turn over an hour ago! What did you do?"

"I didn't do anything except shake your battery cable a bit. You probably need a new one. I'll just clean them up and you should be good to go until you can get it replaced. Though I wouldn't wait very long to do it." I shut the car off and he removed the cables and looked them over. They were clean and tight. As a matter of fact they were so clean and tight he said they almost looked new. He put them back on and I started the car up again.

"Well, I can't find anything wrong so I guess you're good to go."

"Thanks for coming out," I said as I started the car back up. It just seemed to jump to life. I left the parking lot and headed for home.

On the way home I stopped at Key Bank to cash my check. I pulled up to the drive-up window and made a deposit. I only deposited half of my check. I took the other half in cash and then went back to my apartment.

When I got home I opened the door and went in. I headed for the kitchen and deposited my lunch box and thermos in the sink. I then headed for the bathroom where I took a shower and cleaned myself up. Now it was time to eat.

Let me tell you a little about the apartment. It's up on the second floor of a complex. There must be about three hundred other units. There's never any room in the parking lot and you have to park about a half mile away from your door. I stood in the living room and looked around. The place was a real mess. All the dishes were dirty. All the pots and pans were dirty. All the silverware was dirty. All the glasses and all the cups were dirty. Everything was dirty! I decided rather than cook I would go out to Denny's for a burger.

I had no problem starting the car again. When I reached Denny's I parked next to the door and went right in. It was dim inside. I took a booth. Shelly, the waitress for that evening, came over and asked if I wanted coffee. I said that I did and that I also wanted a menu. She brought the menu and the coffee at the same time. I looked the menu over for a minute. There were four types of wine on the wine list. There was a burgundy, rich and rare. There was a rose, delicate and light. That was it for the reds. The other two were white and I don't care for white wine.

I called Shelly back and told her I would have a carafe of the burgundy and a Denny's burger. I told her that it would be just fine if she brought the wine out now because I was thirsty. While I was waiting I sipped my coffee before it got cold. There's nothing worse than cold coffee.

Shelly brought out my wine and at the same time Dreg Harlow walked into the restaurant. He spotted me and came over to my table. "Mind if I join you?" he asked as he sat down.

"Not at all, man, go for it."

"Woody, old boy, how you doing?"

I hadn't seen Dreg in a long time. He hadn't changed a bit; he was still his same old self. "Dreg, shit, man, I'm still alive. How about you?"

Shelly came over to see if Dreg wanted anything. "Well, sweetheart," he said, "just for starters I'll have a double Irish whiskey."

"Is that all?" asked Shelly.

"That's a start," said Dreg.

She brought the drink back right away and my food came at the same time. Dreg picked up his drink. "Here's looking at you," he said as he tossed it down. He looked at my wine and said, "What the hell you doing drinking that red grape juice for? You should be drinking a real man's drink, you know, like one of these." He hoisted his empty glass for Shelly to see. She came over and Dreg ordered two more doubles.

I told Dreg that I really couldn't go on a spree tonight. I had to clean my apartment.

"What!" he exclaimed. "I'll let you know I have just returned from the most miserable voyage that you have ever seen or heard of. Crabbing this year has been awful! And you, my best, oldest friend won't even let me bend your ear and tell you the story. Well, friend, my wife won't listen either, so I guess I'm just going to have to tell you whether you want to hear or not! Shelly," he yelled, "bring two more doubles over here when you can."

The Dungeness crab season had only been open for a week this year and Dreg had only cleared twenty-five thousand dollars above expenses. I listened to his sob story and bought the next three rounds.

Shelly brought my food during that time and Dreg and I picked at the plate until it was clean. By one in the morning my wallet was a considerable amount lighter, and so was I! Finally, I decided it was time to go and I floated out to the car.

It was well after one when I got home. The next thing I knew it was Saturday morning and I was waking up. Somehow I had made it into bed but I still had my shoes on. That's funny because that's all I had on was my shoes. I felt awful. My mouth felt like it was all covered in wool. My head pounded and my stomach was rolling over. After drinking a carton of milk and eating about half a box of crackers I felt a little better. I started to clean my place up. I got it about half done and I was getting hungry again. I looked at the clock and it was four o'clock. The afternoon had just vanished. I needed something else to eat. I got in the car and went down to McDonald's and grabbed a burger. By the time I got back home it was after five.

I kept cleaning and at six the news came on. I flopped down in my chair to watch. After the news came the lotto drawing.

It was a few minutes before seven when they announced the drawing. I sat through several commercials and then Debby Conners came on with the lotto. First they drew for the Quinto Jackpot. Quinto is played just like five card stud but you have to match the hand they draw. After that there were some more commercials. Then Debby came back on for the main drawing. The numbered balls in the machine bounced and she drew the first ball. It was number nineteen. The rest of the balls came up into their chutes and she drew them. They were six, forty-two, seventeen, thirty-four, and seven. I wrote each number down on a sheet of paper as she drew it. Then I went back to the bedroom and found where I had set my shirt with the ticket in the pocket. I dug the ticket out and went back to the living room to compare the numbers. Picture my surprise when the numbers on the second line of my ticket matched the winning numbers! I had a winning ticket!

I couldn't believe it! I checked the ticket again with the numbers that I had written down. The second line still matched. Maybe I had written the numbers down wrong. This couldn't be a winning ticket. My luck just didn't run that way.

I decided that I would have to go down to the Seven Eleven on the corner and get a printout of the winning numbers. You know, just to be sure. I grabbed my coat and the car keys, and then I ran out the door to my car. I drove like mad down to the store. When I got there I climbed out of the car and in my haste I threw the door of the store open. The clerk behind the counter gave me a startled look.

"I need an on-line lotto printout!" I yelled as I dove into the store.

She punched some buttons on the lotto machine and it spit out a printout. She handed me the ticket and I grabbed it and got back out to the car. The door of the store swung violently shut behind me. I sat down and looked at the numbers on the ticket. They didn't match any of my numbers. They weren't even close.

I looked at the printout again. On the top it read, "NO JACKPOT

WINNER." Right under that was printed some more information: "THESE ARE THE WINNING NUMBERS FOR THE LOTTO DRAWING FOR WEDNESDAY NOV. 17." I looked at the ticket again. This wasn't Wednesday it was Saturday! She had given me the wrong printout.

I got back out of the car and raced back into the store. "This isn't the right printout," I said the girl. "It's for last Wednesday. I need the one for tonight."

The girl looked at me and said, "The one for tonight's drawing won't be in the machine for at least an hour. There's a delay, it takes them that long to get it out on-line. Is there anything else I can help you with?"

"No, I think I'll just wait until it comes out then. Is that OK?"

She said that was just fine, so I wandered around the store. I grabbed a cup of coffee, and then I got hungry so I fixed up a couple of hot dogs, too. I paid the girl for the food and kept looking at my watch. It was probably the longest hour of my life!

The hour went by. I seemed to ask the clerk every five minutes if the new on-line lotto printout was up yet. She kept telling me no. After forever she called me over to the counter and said, "I've brought up the printer now, Sir, and you print-out is ready."

"Thanks!" I took the ticket and went out to my car to compare it. I sat there and looked at each number carefully. Across the top of the ticket in bold lettering was "ONE LOTTO WINNER FOR SATURDAY." Not only was I a winner, I was the only winner. That meant that I didn't have to split the pot with anyone else. It was all mine. I had just won six million dollars over the next twenty years!

I just sat in the car and looked at the ticket. I couldn't believe it. I sat and looked at the ticket for a very long time. I mean I just sat there. To tell the truth, I was totally overwhelmed!

I finally looked at the time. It was three in the morning! I had sat in the car and looked at my ticket for almost seven hours. My how time flies when you're having fun! I started the car and decided to head for the bowling alley. I was going to get a cup of coffee and something to eat.

I sat by myself in a booth at the bowling alley and tried to figure out what I was going to do with all that money. I knew for a fact that the first thing I was going to do though was to get Murphy's old truck fixed up for him. Not only was I going to fix up his truck, but I was also going to have it put back into showroom shape!

I went home and in the morning I started calling auto body shops. It being Sunday all the places were closed, though. I finally decided that the project would have to wait until Monday morning.

While I was stewing over the problem of an auto body shop I got to thinking. Murphy was going to need something to drive while his truck was being fixed up. Maybe I should rent him a car while the work was being done. Then I got to thinking, though; hell, I have enough money, why don't I just buy him another one? I could just tell him it was mine and that he could use it while his truck was being fixed, and when his was done I could just give it to him. Wouldn't that be great! Then he would have another vehicle other than that awful old truck to drive. I didn't sleep a wink that night just thinking what fun it was all going to be.

All day Sunday was rough. I sat in the living room and stared at the TV. I didn't want to leave the apartment. What if I lost the ticket while I was out? I just couldn't take the chance.

Monday morning after a restless night I woke up thinking about the ticket. I kept checking my wallet to see if it was still in there. It was. I finally went into the kitchen and mixed myself up a package of instant breakfast and then I started calling auto body shops again. I got hold of a good one and they said that they could take the truck in right away.

That's when I decided I needed a really good tax lawyer. I would need somebody really sharp before I claimed the ticket. I dug through the phone book once again and called Ron Dale, tax consultant. He had a big ad in the yellow pages. His office opened at nine so I called right at the stroke of the clock. His secretary answered and I explained my problem to her. She made an appointment right away and I was on the way to wealth and riches.

The next thing I did was call into my job and quit! Dick, the foreman, said that they would mail my check and he would call the union hall with my termination. That way I didn't have to go back out to the job site to pick it up. I got in the car then, and drove over to the union hall to sign the books. It never hurts to have a place on the dispatching list. When that was all done, Monday was over! It had been quite a day.

Tuesday arrived with quite a fanfare. I went down to Olympia, on the advice of Ron Dale, and collected my first check for two hundred and forty thousand dollars. It was a surprisingly easy thing to do. The lady at the lotto commission took my ticket and verified it with the winning numbers. Once that was done I had to sign a bunch of papers for the IRS, basically stating that I wouldn't even dare to think about trying to beat them out of their percentage. The lotto commissioner then came out of his office and I had my picture taken with him. He shook my hand all the time the cameras were flashing and told me how lucky I was to be the winner of so much money. The whole thing took a little less than four hours. Not bad for six million if you ask me.

When I left the office the members of the press attacked me. Word travels fast when you're talking about huge sums of money! There was a guy from the *Seattle Post Intelligencer*, another guy from the *Seattle Times* and one lone reporter from the *Tacoma News Tribune*. All the local TV stations were represented, too. Of all the reporters, I have to say the guy from the Tacoma paper was the most courteous. He asked pertinent questions and didn't try to get me to put my foot in my mouth.

That night when I got home I called Murphy. The phone rang twice and he answered.

"Hello."

"Hey, Murphy, Woody here. Meet me at Sixth Avenue Auto Body Shop tomorrow at ten. I'll buy you breakfast later."

"Gee, kid, what's so urgent?"

"I'll tell you over breakfast tomorrow morning, OK?"

Murphy showed up at the stroke of ten. The old green Dodge churned into the parking lot of the auto body place, pulled into a parking spot and cast anchor. Jim bounced against the door and climbed out of the truck.

Before he could say a word I tossed him the keys for the new truck I had just bought. I had gotten it down the street at Phillips Dodge on the way to the auto body shop that morning. He snatched them out of the air like a good right fielder going after a pop fly.

"What's this?" he asked.

"They're the keys for your new truck," I told him. I had changed my mind about telling him it was mine.

"No way. You make this sound really important. I even missed a day of work to come down here and have you pull my leg. What're you trying to do, kid?"

"Just keeping up my end of a bargain," I said. Then I told him about hitting the lottery jackpot and I reminded him of the promise that I had made to him just the other day.

He didn't seem too thrilled and told me in not too many words that he didn't need a new truck. "This old Dodge of mine runs just fine. I've been happy with it for years. It just seems a little beat up, but that's just how it wants to be. Somehow this old truck and me just feel right together. I don't need a new truck. I don't need to get this one fixed up, either!"

I said that we should go get something to eat and we could talk about it some more. I told him that we should take the new truck, just to see how it felt. He finally said all right and we climbed in and headed for the restaurant.

All during breakfast I worked on him and I finally talked him into accepting my gift. It took quite a bit more talking to have him agree to have the old Dodge put back together, but he finally agreed to that, too. We finished up breakfast and drove back to the auto body shop. Neither one of us had anything else to say.

It took a total of two months for Sixth Avenue Auto Body to complete the Dodge. It seems that they had some minor problems during the restoration. When they tried to paint it the paint just wouldn't take. There were several spots where it just wouldn't stick. They eventually had to strip the whole truck down to bare metal and paint it over again.

And then came the interior. The seat kept splitting out. They figured that they had gotten a bad batch of material and ordered some more. After the third time it came out right, though. That had been the final part of the restoration.

I made arrangements with the body shop to pick it up the day after it was finished. I got hold of Murphy that evening and told him that we could go and get the truck the next day. Murphy sounded kind of relieved over the phone when I told him it was done. I kind of got the impression that he was just glad that the whole thing was over with. We talked a little and I found out how the job was going. He told me it would be completed by the end of the month and the layoff slips were starting to come out now. Murphy figured that he would get his in a week or so.

Murphy took the next day off and we went and got the old Dodge. He was just tickled with the job that Sixth Avenue had done on it. He said that the truck looked just like it did when it was new. He was so excited he grabbed hold of me and said, "You can see yourself in the paint. Why, this is even cleaner than when it was new!"

Murphy got his layoff slip right when he expected it to be coming. I saw him off and on for the next six months. We would go out to breakfast or something like that once or twice a week.

I opened up my bookstore, just like I said I would, and it was really starting to take off. I figured that maybe I would see some kind of profit come the end of the year. When Murphy came out to see the store he drove the new truck, but you could tell that he really didn't like it. We were outside of the store one day and I happened to catch a glimpse of the odometer. There were next to no miles on it. So it seemed that the only time that Murphy ever drove it was when he came out to see me!

One day Murphy gave me a call. He had just received a dispatch from the union hall. The job was down at a pulp mill on the Columbia River, just outside the town of Camas, Washington. He told me that the job would run for at least a year and a half. That was a long job. "I'll let you know how I'm doing," he told me. That's the last I ever heard from Murphy.

I got a call from Murphy's sister about two weeks later. She lived in Spokane. It wasn't a very good call. She was really torn up! "There's been an accident," she told me.

It seems that Murphy had been on his way back to Camas after work one night and had somehow lost control of his old Dodge. It had run off the road. The truck had jumped an embankment and plunged one hundred feet into the river. He died at the scene. The truck was a total loss. The funeral service was set for Saturday at one o'clock in the afternoon in Tacoma. She wanted to know if I would be coming. I told her she could count on it.

Saturday came and I went to the funeral. Murphy's whole family was there, along with a bunch of his friends. It was a nice service, as far as funerals go. We stood around the casket and people said a lot of nice things about old Murphy. You know, about what a great guy he was and such. The typical things that people say about the recently deceased.

After the service I headed for the parking lot. I had recently purchased a 1985 Mercedes 380 SL. It was sitting right where I had left it. It looked a little dirty for some reason. It shouldn't have been dirty though, I had just washed it before I came. I went to unlock it and the driver's door wouldn't unlock. I opened it from the passenger side. When I got in, the glove box fell open and I bashed my knee into it reaching over to unlock the other door. I slammed the door when I got into the car and tried to start it. The motor turned over real slow like and it made a kind of *no-no-no* noise before it caught and started. I figured that I would have to have it looked at as soon as possible to find out what was the matter.

I pulled out of the parking lot. There was a loud cracking noise that came from the windshield. The glass broke right in the middle of the passenger side. I pulled off to the side of the road and got out. There was nothing that I could have done to cause the window to break. Nothing had hit it. The glass wasn't even chipped, but there was a huge crack on the inside. It looked like it was in between the glass.

I sat in the car and looked at the crack. I looked at it for a long time. The more I looked at it the more familiar it became. Then it hit me. It kind of looked like a tattoo! You know, one of those fancy ones that are done up in several colors. It looked just like a lion!

IMPACT

It was a leftover remnant from the construction of the solar system. It circled in the band of debris that lies between Mars and Jupiter, a billion miles from the sun's feeble light in cold vast space. This piece of flotsam was a nickel-iron meteoroid no bigger than a small car weighing in at a thousand pounds. On this, its last pass around the sun, it happened to have a minor collision with another piece of rubble. This small nudge caused it to move ever so slightly from its long established orbit and the long plunge into the inner solar system began.

Myra cruised the block slowly. She was trying to find a parking spot. After covering six blocks she was still looking. It was almost time for her class to be starting and at this rate she was going to be late. She glanced across the street and the most beat-up Mercedes sports car she had ever seen started to churn away from the curb and into the street. Myra pulled a quick u-turn and pulled her car expertly into the open spot.

She got out of the car and locked the door. Myra dug through her purse for some change to feed the parking meter. When she looked at the meter there was an hour left on it! This was going to be her lucky day after all. She dropped a quarter into the meter, which would give her an extra hour, and headed down the sidewalk for her class.

A white 1973 Lincoln Town Car drove slowly down the street. Marvin, the driver, found a spot to pull the car over. He stopped the car and the gang got out. This was Marvin's hood. He and his gang had put the word out that anything that went on in this section of town was his. He enforced his rule ruthlessly. At one time other gang leaders had thought they could muscle their way in. Marvin had a way to put a stop to that though. He had George, and George was really good at following orders.

Marvin watched as the woman finished parking. She didn't know that she had just taken one of Marvin's spots. She had no idea that there was a problem. The gang watched her as she fed the parking meter and then headed down the street.

"Shit, man, did you see that?" George asked. "That bitch just up and took that parking place. And now she's acting just like she owns it or something."

Marvin turned to George and lay his hand on his shoulder. "Shut up, George," he said. "Just shut up and watch her."

George turned his head and watched the woman as she walked down the street. She moved with a brisk step as if she was in a hurry. She had a large purse that was slung casually over her shoulder.

"You see that purse she's packing?" asked Marvin.

"Sure I do," said George.

"Well, that's a pretty big purse, don't you think?"

"It sure is, Marv," George said as he slowly shook his head.

"You know, she sure could put a lot of stuff in a purse like that. Maybe a cell phone, or a whole shit load of cash. How much cash do you think a lady like that carries?"

"I don't know, Marv."

"Well, I bet you it's a lot! A lot more than any of have right now." Marvin let go of George's shoulder. "Why, I bet she even has a wallet full of credit cards. Do you know what we could do with a bunch of credit cards?" Marvin started across the street. "Well, guys," he said, "it looks like that bag is soon going to become ours."

George quickly stepped up beside Marvin. "Sure, Marv. Anything you say."

The group cut across the street and headed down the sidewalk after their victim. This was going to be a pretty standard purse snatch. They had done it a thousand times before. It would teach the woman a lesson she wouldn't soon forget. Next time she would think twice about coming down to this end of town and taking up all the parking. There never was enough parking in this end of town anyway, with the school and all being so close.

The four gang members grouped up around Marvin. George's job was going to be the grab man. He would grab the purse while Cash and Mike gave the woman the sidewalk two-step. In the ensuing scuffle they would be able to dash off with her purse. Easy!

Myra heard the gang as they pounded down the sidewalk behind her. She knew what was coming and she got ready. Two years of martial arts training and this was the first time that she would actually get to use it. She listened and could tell that the lead man was starting to fret to the right. She ducked to the left and made contact with him. He went down sprawling on the pavement. Two other guys came charging up on either side of her. She dived down low and they ran right into each other, going down on top of the first guy. That only left one more.

George charged down right on top of Myra. He was going to run right over her. That's what he was going to do. The plan hadn't worked and this was all he could think to do to salvage what was left.

Myra moved. She raised her right elbow up to shoulder height and spun around with all her strength. Her elbow made solid contact with George's nose as he passed her by. She was certain that she heard bone break as he passed.

Blood erupted from George's face as he landed on top of the other men lying in the street.

Myra turned and looked at the carnage. Everything had happened so fast. She turned back and kept walking down the street. She was going to be late for class!

Marvin crawled out from beneath his three lackeys. The woman was gone! She was nowhere to be seen. The other two members of the gang disentangled themselves and stood up. George was still down on the ground, though. He sat on the sidewalk and held his face between his huge hands. He rocked back and forth. Blood oozed between his fingers. It slowly dripped onto the ground and formed a little crimson pool. "I dhing dhe bidch broge my dose," he said as he sat on the ground. He removed his hands from his face. "God, Marv, dhe bidch broge my dose!"

Cash and Mike went over to help George up. Marvin looked up and down the street, but the woman was definitely gone. "Shit," he said as he surveyed the situation they were in. "You guys go load George up in the car. Make sure you don't let him bleed all over everything though!"

Marvin walked over to the car that he had seen the woman get out of. He pulled a flat bladed screwdriver out of the inner pocket of his coat. He tested the weight of the screwdriver as he looked up and down the street.

He watched as the guys helped George get into the Lincoln. What a mess. They were going to have to take George someplace to get his nose fixed.

Marvin stepped up to the front of the car and drove the screwdriver into the heart of the radiator. Water and anti-freeze blossomed out from the hole in a bright green stream and pooled onto the pavement under the car.

Myra walked into the lecture hall. The class had already started and she was late, just like she thought she was going to be. This lecture was to be on St. Cyril of Alexandria and the run-in he had with Nestorius The Heretic. It seemed that there had been an altercation between the two over who was permitted to actually pray to God. At the time, the church thought that priests should be the only ones allowed this privilege. This was church doctrine and also the belief of St. Cyril of Alexandria.

The other school of thought was lead by Nestorius. This faction believed that the congregation should be able to converse directly with God without the intervention of the Church.

It seemed that St. Cyril became livid at hearing this point of view and in a rage he pronounced twelve curses against Nestorius. This all happened in the year 431 and is the incident that had caused the split between the Roman Catholic and the Greek Orthodox Churches.

Because she had come in late and had missed the beginning of the class she had not been there to hear the twelve curses. She would have to borrow somebody else's notes so she could go over them. If those punks hadn't delayed her she would have made it in time for the beginning of class. What did they think they were doing anyway? Didn't they know pulling stuff like that could have gotten one or maybe all of them hurt? What gave them the right to hassle people anyway?

She was fuming. She had missed the most important part of the lecture. There was probably going to be a test or a quiz later and she wasn't going to be ready because she had missed the beginning of class. That was all there was to it, she was going to have to borrow somebody else's notes. This just burned her up; everybody else in the class took crummy notes. So even if she could find a set to borrow they probably wouldn't have any of the stuff she needed.

When the class was over Myra collared Jim Sandal. He was a nice guy; he would let her borrow his notes. She asked him and Jim told her that he would be glad to loan them to her, but he would need them back by Tuesday morning.

Myra said that she would return them promptly and that she really appreciated him loaning them to her.

On her way back to the car she looked over Jim's notes. She rifled through the pile of pages as she walked down the street. As far as she could tell everything was there. What a stroke of luck! There was only one small problem though. Jim's writing! He wrote like a drunken chicken that had been out on a Saturday night binge. As hard as she tried she couldn't read half of what he had written down. This was going to take some time. It looked like she was going to have to spend her whole weekend trying to decipher his notes.

She stuffed them into her purse and headed for where she had left her car.

When she got to the block she looked down the street toward where her car was and saw a florescent pool of green icker oozing out from underneath it. The wound in the radiator had quit flowing and was now slowly dripping the remainder of the car's lifeblood out onto the pavement. Almost all of the water that it had once contained was gone. Drops were slowly falling off the frame and splashing into the pool underneath. They made a distinctive plopping sound as they landed.

"Damn those guys!" Myra yelled. "What the hell have they done to my car?" She ran the remaining distance to her vehicle. She stood for a second and surveyed the damage. She looked at the pool underneath and just knew that it wasn't going to be a good idea to try and drive it someplace. She was going to have to get it towed into the shop to get it fixed.

She was mad as hell as she turned around and headed back down the block toward the nearest phone booth. This was just the kind of situation where a cell phone would have come in handy. She was going to have to break down and buy one of them one of these days. The nearest phone booth was clear back on campus. That was at least six blocks away. That would make her entire walk for today eighteen blocks. Her feet hurt.

As she walked down the street she thought about how awful her day had been. Everything had gone wrong. She had been late for class, her car was broken and would have to be repaired, and she was on foot. It all boiled down to some dirtbag punks that thought they could control the street. If she ever saw them again she was going to teach them a thing or two!

Myra just hated to walk. With all the martial arts training and the aerobics classes that she took just to keep fit and stay in shape she still just hated to walk anywhere. If she had to go down the street from her apartment to go to the store she drove. It didn't matter if when she got there she had to spend twenty minutes trying to find a parking place. She still drove. Halfway down the street Myra's anger had come to its peak. She had made her mind up. If she came upon any one of those punks she was going to clean his clock for him! That's all there was to it. She would teach those jerks a lesson if it was the last thing she ever did. Harass people like that, try and steal her purse would they! She was as mad as she had ever been!

Myra turned and looked down the street at her car. It just sat there. Green goo dripped out of it and a small river was running down the gutter toward the drain.

Myra wasn't one to curse but this case just called for it. "Damn it!" she swore as she looked at her car. "May God strike all of you assholes dead!"

The meteoroid had been making its plunge toward the sun for a long time, but it would never get there. There was a small green-blue planet that was blocking its path. Becoming part of this body was its only option.

They had just gotten back from the clinic where they had George's nose fixed. The doctor in the clinic had done a hurry-up job on George. He wanted them out of there as quickly as possible. George's face was a mess of dried blood and dirt. He had pretty much soaked the front of his shirt before the bleeding had started to slow down. He had a shop rag pressed to his face to staunch the rest.

The receptionist had taken one look at him and the group and had rushed them through. The clinic didn't want any trouble with hoodlums. Just patch them up and process the paper. Get them out of there as fast as possible. That was the policy.

The doctor came in and looked at George. He cleaned his face up, and then packed his nose with cotton to stop the bleeding. The cotton also helped to hold George's nose in some kind of shape. This way when it healed it would still look like something resembling a nose. After that he taped the whole mess up. He told George to keep ice on it and to go and see his own doctor just as soon as he could. "That's the worst case of a broken nose I've ever seen," he said. "If you don't want to have trouble with it later you'll do just as I've told you."

"I bill," said George. The gang headed back out to the car.

Marvin wheeled the Lincoln down the road. He was doing just a little under the speed limit. He didn't want to call any attention to himself. They were back on the same street where everything had happened. If that woman's car was still there they were going to trash it good. If she happened to be there they were going to trash her up too!

They spotted Myra's car just where it had been. Marvin gave a knowing look at Mike. "Get the gun," he said.

Mike opened the glove box and withdrew a gun. It was a nine-millimeter pistol. He kept it low so no one outside of the car could see it. He lay the gun in his lap and popped the clip. It was fully loaded. He rammed the clip back home and rested the middle finger of his left hand on the power window control. The window started to come down. "I'm gonna shoot the shit out of that car!" He brought the gun up and rested the barrel on the edge of the open glass.

Myra came to the end of the block. She had her purse slung over her shoulder and was walking briskly back toward the car. She had made the call to the auto club and a tow truck was on the way. They were going to meet her back at the car. She didn't see the Lincoln coming toward her.

Cash, who was in the back seat with George, was the first to spot her. "There she is!" he yelled. "There she is! Get her, man! Get her! Come on man, shoot the bitch!"

Mike saw her and leveled the gun out the window. He took aim. He didn't want to miss.

Marvin saw her too and at the same time he put his foot down hard on the accelerator. The big car responded instantly and roared down the street toward his victim.

Mike had her dead in his sights. His finger twitched as it gently rested against the trigger.

The meteor entered the earth's atmosphere. Its speed was well over fifteen thousand miles per hour! Frictional heat instantly raised its surface temperature to the boiling point of steel. Glowing particles were streaming off it, creating a fiery tail. The fall to earth would only last a second.

Mike's finger was just tightening on the trigger when the meteorite struck the Lincoln. It hit the trunk of the car and penetrated all the way through the gas tank. The gas tank had been full. The ensuing explosion and fire could be seen for miles.

THE VOICE FROM WITHIN

Raymond came out of the front door of the shelter and sat on the steps. He had come outside because he had heard a noise. He looked up and saw the light as it flamed through the sky. As he listened he heard the explosion it made upon impact. He sat on the step and watched the smoke rise up into the early evening sky. Fire engine and police sirens could be clearly recognized as they converged on the scene.

He sat on the steps and waited for the fury to subside. A yellow glow could be clearly seen over the north end of the city. Mixed in the glow was the flicker of emergency lights. It was a big fire. A very big fire! It was going to take all the equipment the fire department had. If it got any bigger they would have to call in neighboring fire departments.

This was the sign that Raymond had been waiting for. This was the portent that the voice from within had told him about.

They were coming!

He had to move and he had to move now. Time was short. He had to get to the other side of the bay, out to the cabin at Belfair. He went back inside and attempted to clean up a little bit. He was going to have to hitch a ride and it was awful hard to hitch a ride when you looked like Raymond. With all the muggings and car-jackings that were going on nowadays nobody wanted to pick up a hitchhiker, let alone a bum.

This was the look that had taken Raymond years to perfect, the appearance of a homeless person. It was a good disguise. Years ago he used to be Ray Langley, one of the top engineers at Boeing, but that was years ago. That was before the voice from within had crept into his dreams. Before it had crawled its way out and clawed its way into his daily life.

It had all started simply enough with a dream. He had been having bad late-night dreams, very bad dreams. The kind of dreams that wake you in a convulsion and leave you covered in a cold sweat. He knew that something was wrong but he just couldn't tell what it was. He couldn't remember the dreams. He just knew that something was wrong. Very wrong!

This went on for months until finally he woke from a dream to hear a voice whispering. Whispering softly and quietly as it reverberated around the edges of sleep. Telling him, warning him.

It was terrifying. He had no idea what to do. He felt like he was going mad. There had never been any trace of mental illness in his family. Going to a doctor was just out of the question. What would the company think? They would think he was having some kind of breakdown, that's what they would think. That would give Joe the grounds to can him. If he were fired, how would he ever locate another position as good as this one? Who would hire a psychotic? He decided that he would just have to puzzle this out on his own.

The longer it went on, though, the worse it got. Eventually it got to the point where he was sleeping only two or three hours a night. He used to sleep eight hours straight, but now he was too busy listening for the voice to sleep. He felt that if he listened hard enough maybe the voice would become clearer, easier to understand. Then he would know what it was trying to tell him.

By now though the lack of sleep was starting to show in his work. Joe finally called him into his office to have a talk with him. "Ray," he said, "it seems there were some design flaws in your last set of drawings."

"What's wrong with them?" demanded Ray.

Joe let him have it plain and simple. "Well, I'll tell you what's wrong with them. They're crap, that's what wrong with them! Why, if that system had been built and installed per your drawings there could have been some major problems! And you know that if that had happened the company would have been held responsible."

Ray sat in his chair. He looked like he didn't even know that Joe was there.

Joe went on, "Ray, you been here what, five years now, and your work has been excellent. That is up until the past few months. You've been slipping lately. Making stupid mistakes." Joe got up from behind his desk and walked over to the window. "You know, Ray," he said, "I think that maybe you've been working too hard. That could be the reason your latest performance has not been up to par." He turned around and looked at Ray. "You haven't been looking too good lately," he said. "Like you haven't been getting enough sleep or something." He walked back over to the desk. "Those mistakes were simple enough, any second-year apprentice could have made them. Somebody would have caught them sooner or later and that system would never have been installed. I think you need to take some time off. Relax a little bit. When was the last time you took a vacation?"

Ray sat in his chair and looked at the wall. After a moment he answered, "I have never taken a vacation."

"Well then it's about time you had one," said Joe. "Why don't you take a month off and just forget about the job for a while. That could be the best thing you could do. When you come back it will be just like you were starting fresh! I've been looking through your records and I see that you have acquired enough time for at least a month. Maybe even a week more. Why don't you put in for it and we can have it start right now?"

Ray sat and looked at the wall.

"Well," Joe said, "you don't have to do it today. All I'm saying is think about it. You can take a week now and make up your mind about using more time later. Though, let me tell you, now is a good time to be taking off. We will be starting to run low on work this week anyway and things could get really slow later. The next major contract won't be coming in for at least six months."

Ray got up from his chair. "I'll take the time off now," he said. He slammed the door to Joe's office on his way out.

At the end of two weeks Ray was a living wreck. All he did was worry about his job. At night when sleep did manage to overtake him it was only for what seemed like sparse minutes. The voice from within his dreams would wake him right back up again.

By the end of the third week he wasn't sleeping at all anymore. He spent all his time sitting on the couch and staring at the TV. He had been awake for the past two days when the voice suddenly became clear.

Wheel of Fortune was on the television. Sleep was as remote now as it had ever been. Ray watched half-heartedly as the contestants spun the wheel and called out their letters. Ray watched as one lady took her turn and the wheel landed on a space marked $1000.

"Pat," she said, "may I have a C?"

Ray watched as Vanna White touched the spaces on the puzzle where the Cs were hidden.

The lady contestant then said, "Pat, I would like to solve the puzzle. Is it—" That's the moment that the voice hit Ray. It hit him with baseball bat precision. It came from the back of his head and tore its way through his mind. A major league home run couldn't have hit him any harder. It was like the voice had sailed right down the middle of his mind and clear over the center field fence.

Ray sat bolt upright as the voice subsided from a booming roar to low tones that vibrated softly through his whole body. He could hear it clearly as it whispered over his right shoulder. He turned quickly, but there was no one there. He tried to get up but it felt like he was pinned down to the couch. He couldn't move! That's when the voice started to tell him about Them.

He sat and listened while the voice told him about worlds that had been totally destroyed and the rape of galaxies. It told him about the fall of civilizations and of the destruction of all life in the universe. Of utter destruction.

It told him about Them. It told him that They hated all living things. That it was Their sole purpose to erase all forms of life, large or small.

It told him that life is what changes the universe. That life caused the universe to be. That life was the reason for the universe. Life caused the universe to expand!

It talked of gravitational forces and how in time, left to itself, the universe would start to contract in upon itself. Draw back to the central core where it came from. Collapse.

It talked of life. How life, if it was intelligent enough, could eventually leave the sphere of gravitational influence and thus avert the collapse. If life escaped then there would not be enough matter in the universe to cause a collapse. This included even the smallest portion of life. If this happened then the universe would go on expanding forever!

It told him that They existed before the collapse and that They existed after the collapse. If They could stop all life then the universe would go unchanged to its final end and collapse. Without a collapsing universe They would not exist. Life would control the heavens. If that happened then life control would be forever!

Then the voice gave him the idea for the machine. The machine of all machines! The machine that could save his world, the machine that could save the universe! He listened as the voice gave him a detailed plan. A plan to build this machine.

The machine would shield his world from Them. That meant that life could continue in this little speck of the universe. If life continued then the collapse would be averted. Their plans then were for not!

The voice stopped just as abruptly as it had started. Ray rose from the couch and turned the television off. He looked down and lying on the floor in the middle of the room were explicit notes and drawings for the construction of the machine. He picked up the pile of paper. He didn't remember making any such sketches and notes but the handwriting was definitely his.

He went into the bathroom in a daze and turned on the tap. He splashed some cold water in his face. This seemed to bring him around and focus his reality. He went back into the living room and gathered up the sheets of paper. He inspected them. They were fascinating. The intricacy and details of the drawings were superb. He spent the rest of the night checking and crosschecking schematics and diagrams. He finally came to the conclusion that this thing could really be built. And that if it were built it would work. He didn't know what it would do but it would work.

He started a cost analysis. If he built this thing as it was shown it would take every cent that he had. He went to the safe in the bedroom and dug through his records and files. If he cashed in everything he would be able to raise about two hundred thousand dollars. This would still leave him short. He would have to cut corners somehow.

The other thing that he had to do was lose his identity. The voice had told him that if he built the machine They would know that it was being constructed. They would be hunting for him everywhere. They would search the here and now until they found him. The only way that he could avoid detection was to become somebody else. That's why he had to become Raymond.

He bought a five-acre parcel near the town of Belfair out on the Olympic Peninsula. That's the first thing he did when he became Raymond. The parcel was ten miles outside of town on a small lake.

It had taken no time at all to cash in his assets. He hid the money and moved out onto the streets. Doing business from pay phones he found a contractor and had a pole building erected out on his property. It was a good size building, measuring sixty by thirty. This was where he would assemble the machine.

With that part of his project completed he started organizing the materials he would need. During this phase the voice came back. It was intrusive. It kept pushing him, whispering in his head. Telling him to hurry. Time was short. Time was relative! They were coming!

It took every dime that Raymond could lay his hands on and over a full year to complete the machine. By the time it was done it completely filled the metal pole building. The machine was extremely heavy and sat on a six-inch concrete slab. Raymond had poured the slab himself.

There was a single garage door at one end of the building. Several windows were evenly spaced down both sides. Another door graced the backside of the structure. The windows were all covered in black plastic garbage bags, which allowed some light in but prevented anyone from looking in.

Every square inch of the building was filled with the machine. It ran across the floor and climbed up the walls. Wiring ran like vines across the rafters. Trusses were hung with panels and tubing. Electrical and hydraulic components festooned the building in a rainbow of colors.

A main control panel sat by itself over by the garage door. Above this was a bank of gauges and dials. To the right side of the control panel suspended in a framework from the ceiling, was a portable power plant. It wasn't portable anymore, though.

Raymond headed for the ferry terminal as fast as he could. He checked his thin jacket to make sure that the walk on ferry money he had stashed was still there. Running his hand down the seam of his coat he felt the two dollars firmly imbedded in the lining. He was pleased. He had placed the money there when he had found the coat.

The two one-dollar bills were his security money. It was all he had left and it was just enough for him to ride the ferry from Seattle to Bremerton. Once he was in Bremerton it was a short hop out to the property in Belfair.

Things were working out just fine! He had enough warning that They were coming. He was just in time to catch the last ferry. The run would take just over an hour.

Raymond sat on one of the seats and watched the other passengers. A group of six was sitting on the port side drinking beer and talking. Raymond wished he had enough money for a beer. It had been a long time since he'd had one. He watched them in silence. He sat quietly and watched.

The ferry left Elliot Bay and headed across the Puget Sound. It rounded Blake Island and entered the mouth of Sinclair Inlet. Evergreen trees lined the shores. The forest was intersected every now and then with costly homes. Spacious lawns and gardens that a master gardener would have been jealous of reached down to the water's edge.

The lights of East Bremerton danced over the bay as the ferry slowed and made its approach to the dock. Raymond left the passenger deck and headed down the stairs for the docking ramp. He threaded his way through the cars as the boat pulled gently into the slip. The deck hands tied off the boat and the engines shut down. The boarding ramp was lowered and Raymond was the first person off the ferry.

He walked up the ramp, past several bars and restaurants, and made his way toward Pacific Street. Noise and laughter wafted out of the doors of the various bars that he passed. The smell of stale beer was heavy in the air.

He walked several blocks up Pacific Street until he hit Burwell Street. He stood on the corner of Burwell and tried to thumb a ride. Several cars passed him. None of them slowed down or stopped.

It was well into the evening. Parked cars lined the street. The parking lots were full. Raymond dipped into one of the lots. It was a small lot just off of State Street. He knew that every once in a while somebody would just happen to leave his keys in his car. After checking ten cars he was lucky enough and found one with the keys still dangling out of the ignition. It was a 1979 Toyota Celica Supra. He climbed in and started the car up.

He threw the car in reverse and backed out of the parking lot. He looked around the lot to see if anyone was there watching. Everything was quiet. There was no one there. Placing the car in first gear he drove slowly through the lot. When he pulled out onto State Street he turned on the lights and headed out of town.

He slouched down behind the steering wheel and drove slowly down the street. He didn't want to call any attention to himself. The speed limit was twenty-five miles an hour. He was doing just over twenty. He was very careful and watched for the cops as he maneuvered his way through the back streets of downtown Bremerton. Finally he made his way out to Highway 3 and headed for Belfair. There was little traffic on the road at this time of night and he picked his speed up. The car glided down the highway easily.

He cleared the Highway 16 cutoff, lost sight of the water and plunged into an old growth forest. The trees grew up right next to the side of the road. They towered up over the highway and formed a canopy over the dark and empty road.

Raymond was concentrating on the road. It took all his effort to maintain control of the small car as he pushed it up as fast as it would go. He was doing well over eighty miles an hour and the Toyota seemed to float down the road.

The voice came out of nowhere and slammed into Raymond's head. Raymond jumped and the car veered across the centerline. "Hurry," the voice said. "They are coming!" He regained control of the car and brought it back into its own side of the road. All the time the voice was chanting. "Hurry, They are coming! Hurry, They are coming! Hurry, They are coming! Hurry, They are coming! They are coming! They are coming!" By the time he reached Belfair it was screaming as it hammered its refrain into the center of his brain. "HURRY, THEY ARE COMING!"

When he got to the dirt road that led to the property he was pushing the car for all it was worth. Blue smoke was coming out of the tail pipe, and the engine was knocking badly. He braked hard, downshifted and shot off the pavement and onto the dirt road. The car slid around the corner. He put his foot to the floor and fishtailed up the road in a cloud of dust and flying gravel.

By this time the voice was earsplitting. His skull vibrated with its increasing sound. Blood oozed from his ears and nose. The pain in his head was explosive! He passed through a clear-cut, took a hard right and followed the track that led to his property. He slammed the car to a stop in front of the pole building and cut the engine.

The voice bounced off the inside of his skull. "HURRY, THEY ARE COMING! HURRY, THEY ARE COMING!"

He crawled out of the car. The voice was so loud, it was so clear. It was the loudest and the clearest it had ever been. He was staggering with pain by the time he made his way up to the door of the building. All the time the voice was pounding inside his head. His spine shook with its reverberation.

He stood in front of the door for a second. He clutched his hands to his ears but the voice wouldn't stop. Finally he was able to reach up on top of the doorjamb. He groped for the key, found it, and stuck it into the lock on his third try. The door unlocked.

The machine sat dead and silent. It filled the building to overflowing. The quiet hung in the air like a shroud. As the door opened, dust circulated on the breeze that gently blew through the building. Raymond reached out his right hand and groped for a flashlight that sat on a beam next to the entrance. When he found it he turned it on. A pure white beam of light cut through the darkness. It struck the generator and lit it up in all its intricate detail.

Suddenly, the voice stopped!

Raymond wiped his nose on the sleeve of his jacket. It left a crimson streak on the cuff. The voice was definitely gone. Its incisive message and the pain that had accompanied it had ended!

This was the instant, the cusp of the moment. He knew that he had to hurry. They were coming! He walked over to the generator and flipped the power switch into the on position. The generator was self-starting. Raymond could hear the motor turn over. It rolled over several times and then caught. The generator roared, the overhead lights came on and the building came to life!

Raymond stepped over to the control panel. He started flipping switches and adjusting knobs. The cooling pumps for the machine came on. The machine created a tremendous amount of heat and without the pumps the machine would be lost.

The pumps came up to pressure and the recirculation valves opened. Coolant gushed through the internals of the machine, bringing a chill to the building. Air that had been trapped in the system banged loudly in the piping as it made its way through the pumps.

By now the machine was up to temperature. Everything was functioning properly. Raymond checked and double-checked his gauge and pressure readings. The machine was ready! When he started the transmission he knew that the solar system would be safe! He stood with his finger poised over the transmitter. All that he had sacrificed and worked for the past few years came down to this one moment!

The voice struck him from behind. Its calling was intense! "Hurry, They are coming! Hurry, They are coming! HURRY, THEY ARE HERE!"

Raymond pressed the transmitter and the machine opened its eyes and came to life. The floor shook with the energy created by the machine. The walls vibrated with its very existence! The building cried out as if in pain and the sound penetrated the surrounding forest. Trees moved in harmony with the sounds of the machine.

That's when the cooling pumps quit, and with the death of the pumps came the death of the machine. Raymond watched as the pressure dropped. He ran to the pumps and tried to restart them, but they were dead. Dead and gone. He jammed at the reset buttons frantically.

The explosion was deafening. Pieces of the building, and pieces of the machine flew into the surrounding forest. The Toyota parked in front of the building was instantly incinerated. Hot metal from the explosion landed in the forest and started fires. Burning embers and cinders floated on the wind and started other fires.

Where the building had been was a glowing pool of yellow liquid. It slowly cooled and took on the color of tarnished silver.

The forest fire that ensued consumed two thousand acres before it could be contained. Smoke from the fire could clearly be seen from Seattle.

BUGS

Mike made the turn from highway nineteen and crossed the narrow old bridge that lead to Indian Island. The semi-truck took up both lanes of the bridge. Any oncoming traffic would have to pull off to the side of the road and wait. After he cleared the span he pulled back over to his own side of the road.

As he drove down the road he checked his map, which told him the next thing that he would come to was the Indian Island Naval Reserve. From the directions he had gotten at the pickup point, the EPA lab should be on the left just after the Naval Base.

Thirty barrels of hazardous waste sat securely in the back of the truck. They were latched in place with half-inch rope and the tops were tightly wired shut. On each barrel was a hazardous waste sticker detailing where they had come from. All the barrels had been collected from the site of a major fire near Belfair. The sticker also identified the contents as unknown. That is the reason they were being shipped to the EPA labs, to be identified.

Each barrel had been carefully filled to within seven inches of the top with a phosphorescent yellow goo that had come from the site. The men that had filled the barrels had been dressed in full anti-contamination gear. After all, with something unknown it was better to be safe than sorry.

The sight had been a charred mess. Only the yellow tar-like substance appeared to be unburned. The team could tell that once there had been a metal building there, but now all that remained was a pile of rubble and a mass of melted metal. Hundreds of acres of forest had been destroyed in the fire. It had been the biggest fire in Western Washington in years.

The yellow tar-like stuff had collected in a pool just south of where the building had been. Everything around the pool was dead. There was no life at all. Even the soil itself was dead!

The spill team had cleaned up and contained the area quickly and efficiently. The ground had been removed to a depth of one foot and all material had been packaged in the barrels for shipment.

Mike was an expert driver. He had been driving a truck now for ten years. The past seven years he had specialized in hauling hazardous waste. Hazardous waste hauling paid better. He had hauled everything from asbestos to zinc chromate.

Most of his loads went to the toxic waste dump in Oregon. Though, when he hauled something that was radioactive it usually went to Hanford. However, this was the first shipment he had ever made to Indian Island.

The roads on the island were narrow and torturous. They were originally built in the 1890s to allow a land access to Fort Flagler and the neighboring village of Nordland. Most of the island is heavily wooded, although at places it is interspersed with an occasional farm or some patch of land that has been clear cut.

The deer ran blindly through the woods. Her terror was all consuming. A pack of dogs had caught her scent and were in the process of running her down. She crashed through the brush with no concern about the noise she was making. All her instincts told her to run. Run or die! Every muscle in her body was dedicated to running. If she had to she would run until her heart burst.

There were five dogs that made up the pack. They came from several of the local farms on the island. This wasn't the first deer that they had run to death and it probably wouldn't be their last.

When they were home they were good dogs. The best of family pets. When they ran free in the woods, though, they reverted to their ancestral ways and became a pack, and as a pack they operated like a finely-tuned machine. If they caught the scent of a deer or other small animal that happened to live on the island they would run it down and eventually kill it. As a pack they worked efficiently.

Mike downshifted the truck as he came into the corner. He was doing forty on the narrow road and that was pushing it. The right side of the road was a steep bank that climbed up into the woods. It was well over eight feet tall and towered above the road. The steep slope angled from the pavement and sheered off up into the woods that were on top. They were dark and thick.

The road made a sharp curve to the left and crossed over Teacher Creek. The creek ran sluggishly north for two miles and eventually ended at Marrow Stone Bog. The bog made up the southern boundary of Fort Flagler, one of the old historic coastal artillery stations on the Puget Sound.

The deer broke free from the woods. She could hear the dogs running behind her in hot pursuit. As she ran she peered over her shoulder and in horror saw the lead dog of the pack

The bank was too steep to run down, and in a state of pure panic she leapt for the relative safety of the road below.

The truck slowed as it rounded the apex of the curve. Mike shifted again and started to pick up speed, just as the deer sailed through the air and impacted with the windshield of the truck. She instantly broke both her front legs as glass and deer spewed into the cab of the moving truck.

Mike pulled the wheel sharply to the left and the truck and trailer went into a long slow slide. The trailer jack-knifed and the truck rolled over with a grinding impact. It slid off the highway and finally came to rest in the middle of Teacher Creek.

Mike lay in the cab of the truck. He was covered with broken glass and flailing dying deer. He was bleeding in several places and there was glass in one of his eyes. It felt like a couple of his ribs might be broken too.

The dogs came rushing from the woods and stopped abruptly at the top of the bank. They stood for a moment and surveyed the situation, then they turned and ran back into the woods. The prey was dead, the chase was over.

Mike crawled out of the wreck of the truck. He knew for positive that he had at least several broken bones. He was beat up and bruised up. The deer had really done a job on him when she came through the windshield.

The truck lay on its side in the middle of the creek. Steam issued from the engine compartment. It blew freely from the ripped and torn hoses under the hood. Smoke hung over the scene in a dirty glycerin haze. One wheel still slowly rotated with the momentum of the crash.

The trailer had ruptured at the seams and barrels were strewn in and around the creek. Most of them had held up pretty well considering the collision they had just been through. Only one of the thirty barrels that had been in the trailer had suffered any damage. It lay in the creek bed and gradually dripped its contents into the unhurried flow of the stream.

Mike painfully climbed out of the creek bed and worked his way back up to the road. When he got there he sat on the side of the road and waited for a passing car. He wasn't going any further. His chest felt like a tree was sitting on it and he wheezed heavily with every breath he took. The pain in his right knee was agonizing and he couldn't move it at all anymore.

He lay there for at least twenty minutes until a family in a Volvo station wagon came by. They were on their way out to see the ruins of the abandoned gun emplacements at Fort Flagler. When they saw Mike on the side of the road they stopped to help. They made him comfortable and called 911 on the cell phone and waited for the police and an ambulance to show up.

The leaking barrel hadn't deposited very much of its contents into the creek before a hazardous clean-up crew arrived at the scene. The hairline crack in the lid only allowed one drop at a time of the viscous liquid to escape the barrel. It would slowly ooze out and collect into a drop. Then it would make the leisurely trip across the lid. When it reached the bottom edge of the lid it would make the short plunge into the slow moving stream, where it would spatter when it hit the water. By the time the barrel had been righted less than a quarter of a cup of the toxin had made its way into the creek. The clean-up crew hadn't noticed the infinitesimal breach in the barrel's integrity.

Toxin and water mixed readily and flowed along the course of the stream. It eventually collected in the calm still pools of Marrow Stone Bog.

The mosquito hatch had started several days before. Tiny clusters of eggs floated on the surface of the bog, while others wriggled with the hatching of tiny mosquito larvae. The larvae were born hungry, they were starving. Upon hatching they started their mad search for food. When they came in contact with the toxin they fed freely on it.

The female larvae thrived on the new food source. They became bigger, larger and stronger than the males in the bog. They matured quicker, and they ate. By the time they had molted four times they had become pupas and had eaten all the males in the bog. As pupas, they quit eating which was fine as there was nothing left in the bog to eat. Now all they had to do was wait, wait to become adult mosquitoes.

Diana Freeman pulled into the parking lot of the Island Cafe in the village of Nordland. She reached behind her and grabbed the camera bag that lay on the back seat. Opening the bag she dug through it and found the Minolta 400SL camera body. She dug some more and extracted a twenty-four by fifty zoom telephoto lens and snapped it onto the camera body. This would work nicely for the shots she was planning to take. She checked the flash and seized two extra rolls of film from the depths of the bag. Now she was ready.

Diana was a freelance photographer who sold most of her work to *Cascade Magazine* and this piece she was planning to do on old Fort Flagler would be picked up in a heartbeat!

She got out of the car and headed for the cafe, camera slung over her shoulder. Sources had told her that Ned Olsen was the owner of the Island Cafe and as far as she could find out he was the last enlisted man to be stationed at Fort Flagler before they closed it down. This interview and photo shoot would be the highlight of the story.

She swung the door open and a little bell sounded. The rich smells of breakfast hung in the air. A man sat at the counter drinking coffee and reading a paper. He looked up at Diana as she came into the restaurant.

Ned Olsen was behind the counter. He had on a chef's hat and a white apron. He was meticulously arranging a mile-high stack of pancakes on a plate. "Grab a seat," he cheerfully hollered at Diana as she came in. "I'll be right with you."

She sat down in a booth by a window. The man at the counter set down his coffee cup and watched her as she sat down. She arranged her camera equipment while Ned finished organizing the order of pancakes he was carefully stacking. When he was satisfied he placed them before the man at the counter. "Enjoy your breakfast," he said as he filled the man's empty coffee cup.

Ned came out from behind the counter and Diana watched him as if through the eye of a camera lens. The light from the kitchen was just right and it shimmered through his fresh military hair cut. Ned was on the high side of sixty. He wore a short-sleeved shirt and the girlie tattoos that ran up and down both of his arms were in plain view. This was something he had done while he was stationed in Hawaii.

"And what can I get for you?" he asked as he set a menu in front of Diana. "You know I make the finest stack of flapjacks on the island, and my coffee isn't too bad either! Would you care for a cup to start off this fine morning?"

As Diana opened up the menu she said, "Yes, please, a good cup of coffee would be very nice right about now. " Ned leaned over the table and with his ever-present coffee pot he filled her cup to the rim.

Diana opened the menu, thumbed through it quickly and then put it down. "I think I'll pass this morning on breakfast," she said. "Though, those pancakes really do look delicious."

"They are," muttered the man at the counter as he chewed a huge mouthful. He set down his fork and took a sip from his coffee cup. "Hey, Ned," he said as he put his cup down, "what's a guy got to do anyway to get a refill around here?"

"Hold on, I'm on my way. " Ned headed back toward the counter with the coffee pot held out like a silver chalice in front of him.

Diana set her camera on the table and turned it on. Once the flash had warmed up she brought the camera up to her eye. It made a whirring noise as it focused in on Ned and the man at the counter. She watched through the lens as Ned poured more coffee for the man. Just when he picked up the man's empty plate to take it back to the kitchen, Diana depressed the shutter button on the camera. The flash went off, lighting up the cafe just like a bomb blast!

Ned turned and dropped the plate he was holding. It hit the counter but did not break, wobbling in tight circles. "What the heck was that?" Ned asked as he scooped the plate back up.

"I was just setting my camera up."

"Camera," said Ned.

Diana pointed at the camera that she had set back on the table. "I'm Diana Freeman from *Cascade Magazine*. I'm up here to do a story about Fort Flagler."

Ned set the plate back down on the counter. "You know," he said, "I was stationed over at the fort when they closed it down."

"That's the reason I stopped in," said Diana. "I'd heard that you would probably be able to give me some information that I could use for my story."

"Why, I'd love to," answered Ned as he picked the plate back up and then gently placed it in the dirty dishpan.

The man at the counter took a ten-dollar bill out of his wallet and placed it under his coffee cup. He looked Diana over one move time as he headed for the door. "Don't let him talk your leg off," he told her as he placed his hand on the doorknob. "If you give him a chance he'll talk for hours about that old fort."

"Crying out loud, Walt," Ned yelled at him, as the door closed, "I can't talk for forty-five minutes about that place, yet alone an hour."

Ned wiped his hands on his apron. He plucked a sponge up from under the counter and wiped down the place where Walt had been sitting. "What would you like to know about the old fort?" he asked.

"Well, for a start," said Diana, "would you mind if I took some more pictures to go along with the interview?"

"No, go right ahead," said Ned. "I could use the advertising!"

Diana took a Walkman sized tape recorder from the depths of her purse. "Do you mind if I use this? It makes taking notes easier," she said. "I hate writing things down."

"That's just fine by me," said Ned.

Diana set the miniature machine on the table and turned it on. "I'd also like to take some more pictures while we talk."

"Shoot all the pictures you want," he said. "If this place gets in your magazine it will do nothing but help my business."

Diana started asking questions and shooting pictures at the same time. "Well," she said, "what can you tell me about the fort?"

"What would you like to know?"

"Everything," said Diana as she continued to snap pictures.

Ned thought for a second. "OK," he said. "Let's see. I enlisted in the Navy in 1951 and right out of basic I got stationed at Fort Flagler. I was there until they closed the place down.

"What a ceremony that was. The fort had been run down over the years but we really spruced it up. That's most of what we did when I was stationed there. Cleaned and painted. There was a fresh coat of paint on everything. If it didn't move we painted it. We had to make it look good for when the captain handed over the keys to the governor.

"When they closed the fort I ended up being stationed as a messmate on the Aircraft Carrier Forrestal. I've been cooking ever since.

"When the state took over they turned the fort into a park. We get a lot of summer people up here now to come and look it over. Some of the old five-inch guns were left and are still in place. If you go down by the bunkers you can see them.

"Every summer the Seattle Youth Symphony uses the dining hall for a practice room. They spend the whole summer living in the old barracks. Those kids can put on quite a show. They offer public performances during the summer out on the parade grounds. All in all the state has taken pretty good care of the place."

"That's great," said Diana. "What do you know of the history of the fort? I understand that it was considered a strategic location during its time."

"You bet it was a strategic location," said Ned. "It made up part of the coastal defense system which was known as The Devil's Triangle. Any enemy ship that tried to sail within range was going to pay hell! In 1896, Secretary of War, William C. Endicott, proposed three forts. These would guard the mouth of the Puget Sound and give protection to Puget Sound Navel Shipyard, which had just opened in Bremerton. Secretary of War Endicott apparently saw that the fifty-year-old forts located in Steilacoom, Bellingham, and Port Townsend were totally inadequate for the defense of the new navy yard.

"The new forts would be Fort Worden, located in the northeast corner of the Olympic Peninsula just outside of Port Townsend, Fort Casey, which was on the western shore of Whidbey Island, and Fort Flagler on Indian

Island. With the construction of these three forts the Puget Sound effectively became impenetrable.

"Endicott had a revolutionary plan to build camouflaged forts of reinforced concrete. These forts would be fitted out with rifled cannons mounted on disappearing carriages. They would rise up to fire and then the carriages would drop back down to ground level. If you were out at sea you couldn't see them. They just seemed to disappear.

"The biggest guns were at Fort Worden. These were massive fourteen-inch guns. They had a range of twenty-two miles! That's almost the same range as the sixteen-inch guns on the Battleship Missouri. The other forts were fitted out with six-inch and five-inch guns. These had an eight-mile range. As I said some of the five inch are still on display at Fort Flagler."

As Ned talked Diana listened and took pictures. He told her all about the efforts of the Naval Coast Artillery Historic Society to try and purchase two of the fourteen-inch disappearing type guns from a salvage yard up in Canada. The salvage company had purchased the guns as scrap from the US government at an auction out on the east coast. It would cost two hundred thousand dollars, they estimated, to buy the guns and have them shipped out to the west coast, but the cost would be well worth it. They were raising donations towards the purchase of these guns and once they had the money they were sure that the scrap yard would sell. It was just a matter of time.

Forty-five minutes and three rolls of film later Diana had all the information she would need to write a first class piece about the old forts. Ned had told her everything she needed to know and then some. She shut off the cassette and loaded up her camera equipment. "Thanks for your time," she told Ned. "You certainly have been a lot of help to me. I really appreciate this."

"No problem," he said. "It was a pleasure talking to you. And as I said before a little free advertising never hurt anything."

Diana dug her wallet out of her purse. She paid for her coffee and then she handed Ned a fifty-dollar bill. "Here," she said. "Let me make a little donation to the historical society."

Ned accepted the bill. "Thank you!" he said as he placed it carefully in a cigar box that sat beside the cash register. "I'll just write you out a receipt for that. That's deductible, you know, since we're a nonprofit origination."

Diana took the receipt and stuffed it in her purse. She thanked Ned once more on her way out of the cafe.

Once she was back in her car she changed lenses and reloaded the camera. This time she set up with slower film. It was still early and a light haze hung in the morning air. With camera in hand she got back out of the car and walked the three blocks that made up the town of Nordland. She took pictures the whole way. The little town was so photogenic. On her way back she got some really good shots of the outside of the cafe. This was going to be a super article. It was a pure stroke of luck that she had found out about Ned Olsen. He was a going to add quite a bit of human interest to the story.

When she was out of film she got back into the car and headed for the fort. The haze was just starting to lift and it was promising to be just one of those beautiful late autumn days!

The town of Nordland is less than two miles from Fort Flagler. The road runs through woods and comes out on the shores of Indian Bay. It runs parallel with the bay and then breaks back into the woods for a bit. There's a small bog, Marrow Stone Bog, on the backside of Fort Flagler and the road skirts it before it comes to the old main gate. Insects buzzed heavily over the stagnant waters of the bog.

Diana drove slowly through the old main gate. There was a guard station and a stone fence that ran off into the distance. She stopped the car and got out to take some pictures of the guard shack and the fence. She took several shots from different angles. She used various cameras and lenses from her bag. She was hoping to achieve the mood of the scene.

A mosquito hummed noisily around her head. She absently swatted at it. The bug was persistent. It eventually landed on her right cheek and bit her. She felt the sting of the bite and slapped at it. "Ouch, what was that?" she asked as she brought her hand down from her face. She looked at her fingers and saw a smear of blood. "God," she said. "That bug must have been as big as a Boeing 747."

She pulled a tissue from her bag and wiped at the spot on her fingers. She touched it experimentally to her face and it came away bloody. She felt a lump that was rising quickly at the location of the bite. "That's going to be huge," she said out loud. "I bet it's going to itch for a week." She scratched tentatively at the spot. It hurt!

She loaded her camera equipment back into the car. All the time she dabbed at the bite on her face. By the time she had reloaded all her equipment the bite had quit bleeding. She started the car and drove into the fort.

What was left of the old coast artillery station was a group of elderly houses that once had been occupied by the officers of the base. This surrounded a mess hall, and a rec hall. There were two, three-story barracks buildings that were located off to one side of the parade field away from the officer's housing. The bunkers and the gun emplacements were a thousand yards farther down the road and right on the beach.

Diana took pictures as she walked around the parade field and in between the old buildings. Several of the houses were open and she went in and looked around. The commanding officer's home was one of these and she took an impromptu tour. When she came out, the morning was still crisp with a promise of sun and warmer temperatures later. Diana headed down the dirt road that led to the gun emplacements. She was hoping that the haze would lift just a little bit by the time she got there. If it did, the pictures of the bunkers and the guns in the morning mist would be spectral. That is, if the weather cooperated, if the light was right, or if it just didn't decide to cloud up all of a sudden and start to rain. If it did just what she wanted it to, you would be able to step right into any one of these photographs!

She walked down the road that ran past the gun emplacements. Once she reached the end of the road she figured she would turn around and come back along the beach. She scratched at the bite on her face once in a while. It itched. As she walked she looked off into the woods on the side of the road and saw that the mist was coming from a bog off in the distance.

She stopped at the first bunker she came to. The building was set into the ground on the side facing the road. The seaside followed the contour of the land and stuck about twenty feet up in the air. One of the old six-inch guns was still in its mount. She took pictures of the gun. Standing on the top of the bunker you could see all the way to the San Juan Islands. The view was exquisite.

She positioned the camera so it looked out over the gun. She placed the islands in the background. The haze was burning off slowly. As she set up the camera she scratched at the bite on her face. There was a leisurely buzzing in the air. It was the murmur of waking insects. She swatted at the bugs as they hovered around her head. They paid no attention to her waving hands. She paid no attention to the bugs as she continued to set up her different cameras and take pictures.

The sun broke through the haze and heated the surface of the bog. As the air warmed, mosquitoes started to rise from the surface of the water. They rose into the air increasing in numbers until they became a dancing swarm, ever thickening, taking on almost a form until they became a solid mass of buzzing, darting activity. A light wind came up from inland and blew softly across the bog. The swarm moved with the breeze.

Diana unloaded the camera she was using. She had used up another roll of film. This was the fourth roll of thirty-six exposure film she had used. If she kept using it up like this she was going to run out pretty soon. "Better slow down," she said to herself as she snapped the back of the camera shut. She hit the shutter button and the auto-load made a buzzing noise as the film loaded. Once it was done she placed the viewfinder up to her eye and stepped back.

She focused in on the last bunker in the row and filled the whole frame with it. She could see the stairs that wrapped both sides of the old facility. They led up to the gun platform. Through the lens she could plainly see the graffiti that covered the steps and the building. There wasn't a square inch of the concrete structure that had not seen the work of a vandal with a spray can. The words and drawings were applied so heavy that the sheer volume resembled camouflage. There was almost a hypnotic effect in the style and placement of them. Diana became absorbed in her work. Nothing existed but what she could see through the eye of the camera.

The insects came out of the woods from the other side of the road. Like a flock of birds they moved en mass.

Diana had just gone through another roll of film. She hit the rewind button and reached into her camera bag for the next roll. A mosquito landed on her hand and bit her. She swatted it.

Other insects started to hover around her head. She dropped the roll of film and swatted at them. They continued to swarm around her. They landed on her face and bit her. They were becoming so thick. They were in her hair, they were in her nose, and they were in her eyes. She slapped and smashed at the biting bugs, but as she did more kept appearing for the feast. They surrounded her. They covered her back and were biting her through her clothing. The air became black as it filled with the tiny bodies of the biting insects.

Diana screamed and dropped her camera and bag. She waved her arms madly as she slapped at the bugs. She ran and the cloud of mosquitoes surrounding her moved with her. She was covered in thousands of hungry, biting bugs! As she ran for the road her foot hit a tree root. She stumbled and fell.

Later in the day, a park ranger was making his rounds and he found the body. As far as he could tell it was the body of a woman and there was camera equipment strewed all around it. As he looked through the windows of his car he could see that the body was mostly concealed by insects. Others buzzed lazily in the air or were so saturated that they just sat on the ground.

He stayed inside his car and called on the radio for help. The insects swooped and buzzed lazily around. They started to swarm around the car. He wasn't about to get out!

GONE FISHING

The *Mary "B"* was tied at the end of the dock. Walt Taylor trudged down the pier toward it. With every step he took little waving motions ran down its length. He had his duffel bag thrown over his shoulder. The weight was securely strapped on his back. It swung as he walked.

The early morning was cool and a light fog hung in the air. Walt was late and he just knew that Pete was going to be pissed! Pete Banks owned the *Mary "B"* and Walt had signed on to work for him for the whole season. Gone fishing, that's how Walt's time was going to be spent this season. Gone fishing with Pete. Shit, he wished he could have gotten on a better boat this year!

Walt reached the boat and he slung his duffel from his shoulder. He tossed it over the rail. It landed on the rear deck with a thud and he climbed quickly over after it. The engines were already up and running. Exhaust rolled up from the stern and mixed with the early morning fog. As his feet hit the deck he called up to the wheelhouse. "Pete, I'm here. Let's get started!"

Pete Banks stuck his head out the wheelhouse door. "About time you showed up," he said. "You're late, we should have been gone ten minutes ago." Pete slammed the door and Walt went forward to untie the boat.

The *Mary "B"* was a forty-foot Monk. She was built in 1952. Pete Banks had bought her about twenty years ago and he had been fishing her ever since. She was an old boat and she showed it. She always needed plenty of work and it seemed like the deck hand was the one who got to do it.

Pete usually fished for salmon. This year was going to be different, though. The salmon season had been cut short and Pete figured that it just wasn't going to pay. This year he was going to fish Ling Cod. Ling Cod was going to be the ticket. You could get at least two dollars a pound, maybe more if you were lucky.

When Walt returned to the stern to continue untying the lines, Pete once again opened the door of the wheelhouse. He just stood there looking down at Walt. His bulk filled the door. He had a donut in one hand and a cup of steaming coffee in the other. Cigarette smoke rolled out of the open door. Its accrued scent filled the air. Just by looking at Pete Banks you could tell that he definitely wasn't one of the jolly, fat man types. It was obvious, though, that he was one fat son-of-a-bitch and he didn't care who knew it either.

He took a huge bite out of his donut, almost engulfing half of it. Crumbs ringed his mouth and bits of powered sugar rained down onto his shirt. "Where the hell have you been?" he roared. "I've been here all the damned night trying to get this scow ready to go and you just take your own sweet time in getting here." He took a swig from his coffee cup and looked at his watch. "You were supposed to be here at six. It's now ten after!"

Walt had dealt with Pete before and he knew that all of this yelling was mostly spouting off. Pete could actually be all right some of the time. He opened the lower hatch in the deck and tossed his duffel bag down. "I stopped over at the cafe to grab a bite of breakfast before we left. You should have been there, Pete. There was this gal and she was asking Ned all sorts of questions about the old fort."

"I don't give a shit about Ned Olsen or who was asking him what," Pete said. He took another swig from his coffee. "You shouldn't be eating in that greasy spoon anyway. You could catch hepatitis or something. Who knows what he's doing back behind that grill. Now get your ass over to the fuel dock and let's get this show on the road."

Walt climbed off the boat and wandered down the pier to the fuel dock. As he walked he thought that this trip was going to be the same as all the others he had made with Pete Banks, and that was a pain in the butt. Though, he had done it before and he would probably do it again. Pete could be a real prick if you let him, but once you got him figured you could handle it. Besides, when you were out with Pete you ate well and when you cashed one of his checks it never bounced.

Pete maneuvered the boat up to the fuel dock. He came in fast and reversed the engines hard. The bow gently nudged the dock. Walt reached out and grabbed the bow rope just as Pete cut the motors. He pulled on the rope and hauled the boat around so it was lying up against the dock.

Pete opened the door of the wheelhouse and sidestepped out. He climbed down the ladder to the main deck and tossed Walt the stern lines. "Tie her up good," he told Walt. "I don't want her to come loose, you know how she did it that one time and ended up in the middle of the marina."

Walt caught the lines. "No problem," he said as he lashed the lines tight to a cleat on the dock. "How much fuel you want to put in her this time?"

"I'm going to splurge, fill it all the way. She should take about a hundred gallons or so, and don't you dare spill a drop. They'll fine the shit out of me if you spill any fuel oil in the damn water! You know, they watch that shit like a hawk now."

"Don't worry."

Pete eased his legs over the side of the boat. His feet touched the dock and it groaned in protest. "When you're done come on up to the office," he said. "And make it quick," he yelled over his shoulder as he plodded down the dock toward the marina office.

Walt clambered back on board the boat and started hunting up the toolbox. It had the fuel cap wrench in it. He found the wrench and opened up the fuel tanks. Then he climbed back onto the dock and hauled the hose from the fuel pump back on board. Once he had the hose securely in the spout of one of the fuel tanks he climbed back onto the dock and started up the pump. He repeated this same process with the other tank. Each tank took exactly fifty gallons. When he was done he tightened the caps back up on the tanks and tossed the wrench back into the toolbox. He made sure that the pump was turned off and the hose had been hung back up. Then he pulled a pencil and a note pad out of his shirt pocket and wrote down the pump reading. He knew that if he didn't have the pump reading written down Pete would change what the guy in the office said they were and Walt would have to come back down to the dock and verify everything. He stuffed the pad back into his pocket and walked back up the dock to the marina office.

Pete poured a cup of coffee out of the coffee pot in the marina office. "What do mean you want a dollar a dozen for frozen herring!" He dumped three large spoonfuls of sugar into his cup and slowly stirred it. "Why, I ain't never paid more than seventy-five cents a dozen in my life!" He dumped a spoonful of powdered creamer into the super sweet liquid in his cup, which turned it the color of burnt oak.

Bob Zerflu was the dockhand that was working the counter. He fumbled with a handful of pre-tied fishing leaders that Pete had tossed on the counter. "That's what Mr. Dresden says they go for. So, that's what they go for. Why if I made you any special deal Mr. Dresden would kill me."

"That's a bunch of bull," said Pete. "I know for a fact that I could make the run to Tacoma and get the same damn bait for fifty cents a dozen. The only reason I do business at this dump is because it's close."

Bob stuffed the leaders into a bag. "Well," he said, "just how many dozen were you thinking about buying?"

"I ain't talking about a dozen damn herring. I'm talking about a hundred and fifty, maybe two hundred pounds of the stinking things."

Bob closed up the bag and handed it to Pete. "Let me call Mr. Dresden and I'll see if he would maybe do you a favor this time."

Pete picked up the bag. "You just do that," he said.

Walt opened the door and came into the office. "Hey, Pete," he said as the door banged closed, "I got both tanks full. They took a hundred gallons on the button."

Pete folded the top of the bag he was holding. "Did you double check the gallons?"

"Sure enough," Walt said. "I got it written down right here." He handed the piece of paper to Pete with the pump number and the total gallons written on it.

Pete took the paper and looked it over, and then he wadded it up and stuffed it into his pocket. "This better be right," he said. "Get over to the freezer and start loading up bait. I'm going to want two hundred pounds at least."

Bob came back to the counter and hung up the phone. "Pete," he said. "I talked to Mr. Dresden. He told me that if you were still going to buy as much as you said I could let you have it for the same price that they get for it in Tacoma at Narrows Marina. So I called down there and found out that right now they are getting seventy-five cents a dozen. I think that sounds more than fair."

"Fair," said Pete. "Hell, that's robbery!" Pete dug out his wallet and counted out two hundred and twenty-five dollars. "I'll take two hundred pounds of the damned things just so I don't have to load them later. And I'll tell you that they had better have been fresh frozen."

"They're the freshest," said Bob as he took the money from Pete. "Caught and frozen yesterday."

Walt was just pulling a ten-pound case of bait out of the freezer when Pete yelled over at him.

"Get two hundred pounds and not an ounce more," he yelled. "I don't want to give these bastards any more then I have to."

"You got it," Walt said as he grabbed three ten-pound cases and headed out of the office and back down to the boat.

Pete stood and watched as Walt left. When the door slammed he poured himself another cup of coffee from the pot on the counter. He dumped three spoonfuls of sugar into his cup and stirred it slowly. "You know, Bob," he said, "seventy-five cents is still a mighty big rip-off. You just tell Harry Dresden that this is the last time I'm ever going to buy bait here. I've done a lot of business here over the years and this is it. I'm done!"

"I'm sorry you feel that way," said Bob. "If there's anything I can do to keep you as a customer let me know and I'll try my best to make you happy."

"There's not a stinking thing you can do," said Pete. He reached for the container of powdered creamer on the counter. It was empty. "Why, hell, you don't even keep a decent coffee mess." He slammed his cup back down on the counter and stormed out of the office.

Walt had just finished loading the last of the cases of herring into the freezer on the boat when Pete came swaggering down the dock. "Lets get started," he yelled as he climbed on board. "Time's a wasting, and you know that we sure ain't catching any dammed fish sitting here." He worked his way across the deck and crawled up the ladder that leads to the wheelhouse. He threw open the door when he got there and it smashed loudly against the bulkhead.

Walt looked up and winced as the boor banged open. *That fat son-of-a-bitch is going to destroy that damned door one of these days*, he thought. *Then I'm going to have to try and fix the stinking thing*. He went back and finished securing the freezer door and then started in on rigging up some of the fishing gear that they were intending on using for this trip. There were six downrigger-type fishing poles in the gear locker. Pete ordinarily liked to try and run a sane net rather than actually fish for something. The poles hadn't been used in at least a year. Walt hauled them out of the gear locker and laid them out on the back deck.

A high-pitched squealing came from below the deck. It was the starter motors turning over. The engines finally engaged and rattled to life. Pete stuck his huge head out of the wheelhouse door. "Untie it," he yelled at Walt over the noise. "Let's get going! Come on now, put a move on it!"

Walt jumped lightly onto the dock. "OK," he hollered back at Pete over the roar. He disconnected the bowline from its cleat and gave the prow a gentle push away from the dock. Then he walked back aft and undid the line that was tied to the cleat there. Hanging off the back of the boat like an afterthought is a small landing. It sits right at the water line and is called a gut platform. It's used for cleaning fish so you don't get any of the mess inside the boat. Walt stepped onto this dais and gave the boat a strong shove away from the dock. "She's all clear," he yelled back up to Pete as he clamored back over the stern rail.

Pete revved up the engines and dropped them into gear. They pulled smoothly away from the marina and started their southbound trip toward Tacoma. The run would take all day, provided that the weather held. If it got rough it could be midnight before they got in. The weather report had said that today would be clear and mild with highs from sixty-five to seventy, but there was a low pressure zone moving in from off shore that could bring winds with gusts up to thirty miles an hour. That wasn't supposed to happen until later tonight though.

Walt returned to straightening out the fishing poles. Each pole held a thousand-foot spool of clear monofilament fishing line. The line had sat so long that it was rotten. It would have to be replaced. The reels were stiff and in need of lubrication. Several eyes on each of the poles were coming loose and would have to be retied. There was a lot of work before any of the downriggers would be ready to use. Walt sat down and started in.

Pete slammed the door to the wheelhouse open. "Hey, Walt," he yelled, "get me a cup of stinking coffee up here and make it pronto!"

"Sure thing," Walt said as he laid the pole he was working on back down on the deck. "Have it up there for you in just a jiffy."

Pete slammed the door again as he went back inside the wheelhouse.

Walt went down into the galley and started the stove. He filled the coffee pot with water and threw eight spoons of coffee into the basket. Then he set the pot on the stove to perk. While the pot was heating he went over to the gear locker and pulled out a new spool of one hundred and fifty-pound test fishing line. He set it down on the counter and waited for the coffee to finish brewing. When the pot was perking heavily he grabbed a cup from the sink and filled it. He turned the stove down and left the pot to simmer. He picked up his line and the cup and headed back out on deck.

Pete was standing in the door of the wheelhouse when Walt got there. "About time," he said as Walt handed him the cup. He took a sip and made a face. "There ain't no sugar in this shit," he said. "You know I can't drink this stuff without sugar." He opened a drawer and pulled out a handful of sugar packets. He tore three of them open and unceremoniously dumped them into his coffee. When he was done the empty packages went sailing to the floor. "Next time you put some sugar in this shit before you bring it up, you hear?"

"OK," said Walt. He turned and headed back down to complete working on the poles.

The run to Tacoma went as smooth as glass. The weather didn't even think about clouding up until Pete slid the *Mary "B"* up to the dock at Narrows

Marina. Walt had spent the entire trip rebuilding the fishing rods, and when he was done with that he cleaned the whole boat from stem to stern.

Pete wasn't one to keep things neat, let alone tidy. As Pete saw it, his job as owner operator was to run the boat and complain endlessly about stupid pleasure boaters and ignorant tugboat captains.

After Walt had tied up and refueled the boat he went up to the marina and made some phone calls. When he came back Pete was digging through the refrigerator.

"Where the hell did you put the beer? You didn't take it out of the fridge or some dumb-ass thing like that, did you? You know I can't drink it unless it's ice cold."

It's in the back on the bottom shelf," Walt told him. He bent down in front of the fridge and reached around Pete to grab a six-pack out of the back. "Here you go," he said as he set it down on the galley counter.

Pete extracted a bottle from the six-pack and snorted, "Thanks." He opened the bottle and asked, "Anything going on up at the office I should know about?"

"Nothing major," replied Walt as he took a beer. "Just this old guy."

"What old guy?"

"Well I think he was Irish or something. You should have heard his accent. We were up in the office and he got to talking about something that he kept calling a Kelpie."

"What the hell is a Kelpie?" Pete asked as he lifted the bottle to his lips and took a swig.

"Well, from what I understood, it's some kind of a sea monster or something."

"A what?" asked Pete.

"A sea monster," answered Walt. "The old boy was saying that he saw a sea monster! He said it was a certain type of a Kelpie."

"Kelpie?"

"Yeah, a Kelpie is a sea monster. It sometimes appears as a hairy man, but most of the time if you see it, it is in the form of a young horse. He said that when he was growing up he knew of one that lived in a loch near his village. From what he was saying I guess these things can be really dangerous."

"Really dangerous," said Pete. "What are they supposed to do, bore you to death or something like that?"

"No," said Walt. "They take a victim and carry him out to sea where they tear him to pieces and eat him. The old boy said that the only part of the victim that doesn't get devoured is the liver."

"Don't like iron I suppose," said Pete. "What the hell brought up this conversation anyway?"

"I asked the counter man how the Ling Cod fishing was this season and the old boy jumped right into the conversation and said to be careful down by Devil's Head. He said that he had seen one of those Kelpies down there just last week."

"You don't say," said Pete. "What a crock of shit!" He reached for his second bottle of beer and pulled it out of the pack. "What you planning on doing tonight?" he asked as he twisted the cap off the bottle.

"Well, I made a call down to More Books. They've got a copy of a book by Philip K. Dick called *Ubik*. I've been looking for it for quite some time. She said she would hold it for me so I think I'll call a cab and go on down and pick it up."

"Well, don't be out all the damned night," said Pete. "We're leaving at six a.m. sharp, so if you ain't here I'm leaving without you."

"I'll be back in plenty of time," said Walt. He climbed the stairs from the galley to the back. He jumped from the deck down to the dock and headed back up to the marina office. When he got there he called a cab from the pay phone. It took about twenty minutes for it to show up. It stopped right in front of the marina office. The driver sat behind the wheel looking around as Walt came over to the car.

"Where you going?" he asked Walt.

"Walt got in, closed the door and took in his surroundings. It was an almost new car so it hadn't had time to become too torn up. The seats were still intact and there wasn't an over amount of chewing gum stuck to the floor. It would do. "I'm heading over to a place called More Books. It's down on First. Do you know where it is?"

"Yeah, sure. I know how to get there," said the cabby. "I'll have you there in about a half an hour, OK?" He dropped the car into drive and pulled out of the marina parking lot in a cloud of dust and gravel. True to his word the car came to a complete stop at the front door of the bookstore. "That will be ten bucks," he told Walt as the car stopped.

Walt reached into his wallet and handed across a ten dollar bill and two ones for a tip. "Thanks a lot," he told the driver as he got out of the car.

"It was my pleasure," said the cabby as the door slammed shut.

Walt watched as the car took off down the street. A fine mist of oil smoke followed it. What a jerk, he thought. When he went back to the boat he would rather catch a bus then take the chance of having to ride with that guy again. He drove at fifty miles an hour the whole way and tried to get lost at least twice by taking wrong turns. Walt had to set him straight or they would still be driving around Tacoma.

As Walt came into the store a little bell over the door chimed. Mrs. More was sitting at a large ornate desk. She was watching a computer monitor and was in the process of checking over orders that were coming in for a book search. "Can I help you?" she asked as Walt closed the door. She didn't look up from the monitor.

"Yeah, you sure can," he said. "I'm the guy that called about the Philip K Dick book. You were going to hold it for me."

"Just a minute," she said. "I've got it right over here." Mrs. More turned from the computer and pushed her chair out from under the desk. She swung her feet around and reached for the corner with her right hand. She clutched the center of the desk firmly with her left hand and levered herself up. "I put it right over here," she said as she ambled over to the counter.

The book was lying on the far right hand side of the counter on top of a pile of books and magazines. The cellophane over-jacket gleamed in the light. It was a first edition, printed in 1969 and in extra fine condition. The picture of the spray can that was the main feature of the dust jacket, stood up in stark relief beneath the cellophane.

"This is a beautiful book if I say so myself," said Mrs. More as she handed it across the counter to Walt. "A very nice piece for any collector."

Walt took the book and looked it over. Not only was it in admirable condition, but also, it was signed. This was more book than Walt had been looking for, but it would add nicely to his collection. He thumbed through the pages, first running them forward and then running them backward. None of the corners were dog-eared. There was no staining. Even the binding was tight. The only mark in the book had been lightly penciled in by Mrs. More. It was price of one hundred and seventy-five dollars. Walt looked at the price and thought a bit. "One seventy-five is a little bit high, don't you think?" he said. "Would you consider, say, one twenty-five?"

Mrs. More put her hand out and took the book back. She turned and hobbled over to a locked bookcase behind the counter. "One seventy-five is what I want," she said as she unlocked the case and slipped the book inside. "That's more than fair. This happens to be a very rare piece. It was signed by Mr. Dick when he was up at a science fiction convention in Vancouver, Canada. That was in 1970. He was one of the guest speakers at the convention and nobody knew who he was. That was before they made a movie out of Blade Runner you know. After that everybody knew who he was. Well, on a lark, some of the books that he signed during that convention he signed with a full-page inscription. Those are really rare and expensive! This one doesn't have one of the full-page inscriptions, though, but it is signed and dated with a small inscription. Best wishes from Philip K. Dick. So that's why I'm asking one seventy-five."

Walt watched as Mrs. More closed the door to the case and he did some quick calculations. One hundred and seventy five dollars would just about max out his Visa card. So if he couldn't talk her down he could still get it, but if he could talk her down and they could do some dealing that would be better. "I'll give you one fifty."

Mrs. More locked the case. "No," was her answer. "A hundred and seventy-five is what I'm asking." She turned around and that's when she knew she had him.

They continued to discuss the book and haggle over the price. A half hour later Walt walked out of the store a hundred and seventy-five dollars lighter and with the book under his arm. Mrs. More had been hard to bargain with and she had stuck to her price, but he was satisfied. It was more than he had wanted to spend on a book, but it would become the premiere piece of his collection. She was right about that.

It was cold and there was a light drizzle coming down. Bill was starting to get hungry. He could see the sign from The Right Spot restaurant that was two blocks down from the bookstore. He figured he should go in and get something to eat before he went back to the boat. A couple of drinks would be good too! By the time he got there his coat was damp.

He sat down at the counter and looked at the menu. The waitress came over and asked if he wanted coffee. "No, I think I'll have a shot of bourbon though. After that I should be able to make up my mind about what I want to eat." She went to get his drink and he kept looking at the menu. On the table was a display. It read: "PRIME RIB WITH ALL THE FIXINGS $15.95." When the waitress came back with Walt's drink he ordered that.

The food came and it was delicious. There was more than he could eat. He finished his meal and downed his second drink. He paid the waitress and then went into the bar for another drink and to watch the wildlife that was haunting the bar at this time of night.

He sat down and ordered another shot of bourbon. Then he kicked back on his stool to watch the crowd. He sipped his drink and spotted two girls out in the middle of the bar. They were throwing darts. Or at least it appeared that they were throwing darts. He watched them for a while and then came to the conclusion that they weren't out there playing a game of darts as much as they were out there performing. One of the girls would make a throw and then she would giggle. Then the other girl would do the same. The show was repeated over and over. It was as if they were standing there saying, "Look at me, aren't I cute!"

He watched this show through three more drinks and then decided that the girls would be more trouble than they were worth. Besides, he was going to have to get up early tomorrow. He had different fish to catch. He picked up his book and left the bar.

The buses in Tacoma run on the half hour. He waited for about ten minutes before a west end bus came. He climbed aboard and rode back to the marina. When he got there it was just after eleven. There was no sign of Pete.

Walt went below and decided that it was time to go to bed. It would be an early morning tomorrow if he didn't.

Pete didn't come in until one thirty. He had been over to the Sands Tavern and he was smashed. He must have downed at least a case of beer, not counting the empty six-pack that was sitting on the counter in the galley. He slammed stuff around and made a general racket before he went over to his bunk and passed out. Walt woke up and didn't get back to sleep until about three.

Pete was up and ready to go at five thirty sharp. He hollered at Walt, "Time for breakfast! Get up off your dead ass and let's get started. We've got fish to catch!" He hurled open the door to the galley. The shades of dawn poured in. "Get your lazy ass out of the sack," he bellowed.

Walt rolled over and opened one eye. "What time is it?" he asked.

"It's time to eat," Pete roared. "Get up!" He turned the gas on for the stove and started a pan heating up. "How many eggs do you want?" he asked Walt.

Walt opened his eyes the rest of the way. "I don't know," he said. "How about two."

"You'd better eat good this morning," said Pete. "The way I figured it we ain't going to have time for lunch. Hell, if the fishing is good we ain't going to have time for dinner either." He started cracking eggs into the pan. They sizzled as they hit the hot oil. The smells of breakfast filled the galley. He threw another pan on the stove and started dropping link sausages into it to fry. Grease spattered across the counter as they heated up.

They ate and when they were done Pete headed topside and Walt stayed below to clean up the mess. By the time he had the galley back in order Pete had the boat running and the engines were warmed up. Walt went up on deck and untied the lines. It was six thirty by the time they left the dock of the marina.

The boat moved smartly out of the marina. The water was dead calm and reflected the overcast sky. It was starting to look like it was going to rain. White wake curled up from behind the stern of the boat and washed in an unbroken wave against the docks as they left.

Two hours later they had completed the run down to Devil's Head. Walt had kept himself busy during the trip setting up poles and packing coffee up to Pete. The rain hadn't come yet but the sky appeared like it would open up any minute. Dark clouds hung low over the water and a breeze, which had started at dawn, was now blowing at a steady ten knots. Whitecaps slapped against the hull. The boat slowed down to a trolling speed. Pete started to run a circular course that would cover about a mile in circumference.

Once the course had been set Pete slammed open the door to the wheelhouse. "Get them damned lines in the water," he howled at Walt over the wind. "We ain't catching no fish if the damned line is still wound up tight on the reels. Move it!"

Walt moved around the boat, baited up hooks and lowered lines into the water. There were six downrigger setups spread around the boat. Two on the stern and two on each side. The line was running out smoothly from each reel. "How deep?" Walt hollered back up at Pete.

"Let him run out about three hundred feet, but don't let him go over three fifty. There's a cliff out here and I want to try and work the edge of it!"

The five-pound torpedo weights on the end of each line made the reels spin at the speed of light as they plunged toward the bottom. Walt stopped each reel at exactly three hundred feet. The lines played out gracefully behind the boat. They moved slowly along with the line of the beach. Walt checked the drag on each reel and saw to it that they had been set a little toward the heavy side. They were going after big fish and he didn't want the reels to run out too fast after a hit. If the drag was set too loose and a really big fish took the bait you could run all the line out of the reel before you had a chance to bring him in. As the lines cut through the water they made their own wake. Little ripples spread out in a v-shape from behind them.

Pole number two was the first to come to life. The top of the pole dipped suddenly and bent down below the side of the boat. By the time Walt got there it was threatening to touch the water. The line fed off the reel fast. A lot faster than Walt had wanted it to. He grabbed the crank and started reeling it in.

Pete stood at the top of the ladder and started yelling. "Fish on! Fish on! Damn it, move your ass or you're going to lose him!"

Walt was cranking the reel for all he was worth. He could tell this was going to be a really big fish. At least a hundred pounds. He didn't dare try to reset the drag with that big a fish on it or it would snap the line for sure. His only chance was to try and fight him in, so Walt kept cranking in on the reel.

All of a sudden the line went dead slack. Walt finished reeling it in and saw that it had broken off just below the torpedo weight. The leader had done what it was supposed to do. He had lost the hook but he had kept the sinker.

Pete came down the ladder. "What the hell are you doing?" he yelled. "Tie the shit up right next time and you won't lose him. You lose one of them weights and I'm going to take it out of your hide!"

Walt set up another snubber and leader. He baited it with a cut plug herring. "Cryin' out loud, Pete," he said as he was setting up. "I rigged it up. I rigged it up right. He was just a big fish. We'll get him next time." He tossed the weight overboard and sent the line plunging toward the bottom.

"Damn it, just do it better!" Pete stormed down to the galley and got himself another cup of coffee. *That son-of-a-bitch had better not be throwing a bunch of gear away or I'll kill him*, he thought as he threw sugar into his coffee. *I'll take it right out of his hide.*

He came back on deck and Walt was hauling in on number five. As he watched, it did the same thing that number two had done. The line paid out like there was no tomorrow and then just went slack. Before Walt could finish bringing in number five, number four came to life. It did the same thing.

"Haul them in!" yelled Pete. "Check the set up. We shouldn't be losing all these fish. Something's wrong."

Walt reeled in the other lines. He checked them over and everything was perfect. He changed out for fresh bait and sent them back down. Then he rigged up the other lines and sent them back down. For the rest of that pass they didn't have a bite.

Pete was really pissed. They should have had at least two, maybe three hundred pounds of fish on board after that first pass. As he saw it Walt was sloughing off. That lazy son of a bitch wasn't coming out with him the next time. He was sure of that. He would go and find some kid to deck hand for him instead. One that would jump when he said jump. Not that slough-off son of a bitch, though. Never again.

They started to make their second pass along the beach. Pete figured that there had to be some big fish living there. He knew it for sure. He had seen them in action. He wasn't going to lose them this time. "Hey, Walt," he yelled, "go below and get me another cup of mud. Bring up my pack of smokes, too, while you're at it. I'll watch the poles and if one hits he won't get away from me."

Walt abandoned his pole. "Sure," he said as he headed down below. "You're the one paying the bills." He knew what Pete was doing and he didn't like it one bit. He had hired on for this trip to catch fish and that's what he was trying to do. It wasn't his fault that they had lost the first bites they had. He had never seen anything like it, a fish just to haul off and take one line after another, just like that. He knew that once you hooked a big Ling like that you either brought him up or you never saw him again. He just didn't go for another bait. Once hooked they became bait shy. This fish was acting strange. Maybe it wasn't a Ling, but being as deep as they were it had to be a Ling, and a huge one. He was sure of it. Then, on the other hand, the only other game fish that lived that deep was a Cabezon. They could put up one hell of a fight, but they became more bait shy after being hooked then a Ling ever did.

He found a carton of Pall Malls in the cabinet under his bunk, pulled out a pack and stuffed them in his pocket. He went over to the stove and poured a cup of coffee and threw some sugar in it. The sugar foamed as it hit the hot liquid. It was the last of the pot and it smelled burned. It was pretty thick. He set up another pot. Pete would want another cup, that was for sure. Just as he was measuring the grounds into the basket he heard Pete yelling on deck

"Fish on! Fish on! Damn it, Walt, get your ass up here and crank him in!"

Walt set the basket of grounds down on the counter and started for the hatch when there was a crash and a shudder that came from under the stern. It sounded as if something had collided with the bottom of the boat. Maybe they had hit a submerged log or something. Water sloshed through the bilge and quickly ran into the galley. Instantly it rose over the deck plates and Walt was standing in water. The bilge pumps had come on but they couldn't keep up with the volume of water that was gushing into the boat. Walt knew in an instant that they were going down.

He ran for the stairs that led out of the galley as water splashed over his boots. Just as he grabbed the handrail the boat took another jarring blow. He could hear the planks of the hull breaking as the boat heeled over toward the starboard side. The stairs went out from underneath him but he had a firm grip on the handrail. He pulled himself up the handrail with both hands. It seemed like it took forever to reach the hatch. He placed one hand on the hatch and pushed. It was jammed! Water was rising quickly in the galley. Bedding, clothing and assorted garbage swirled in the black eddies created by the incoming water.

Walt rattled the handle on the hatch and pushed with all his might. Nothing happened. He knew that he could drown in here if he didn't get out. There was no other choice; he went down a step. This would give him momentum. He raised his right shoulder and threw himself at the hatch. Wood broke but the hatch didn't give. He kept trying. The water was up to the step he was standing on when the frame finally broke.

He staggered out of the hatch and landed flat on the deck. When he looked up he saw that the transom was cracked all the way to the rails. There were broken poles and gear strewn everywhere. Bait was awash in the water that ran over the deck.

He started looking around on the deck for Pete. He wasn't there. Walt figured maybe he was still up in the wheelhouse. He climbed the ladder to check but Pete wasn't there, either. "Pete," he yelled, "where the hell are you? This ain't no time to be playing any damned games!" There was no answer.

Water was rushing over the transom and the boat was going down. It was obvious to Walt that Pete wasn't on board anymore, so he must have gone into the water. Walt didn't want to get trapped in the wheelhouse of a sinking boat. When a boat went down the suction it created could drag you with it all the way to the bottom and they were over at least four hundred feet of water. He had to get out and clear before that happened. He dashed out the door and flung himself over the side.

The drop wasn't far but it seemed like it took several minutes before he hit water. When he hit he must have gone down four or five feet before he regained his buoyancy and started back up. He came up coughing and sputtering water. The water felt like ice and its temperature wasn't much above that. Forty-degree water could sap the strength right out of you but it still beat the hell out of drowning in a sinking boat.

Walt turned around and found the beach. It looked to be about a quarter of a mile away. He started swimming. Each stroke he took was a labor and the cold sunk clear into the bone. As he swam he kept looking for Pete. He would call every fifth or sixth stroke. There was no answer. A slowly spreading crimson stain darkened the water off to his right but he didn't see it.

He finally reached the beach and crawled out of the water. As he did his hand touched a piece of something that was soft and liver colored. He didn't notice it and pushed it out of the way without seeing it. He turned to look back at the boat. As he watched, the bow rose majestically into the air. It hovered there for a second and dropped abruptly beneath the waves. He yelled some more hoping that Pete had made it to the beach somewhere, but there was still no answer. Only the sounds of the wind and the water met his ears.

Walt looked around at the small section of beach he was on. It was a rock-strewn strip about ten feet wide and three hundred feet long. A steep cliff was at its back. The cliff was fairly sandy and ascended well over a hundred feet. Walt noticed that the high tide mark came up its face at least six feet. He also noticed that the tide was coming in. He studied the cliff and he knew that he could climb it, maybe, but it would be a tough go. He was soaking wet cold and he had just swam a quarter mile. He was beat to death.

He turned to the bank and made ready to begin the climb when it started to rain. Not just rain but a real downpour. The wind picked up all at once and blew so hard that the rain came down horizontally.

Walt turned his head to keep the water out of his eyes and glanced down the beach. There in the water plodding toward him was a figure. "Thank God," he said to himself. "It's Pete, he made it!"

"Hey, Pete," he yelled. "You OK? I thought you'd drowned or something."

The figure didn't answer, it just proceeded toward him.

Walt yelled again. "Hey, Pete!" There was no reply.

Walt stopped yelling and stared at the figure coming toward him. There was something wrong with it. It didn't walk like Pete. Pete shifted his weight from side to side as he walked. This thing kind of fell forward with each step. Like something that lived in the water but could come to the land, but you could tell it didn't come to the land very often.

Walt wiped the rain out of his eyes and stared harder at the thing. It was still plodding its way down the beach toward him. He could definitely tell now that it wasn't Pete. It was too tall, too thin to be Pete.

It stayed at the water's edge and kept coming. It was closer now and Walt thought that it looked like it was covered in seaweed. A man covered in seaweed, but then, no, it wasn't seaweed it was hair. Coarse hair. A hairy man!

The tide was still coming in and Walt was standing in water up to his calves now.

The air shimmered and the man disappeared. In his place was standing the finest horse that Walt had ever seen. It stood and looked at Walt for a minute and then started trotting through the surf toward him. Rainbows of spray danced from its flying feet.

By now Walt knew what it was. It was the Kelpie that the old man had told him about. Walt knew this for certain. He screamed and started to attempt to clamber up the bank.

The horse trotted right up to him and stopped. The air shimmered and once again there stood the hairy man. "I'd ask you out for lunch," it said, "but right now I'm just stuffed." It laughed a little at its own joke. "Maybe later, though, we can go for a swim. I'd like that." With that it turned and dove into the water.

Walt kept trying to climb the cliff. The bank was steep and every time he seemed to be gaining, the ground would slip out from under him and he would slide back toward the beach.

The tide was coming in.

THE BOOK

The bell on the door chimed and the man entered the store. He walked slowly through the store as he inspected the rows upon rows of books that lined the shelves. He was an elderly gentleman, dressed in a dark gray pinstripe suit. It was cut to perfection and fit him with a certain kind of elegance, even though it was twenty years out of style. If he had worn something more current it would have seemed out of place.

He walked with a silver-headed cane and in his left hand he carried a large package. It was wrapped in brown paper.

Mrs. More, the owner of More's Used Books, sat behind the counter at an ornate oak desk. It was well over a hundred years old and had come around the horn. The dark oak finish glowed with age as the light from a computer monitor shined off of it.

She was busy surfing the Internet. Not looking for anything in particular, just killing time. In all actuality she was just plain bored and she was hoping to find someone on the net to talk to. She had just had her seventy-third birthday and lately she had found herself doing this kind of search quite a bit.

When she had first purchased the computer she was a little bit afraid of it. She had no idea what it could do or how to actually use it. Her reason for getting the machine was for use in the store. She could do book searches on it and increase her business. It worked just fine for that. There were thousands and thousands of stores out there. They were all on the net. At the touch of a finger she could find copies of rare and out-of-print books. If she ran the proper kind of search she could locate just about anything. Lately, though, she had found herself spending more and more time in the chat rooms.

The more she used the computer the more she began to understand how it worked, and once she started to learn how it worked she became braver and braver with how she used it. Soon she found herself checking out different web sites and locations. She was cruising the net and there was so much out there, she was just amazed. She was fast becoming a computer junkie.

The gentleman approached the counter and gently set his package down. He fiddled with the paper wrapped around it for a second and then cleared his throat so he could get Mrs. More's attention. "Ahem, a...Mrs. More, if you please, could I have a moment of your time?"

Mrs. More turned in her chair and saw the man standing at the counter. She'd noticed him when he had entered the store but she had been so involved on the Internet and the site that she was on that she had completely forgotten that he was there. "May I help you?" she asked as she made a movement to hoist herself up from her chair.

"Please," he said. "If it's no trouble, I have something I would like to show you." He unwrapped the package and set it on the counter. A large book sat in a clutter of string and brown paper. "I would like you to perform an appraisal on this item if you please."

It was a beautiful book, and had been bound in a rich brown hand-tooled leather. The edges of the pages were done in gold leaf and the cover itself had been inlaid in gold, as well.

Mrs. More hobbled over to the counter and took a look at the book. She had heard about these but she had never seen one. It was a copy of the *Necronomicon*, by Abdul Alhazzed. She gingerly opened the book and found that it was in Latin. It was from a Spanish printer and had been published in 1620.

"This is a very old piece," she said. "It could take some time to do the research to come up with a current value. You would have to leave it for me to do it properly."

"I have nothing but time," the man said as he refolded the paper around the book. "I won't be needing this for a while so I could leave it as long as is necessary."

"Well, in that case," said Mrs. More, "I'll need your name, an address and a phone number where you can be reached." She took a notebook and pen out from under the counter. "For an appraisal I charge a hundred dollars for the first three hours of research with a three hour minimum and twenty dollars an hour for every hour after that."

"That will be fine," said the gentleman.

Mrs. More opened the notebook. "I also require a fifty dollar deposit," she said.

The man nodded his head. "That's reasonable," he said. He reached inside of his jacket and removed an exquisite black eel skin leather wallet. He carefully opened the wallet and extracted a brand new fifty-dollar bill. "This,

I am sure, will do nicely," he said as he handed the bill across to Mrs. More.

Mrs. More set the notebook down on the counter and took the bill. It was new bill, fresh and crisp. She looked it over just to check. You never knew when someone would try to pass a counterfeit bill off on you. Though, usually it was hundreds instead of fifties that they tried to pass. She had seen a lot of fifties in her time and she decided that this one was real. She placed it in the cash register. "Thank you," she said. "Now, let's get your name and number and I can get started."

"Belial, Jonathan Belial," he said.

She wrote down his name, address and telephone number as he gave them to her. As she looked at his name on the page she thought there was something familiar about it. She had seen it or heard it somewhere. "I've heard you name before," she said.

"You may have," he said. "It is a very, very old name."

Mrs. More thought for a moment and then she had it. Even at her age her memory was very sharp. "Now I've got it," she said. "That's the name of a monster or some such thing from the middle ages, isn't it?"

"No, Madam," replied Mr. Belial, "but, you're very close. It happens to be the name of a demon."

"Well, isn't that something. I knew I'd run across that name some place before."

"As I said it is a very old name."

Mrs. More bundled up the book. "I'll just take this over and lock it up in the safe. I'll be right back with your receipt."

She carried the book over to an old Chubb safe that sat off to one side of the store. The safe was even older than her desk. It was built in 1850 and during its time it was the state of the art. Chubb had built the finest safes in the world. As a matter of fact it was still considered a pretty fine strong box.

It sat open, as the door had not been latched for the day. She placed the book gently inside and closed the door. She could hear the lock engage as the door shut. Now that she had completed that she could tend to business and get this man his receipt. She turned to make her way back to the counter and she saw that the man was gone.

"Well, I'm sure I'll be hearing from him," she said to herself. She made out the receipt and placed it in her notebook. "I'll start the research on that book this very evening."

She sat back down at the computer to resume her quest for someone to chat with.

It had been a slow day so by closing time Mrs. More was looking forward to starting her quest with the book. She got up from behind the machine and hobbled over to the door. Once it had been closed and locked she returned to the machine and started hunting.

The first site she accessed was the record of auction from Christie's of New York. She ran the book auction records back for ten years to see if this particular book had ever come up on the auction block, and if it had, what it had sold for. It wasn't there.

Her next task was to run a library search. Every library that was tied into the Web could be accessed. It would just take time. She looked at the clock on the wall of the shop and saw that it was eleven thirty. She had just spent her first three hours on the project. She left the machine to perform its search as she headed for bed. As she entered her room she thought to herself that this project could turn out to be very profitable.

She got up at six the next morning, dressed and crept down the stairs into the shop. She promptly went over to the computer and checked its progress. The program had completed running. She went and made herself a cup of coffee and a piece of toast.

She came out of the back room where the kitchen was, eating her toast. She sat back down at the computer and looked up the answers the program had giver her on the search. What she found amazed her. There were five copies of this particular book in the entire world and she had one of them in her hand!

She found that all of the copies were owned either by museums or universities, and that none of the copies had been on public display in close to a hundred years. They were located at The Widener Library at Harvard, The Bibliotheque National in Paris, The British Museum in London, The University of Buenos Aires and one copy used to belong to The Library of Miskatonic University at Arkham, Massachusetts.

As she read she discovered that the copy that belonged to Miskatonic University had been stolen from the library in 1928. It was believed that the librarian, one Henry Armitahe, was the thief. As she read she found that the book had been bound in a rich Moroccan leather, was printed by Olaus Wormis, and was a Latin version. From what she could find this had to be that book, and it was a major find!

The rest of that day she didn't bother to open the store. She spent all of her time at the keyboard running different reference sources about the book. It was intriguing and at the same time maddening. One thing that she did find, though, was that almost all of the sources called the author, Abdul Alhazzed, mad.

She checked every reference that she came across against the book in front of her. She would open it and analyze the print, noting the fine characteristics of it. She could compare the illumination against other books of its time. She came to the conclusion that this book was extraordinary, that there was nothing to even compare with it. She found that the binding was done in a rare and almost forgotten process. The more she researched, the more she was impressed. This was most likely the finest book she had ever seen.

The more she thumbed through the book the finer it seemed. She had to have it! Every time she touched it, it called out to her in needing want.

Finally after she had spent a full day of searching she came across a reference that the Smithsonian had a standing offer of one million dollars for any copy of the *Necronomicon*. She now had established the value for the book.

The plan hatched in her head. She wanted the book. She would make Mr. Belial an offer, that's what she would do. If she scraped she could come up with maybe one hundred thousand dollars. Experience in the business told her that if she made that kind of offer he would jump at it. Then she could sell the book to the Smithsonian and make a clear nine hundred thousand dollars, and that wasn't a bad days work!

But the more she handled the book, the more she wanted it, and the more she wanted it the more she handled it. As she leafed through the pages she realized that it was written in an odd form of Latin. One that had never been in common usage. She would have to brush up, study her Latin before she would be able to even read more than just bits of it, but that didn't stop her, she knew she wanted this book. She wanted this book!

Now that she had her mind made up and she had decided to purchase the book she thought once more about all the money she could make when she resold it. But then once she had it and it was hers how could she ever part with it?

She just knew that Mr. Belial would accept her offer. Why, he would be stupid not to take an offer like that for this book. He couldn't possibly get what the Smithsonian was offering. Her offer would be the best price that he could get for the book. She would see to that.

The rest of that week she didn't open the store. All of her time was spent in drawing up an appraisal for the book. By the time the assessment was complete it ran for eight pages. All the history she could find was incorporated into the document except for the standing offer from the Smithsonian. By the time she had worked out the final details she had well over sixty hours into it. That would bring a nice piece of change just for the appraisal.

She waited until Friday evening to call Mr. Belial. All day she kept putting it off and putting it off until it was dark. Even after it got dark she didn't want to call him but she knew she had to. For some reason it just didn't feel right to let him come and get the book from her. But then, after all, the book would belong to her after she had made him the offer. She was just sure of it.

She finally pulled together enough courage and made the call. The telephone receiver weighed a ton as she held it in her hand. She dialed the number and the phone seemed to ring forever. Time was standing still. The dead space between rings lasted forever. She was just ready to hang up and try again tomorrow when her call was answered.

Mr. Belial stood in his dining room poised over the telephone. On the fifth ring he picked it up and answered it. "Hello," he said slowly and calmly.

"Hello, this is Agnes More from More Books. May I please speak to Jonathan Belial?"

"This is he speaking. How may I help you this fine evening, Mrs. More?"

"Well, I thought you would like to know that I have finished the appraisal of the book you brought in. You should be very pleased with the outcome. When would you be able to come over and pick it up?"

A smile crossed Jonathan Belial's lips. "How about first thing in the morning?" he asked. "If that would not be too much of an inconvenience."

"Why, that would be fine," answered Mrs. More.

"What time do you open?"

"At nine sharp."

"Excellent, I'll be there then."

Mrs. More hung up the phone. It was as if she were in a daze. She was thinking about the book. How lovely it was going to be to own. She had found out that one of the community colleges offered a class in Latin. She had already signed up for it. That way she would be able to read the whole book once it was hers.

That's when the worry started to set in. The thought alone gnawed at her. That whole night she didn't sleep. It was devastating! What if he didn't want to sell the book?

She got up extremely early the next morning and puttered around the shop until it was time to open. At nine-o-clock sharp she went to the door, opened the blind and turned over the door sign. She was now ready for business.

As soon as she opened she started looking for Mr. Jonathan Belial. There was no sign of him. Maybe, she thought, he would not come for the book today and she would get to keep it over the weekend. The minutes seemed to drag. She thought about the book. What if he showed up and wouldn't sell it? What would she do? She just had to have it! She must have it! The minutes dragged into a quarter hour. The quarter hour dragged its way to the half. There was still no Belial. She waited and worried.

More time passed and she started to think that just maybe he really was not coming. He could have had something come up and so he was not going to pick up the book today after all. That would be just wonderful. Or maybe he had an accident and he would never come to get the book. Then she could hide it away and it would be hers, it would be hers. No one would ever know.

She was indulging in this fantasy when the bell on the door chimed and Mr. Belial walked in. He came straight to the desk. He didn't browse the shop like he did the last time. "Mrs. More," he said. "You called yesterday and told me that you had my appraisal ready. I am here to pick up my book."

"Why, Mr. Belial," she said. "No need to be in such a hurry. I have it right here." She was clutching a bundle of papers in her hand. She handed them across the counter to Jonathan Belial. "Here is the appraisal. Just give me a minute and I will go and get your book." She started to hobble over to the safe and then she stopped. She turned back to Mr. Belial and said, "By the way, you wouldn't be interested in selling, would you?"

Jonathan Belial looked Mrs. Agnes More dead in the eyes. "Only if the price I am offered is right," he said. "Are you by chance making me an offer?"

Mrs. More's eyes lit up and she shuffled back over to the counter. "Well, to be fair and honest about it, this is a very old and rare book, and it is in extremely fine condition. I would be willing to give you, say, thirty thousand dollars for it."

"Oh, Mrs. More," he said. "I couldn't possibly accept that for it. It has been in my family for a very, very long time and it is worth so much more to me. How much do I owe you for your appraisal?"

She picked up the appraisal forms from the counter. "Five hundred and sixty dollars, plus tax," she said. She clutched the appraisal tightly. "I could up my offer to, say, thirty-five thousand."

"No," he said. "May I ask you what the book appraised for?"

Mrs. More set the appraisal forms down on the counter. "You'll have to read the work up for that," she said.

"Well, thank you for your time," said Mr. Belial.

Mrs. More tried the last gambit. "You do know that it may have been stolen from a university library at one time, don't you?"

"Why, yes," said Mr. Belial. "I've known that bit of history for quite a number of years." He reached into his jacket pocket and produced his wallet. He opened it and took out six new one hundred dollar bills. They were sharp and crisp, almost iridescent with their newness. "Keep the change for you trouble," he said. "You've worked for it."

Mrs. More took the money.

"May I have my book now?" he asked.

Mrs. More set the money on the counter. "I'll make you one final offer for that book. I can give you thirty-seven thousand dollars for it! That's as far as I can go."

Mr. Belial stood still for a second as if in thought. "No," he said. "But, thank you very much for so generous an offer. May I have my book now?"

Mrs. More picked the money back up from the counter and hobbled over to the safe. She extracted the book from its depths and returned to the counter. "I could turn you in to the police for possession of stolen property," she said.

Jonathan Belial looked right through her. "You could, but you won't," he said.

Mrs. More set the book down on the counter. "You're right," she said. "I wouldn't." She slid the book across the counter to him. "Really," she asked, "what would you take for it?"

Jonathan Belial scooped the book up with one arm. "Why, Mrs. More," he said, "you would have to sell me your soul." He gathered up the appraisal forms and headed for the door.

Mrs. More watched him as he left. His refusal to sell the book had been devastating. What could she do? This was the thought that had haunted her day and night for a week and now it had come to pass. She sat hunched over the computer keyboard at her desk and cried. She hadn't cried like this since her husband Marl had passed away ten years ago.

After a while she calmed herself down. *It would be no good trying to keep the store open today*, she thought. She just didn't feel much like doing business today. She went over to the door and turned the sign over. The word "CLOSED" blared out into the street. It was like a sentinel that had been stationed to bar the entrance to a tomb. She sat back down at the desk, pulled out the keyboard and before long she was once again cruising the internet. The urge to find someone to talk to was overpowering. She just had to find someone. There had to be somebody out there she could talk to about what had happened. If she just talked about it maybe she could come up with an idea of what she was going to do. She searched and found a chat room. She entered and started checking out the other people that were there.

The first person she made contact with turned out to be someone in Arizona. She chatted with him for at least fifteen minutes before she decided that he wasn't the person she was looking for. She went on and found another, and then another. It kept going on like that, contact after contact until she found Quinn.

Quinn lived in Portland, Oregon. He was nineteen years old and was looking for the same thing that Mrs. More was, a confessor. She told him of the book and her failure to acquire it. He listened and offered some words of consolation. He said that he understood just what she was going through. That he had the same wants and needs, only his were different. He talked of a need. His need was deep, maybe deeper than Mrs. More's. His need was murder. He liked to dispense death.

For some reason Mrs. More wasn't shocked by this. She felt she should have been but she just wasn't. She sat quietly and calmly and read the words on her computer screen.

It seems that Quinn had committed at least three murders. Two of them had been for hire. The first was just for a thrill. For the second he had received a hundred dollars. By the time he was ready for the third his prices had gone up. He charged a thousand dollars for that one and got it. He figured that was a fair price and now he was calling himself a professional.

He told Mrs. More that he was very good at what he did, that he knew this was his calling. His life's work! The thrill, the power. To be able to extinguish a life. That was power! And he loved the money, but it just wasn't enough. He felt there was something missing. Something wasn't there that should have been. He needed more!

That's when the idea struck Mrs. More. She could offer Quinn more, she could hire him. That was it! She would hire him to steal the book, and if Mr. High and Mighty, Jonathan Belial, happened to get in the way, well, so be it. She carefully approached Quinn with her idea. What he was sending her could be just a bunch of bull for all she really knew. She crept around the subject until she felt sure and finally she came out with the question she was dying to ask him. Would he be interested in performing a small job for her?

Quinn's reply was that he would love to perform a small job for her and that he was sure they could come to some kind of arrangement. He would need one hundred dollars in cash sent to a post office box in Portland. Once he received the money he would make the trip to Tacoma and collect another four hundred for his trouble.

When they concluded their agreement she exited the chat room and shut down the program. She went straight to the safe and removed one of the crisp new one hundred bills that Mr. Belial had given her. *What sweet justice,* she thought, *that Mr. Belial's money should be paying for this.* She hurriedly wrote the post office box address on an envelope and stuffed the bill inside. She decided that she would leave the shop and go to the post office and mail the payment now. That way it was sure to get to Portland by the next day.

She went straight to the post office. This was so exciting. She had never done anything like this. Why it was right out of the pages of a book! She was sure that she was in control. Quinn was right, this was power. The book would be hers very soon now. She was so thrilled. She hadn't felt this alive in years. She just knew that hiring Quinn would solve everything!

Quinn went to his post office box the next afternoon. When he went it was always late and he always took care so no one could follow him there. It never paid to let too many people know what you were doing. He drove through cross-town traffic, checking his rear view mirror constantly. He drove around the post office three times before he decided that the coast was clear and he hadn't been followed. He parked the car in a lot and got out.

He walked slowly as he entered the lobby of the post office so as not to call any attention to himself. There were people standing in line mailing things and picking up packages. He finally assured himself that there was no stakeout in the post office watching for him and he went to his box.

He looked around. No one was watching him. He inserted his key and opened the box. It was stuffed full of junk mail. He hadn't checked it for at least a month. He dug through the advertising and came upon Mrs. More's envelope. On his way out of the post office he threw the junk mail into the trash and pocketed the envelope with the money. He knew that there was money in the envelope even though he hadn't opened it yet. He just knew it. When he got back to his car he opened the letter. The new one hundred dollar bill floated out and landed in his lap. Quinn started to laugh. He laughed and laughed. This was going to be a piece of cake. He started the car and headed out of town. He was on the road to Tacoma.

The drive took a little over three hours, and it was a little after eight when he arrived. He pulled off the freeway and stopped at a burger stand to grab a bite to eat. Then he headed for the store. Quinn spent the rest of the night in the car down the street from Mrs. More's bookstore, watching.

Dawn came wet and early and by now he was cold and tired. Nothing had happened at the store over the night so he was satisfied that the place was clean. It wasn't a setup. He closed his eyes and slept a little.

He woke just as the lights in the store came on. Mrs. More was up. He zipped up his flight jacket and pulled his ball cap onto his head. He made sure that the bill was pointing down his neck at just the right angle and then he cinched it into place. He lit up his last cigarette and got out of the car. Now, and only now was he ready.

Quinn walked down the street to the shop. He tried the door. It was locked and the closed sign pointed its accusing finger out at the street. He knocked loudly on the glass of the door. There was no answer. He knocked again. After a few minutes a frail voice issued from within. "It's too early, I'm not open yet. Can't you read the sign? Come back after nine. I'll be open then."

Quinn looked at the sign on the door. It gave the hours of business from nine to six, Monday through Friday and from ten to five on Saturday. He knocked again. The shade lifted a little and an eye peeked out at him. "Didn't you hear me? I'm not open yet!"

"Are you Mrs. More?" Quinn asked in a loud whisper. "If you are I think you want to talk to me. I'm Quinn. Open the door or I'm leaving right now!"

Mrs. More cracked the door open to the stop on the security chain. "Yes, I'm Mrs. More. Just a minute and I'll let you in." She made to close the door and unhook the security chain when Quinn gave a heavy push. The chain snapped and the door sprung open. Mrs. More stepped back just as the door smashed into the wall. Quinn stepped in and closed the door behind him.

"Is there anyone else here?"

"No," said Mrs. More. "Just me and the cat. I live alone, you see."

Quinn glanced quickly around the store just to make sure that there was no one else there. Once he was satisfied he moved over to a rack of comics that was sitting at one end of the counter. He turned his back on Mrs. More and slowly started thumbing through the rack, rotating it as he went.

"Hey, lady, you got any *Spider-Man* in here? I just love reading about the Webhead. He gets into some of the most terrible jams, but you know, he always seems to find a way out of them." He kept turning the rack and found the comic book he was looking for.

Mrs. More glared at him. She was wearing an old blue cotton bathrobe.

She still stood over by the door. "What the hell do you think you're doing, young man! I told you that I'm not open. Get out now before I call the police."

Quinn took a magazine from the rack. He rolled it up and put it into his back pocket. "Lady, we talked earlier. The name's Quinn." He turned and looked at Mrs. More as if he could see right through her. "You said you had a job for me. So here I am."

"You're really the Quinn I talked to on the computer?" asked Mrs. More. "For some reason I thought you would be older."

"Hey," said Quinn, "what you see is what you get." He held his arms out straight at the shoulder and sang softly as he swung in a circle. "Come all without, come all within. You've not seen nothing like the mighty Quinn." He came to rest in the center of the floor and tugged his hat farther down on his head. "Time is money, lady, and money is time. So far this little encounter has cost you five hundred bucks. So if you want to slow down on the negative cash flow why don't you just tell me what it is you want done."

He was really here. Mrs. More realized that he hadn't just taken the hundred dollars she had sent him and done nothing for her. He had actually shown up. For that she would gladly pay him the other four hundred dollars she owed him. It was rare today in the business world to find someone who would show up when they said they would, and even rarer to find someone who would do what they said they would do.

She told him about the book and gave him the address of Mr. Jonathan Belial. She told him everything she knew about Mr. Belial. His height, his weight, and the neighborhood he lived in. When she had finished she said, "I don't want any kind of a trail that will lead back to me. Do you hear? If there is anything, anything at all that ties me in with this, I'll make a point with the police that they know about you."

Quinn shrugged his shoulders and said, "I'm sure you would, lady, but I don't see how a thing like this could go wrong. This old guy, from the way it sounds, will go out like a light. I'll make sure of it!"

"I don't care how you do it, but I must have that book."

"No problem. I'll get you your book. And the beauty of it all is that it's only going to cost you five thousand bucks to have me to do the job."

"Five thousand dollars? Why, that's a lot of money. I thought we had agreed on a thousand."

Quinn sauntered around the store. He picked up a book, thumbed through the pages and tossed it down. "No, lady," he said. "Six thousand dollars is a lot of money. You still owe me. Four hundred for coming up here and another five for taking the deal. A thousand now and the other five on completion." He stopped pawing through the piles of books and looked straight at Mrs. More. "Take it or leave it," he said. "I still get a thousand any way you look at it."

Mrs. More didn't have time to think before she found herself saying, "All right, six thousand dollars it is. But for that I get the book just as soon as possible."

"Sooner, if I can get it for you."

Mrs. More started to move to the back of the store. "Let me get my checkbook and I'll write you a check for it."

Quinn stopped her. "No checks, lady. I deal strictly in cash."

Mrs. More looked confused for a second and then she said, "I don't have that kind of money in the store. I never keep large amounts of cash."

Quinn took a pack of cigarettes from his shirt pocket and tapped it on his palm thoughtfully. He flipped the top of the pack open and withdrew one of the smokes and placed it in the corner of his mouth. "Lady," he said, "I'll be back later. You just have my money ready or you won't be able to imagine what's going to happen." He lit the smoke with a Zippo lighter and stuffed the lighter back into his pants pocket. "Later," he said as he turned and opened the door.

Quinn left the store and headed the long way around the block to his car. He knew you had to be careful in his business. He turned around quickly a couple of times as he walked to see if the old lady was watching. There was no sign of her. After he made the corner he ducked into the first doorway he could find and waited. He pulled back into the shadows and stayed there quietly for several minutes. There was no sign of any pursuit. He knew now that he was in the clear. He pulled his hat further down on his head and started back down the block to his car. As he walked his face broke out into a wide grin.

That was simple, he thought as he walked. *What a piece of cake. This will be some of the easiest money I've ever made.* He started to giggle softly to himself as he stepped off the curb and unlocked his car. He fell onto the front seat in a fit of laughter. He managed to close the door and then he pounded his fists in a rapid tattoo on the dashboard as he laughed.

"What a deal!" he chortled. His ribs were starting to hurt, he had been laughing so hard. "What a stupid old witch. Six thousand bucks just like that! Quinn, man, you're the best. The very best!"

Once he regained control of himself he decided that breakfast would be an excellent idea. He hadn't eaten in at least ten hours. There was a Denny's over next to the interstate. He had seen it on his way into town. He got back on the freeway and drove to the restaurant. Traffic was light and he had no problem getting there.

There weren't a lot of people in the restaurant when he got there. The breakfast rush hadn't really started yet. He sat down in a booth off to the side of the counter. This was so his back wasn't facing the door. He knew that you shouldn't sit with your back to the door. Why, that's how Wild Bill Hickok had got it, and Quinn could learn from history.

The waitress came over to his table. "Coffee this morning?" she asked.

"Sure," said Quinn as he shook a smoke out of his pack.

She poured a serving of steaming black tar into the coffee cup on the table. "Would you like a menu?" she asked.

"Nah," he answered. "I already know what I want. Just bring me a Grand Slam, and make the eggs sunny side up. That's the way I like 'em, sunny side up."

She wrote down the order in her book. "It will be here in a little bit, Hon," she said as she was leaving to take the order to the kitchen.

Quinn sipped his coffee as he watched her walk over to the counter. He set the cup down and took out the *Spider-Man* comic book and started to read it as he waited for his food. By the time his breakfast had arrived he had read most of the magazine.

The waitress set his food down and asked if he wanted anything else. He said no and she left his check on the table. He set down the magazine and ate in silence. When he was finished he started looking through a *Little Nickel Want Ads*. He had picked up the paper from a stand by the door when he came into the restaurant. He was going to need a gun for this job and the Little Nickel was a good place to find one.

He cruised the ads carefully. There were quite a few to look through. Tacoma seemed like a gun kind of town. There was everything from gun shows to shotguns. Quinn read each ad. He finally found one for a twenty-two that looked promising. The ad said that the gun came with an extra clip and a holster, and the asking price was right up his alley. It was two hundred dollars. At this price he could afford to toss the gun after the job and he wasn't out much. There was a pay phone in the foyer of the restaurant where the rack with the *Little Nickel*s was. Quinn went to the phone and called the number in the ad. It was still a little early but he called anyway. "What the hell," he said out loud. "If they want to sell the stinking thing then they had better answer."

The phone rang three times and a groggy voice answered. "Hello?"

Quinn folded the paper and said, "Is this the guy with the twenty-two for sale?"

"Yup. I still have it and I'll tell you up front I want a firm two hundred dollars for it."

Quinn waited for a second for effect and then said, "Well, when can I come over and look at it?"

"Any time will be good, but why don't you let me wake up a bit first."

"How about around ten, would that be OK?"

"Sure, ten would be fine, just fine."

Quinn got the address from the guy and hung up. He figured he still had lots of time to kill before he went and got his money from the old lady. He decided that he could drive by the target's home and look it over. By then the old lady would have his money and he could go and get the gun.

He got back to his car and dug through the glove box until he found a map of Tacoma. He had lots of maps in the glove box. There were maps for every major city on Interstate Five stuffed in that glove box like sardines in a can.

He unfolded the map and looked up the street that the target lived on. It was in the North End of town. Then he looked up the address of the guy with the gun. It turned out he was clear over on the other side. Quinn planned out his route and headed for the target's house.

He drove by the house slowly, but not so slowly as to draw attention, and looked over the house. It was one of those old towering monsters built for a timber baron around the turn of the century. The house sat well back from the road and it had a huge front yard full of rhododendrons. He drove down to the end of the block and found an alley that led behind the house. Down the alley he spotted a garage. It was tucked nicely into a Laurel hedge. The hedge had to be at least fourteen feet tall. He looked for any movement, but there was no sign of life coming from the house. It was dead quiet. The houses on either side of the target's were for sale and they looked empty. This was going to be a perfect set-up!

He stopped in front of the garage and looked it over. As he figured it, he could slip into the yard from between the garage and the hedge, do the job and slip out again totally unobserved. This was really going to be a piece of cake.

He sat and formulated his plan as he looked at the garage. After dark, once he was in the yard, he could creep in through one of the back windows.

If he timed it right the old guy should already be in bed. Old people went to be early. Once he was in the house he would just walk right into the bedroom and stuff the gun in the old boy's ear. That would get his attention. Then he would ask him really nicely where he kept the book that the old lady wanted. If the old fart wouldn't tell him he would get to beat on him a little. Nobody would hear a thing since there was no one else around. A couple of thumps and he was sure that the old man would tell him where everything was in the house.

Once he had his plan he started the car up and drove out of the alley. He drove around for a little while looking the neighborhood over. He needed a good place to dump the gun once the job was done. Only a dumb creep would keep a weapon after a job. It would not be any good if the cops stopped him, say, for some minor reason, and found a murder weapon in his car.

As he drove, he came to a small park down on the waterfront. It was under a bridge. He pulled in. It looked like the kind of spot that only a wino would hang out in after dark. There was trash everywhere. He parked the car and got out. The water was right there at the end of the parking lot. He stood there and looked out into the bay. The water looked mighty deep! This spot would do fine, just fine.

He guessed that the old lady should have his money by now. If she didn't then maybe he would beat a little out of her, too. He got back into the car and headed back to the store.

Mrs. More had been expecting him, so, when he came into the store she handed him a plain envelope. "Here you are," she said.

He opened the envelope, stood right there and counted the money. "Hey, there's only nine hundred bucks in here. Where's the other hundred?"

"I already sent you a hundred. Don't you remember? With the nine hundred that's in the envelope I just gave you that makes an even thousand."

Quinn thought about it for a bit and then said, "OK, lady, I'll buy that. I'll be back later with the book. You better have the rest of my money when I do."

"If you bring me the book you won't have to worry about getting the rest of your money."

Quinn left the store and went to see a man about a gun.

The apartment where the guy with the gun lived was on the second floor. The building was about twenty years old but it looked at least a hundred. Some kids were riding skateboards in the parking lot. They had built a jump out of a half sheet of plywood and some concrete blocks. Each kid took his turn making a run at the ramp and sailing into the air. Each seemed to defy gravity for about six feet before landing. Then it was the next kid's turn. This appeared to be a constant process.

Quinn checked the number of the building. Once he was sure, he parked the car and walked up the flight of stairs to the apartment. He found apartment 14 two doors down from the stairwell. He rang the bell and took his hat off running his hand through his hair. He then put his hat back on and pulled it down so that it covered his eyes.

The man who answered the door didn't look none too awake!

"Hi," said Quinn. "I'm the guy who called about the gun."

The man yawned and scratched his stomach. "Well, I got it right here," he said. He walked into the apartment with Quinn following. He picked the gun up off of a table in the living room and handed it to Quinn. Quinn looked and there was no clip in it.

"I want two hundred dollars for it, firm," he said. "It's a really nice gun and I got two clips and a holster for it. To tell you the truth I didn't even run a full box of shells through it."

Quinn looked the gun over, checked the action and looked down the barrel. "I'll give you a hundred and seventy for it," he said.

The man thought for a second. "I'll tell you what. You give me two hundred bucks and the gun is yours."

Quinn reached for his wallet. "Good enough," he said. "You just sold a gun."

The man took the money and stuffed it into his pocket. He then handed Quinn a shoebox with the rest of the stuff that came with the gun.

Quinn opened the box and looked through it. There were no shells for the gun in it. "You got any shells?" he asked.

"Nope," said the man. "My wife won't let me have them in the house. That's why I'm selling the gun. It ain't no good if you don't have any shells for it. There's a gun store just over on the avenue. You can get some shells for it over there."

Quinn placed the gun into the shoebox. "Thanks," he said as he walked out the door and headed back for the car.

The kids were still rolling the skateboards though the parking lot.

Quinn found the store with no problem. The painted sign in the window read "WELLER'S GUNS, In Business Since 1960."

Weller had been in business in the same location for a long time and he wasn't planning to go anywhere. If he ever did decide to retire, then his son would take over the business for him and the store would go just like it always had. Weller figured that he at least owed that much to his customers.

Weller stood behind the counter and watched the punk kid that had just come into the shop. He was roaming around and Weller didn't like the look of him. He looked like trouble. The kind of trouble that Weller didn't like. The kid was dressed in a pair of old jeans and a dirty Raiders sweatshirt. The cap he wore on his head was turned around backwards and pulled down tight across the bridge of his eyes, the bill pointed sharply down his neck.

Weller'd had it with kids just coming in and wandering around. They tended to drive off paying customers. If this kid wasn't going to get something then he was going to kick him the hell out of the store. "Can I help you with anything?" he asked the kid, none too nicely.

"Sure, Pop," said the kid. "I need four or five boxes of twenty-two shells."

"I ain't your Pop and twenty-twos go for five dollars a box. How many did you say you wanted?"

"Get me four of them. That should do it."

Weller put the shells in a bag and set the bag on the counter. "That will be twenty dollars plus tax so your total comes to twenty-one dollars and seventy cents."

Quinn reached into his pocket and started digging for some money.

Weller really didn't like the way he was doing it, something looked funny. He casually slipped his hand under the counter and rested it gently on the butt of a loaded Smith and Wesson .357 magnum. He kept the gun under the counter in case of emergencies, and the way the kid was acting Weller was sure there was going to be an emergency. The kid was going to try something. *Well, just let him*, Weller thought. It never hurt to be prepared.

The kid had his hand in his pocket. He was rambling around on the counter with the other. Weller wrapped his hand firmly around the gun. *This is it*, he thought. *Come on kid, make your move.*

The chime on the door sounded as it opened and broke the tension. "Hey, Weller," said the man as he entered the store, "my gun come in yet? I been waiting for it for months."

"Why, Jim," said Weller. "I was just going to call you as soon as I was done with this customer. Your gun just came in yesterday and I haven't had the chance to get a hold of you yet. Let me finish up and I'll go and get it for you. Just be a minute."

"That's great," said Jim. "I been waiting for that gun seems like forever."

Weller looked at the punk kid. "Well, kid, you going to buy them shells or not?"

The kid took his hand out of his pocket. He reached for his back pocket and pulled out his wallet. He opened the wallet and took out a hundred dollar bill and laid it on the counter.

Weller rang up the sale and gave the kid back his change. "Pleasure doing business with you," he said. "Come back again."

Quinn grabbed the sack of shells and hurried out of the store. He was so mad he was just steaming. He had just about been ready when that fat jerk had come in and spoiled everything. He just knew that the counter man wouldn't have been any problem. He would have been easy, real easy. All he would have had to do was pull the knife that was in his pocket and stick it right in the guy's fat gut. Wouldn't that have made his day? Then Quinn was going to clean out the till and be gone before anybody was the wiser. But that other jerk had come in and ruined it all.

Quinn pulled the car into an Arco mini-mart, got out of the car and went in. He looked around the store for a minute, before grabbing a couple cases of beer. He paid for the beer and left. When he got back into the car he decided that it would probably be a good idea to go out and shoot the gun someplace. He got back on the freeway and ended up out on the other side of the Narrows Bridge. He pulled onto a promising looking off-ramp and started searching for a good place to shoot.

He was on his fourth beer when he found the gravel pit. It was two, maybe three miles from the freeway and it looked like people had used it for target practice before. There were cans and broken bottles lying around everywhere. A paper target stuck on a stick fluttered in the gentle breeze.

The pit itself was about sixty feet deep and three hundred feet long. Old fir trees surrounded the rim. There was an old dirt road that led down into the bottom of the pit. No one would mind if he shot off a few rounds.

He finished his beer, cracked open a new can and tossed the empty down into the pit. He slammed a fully loaded clip into the gun, loaded the first round and shot at the can. He missed. He spent the rest of the day drinking beer and shooting at cans out in the pit. By late afternoon he was out of beer but that was all right. The gun had started to feel like an extension of his hand. He was good enough to be able to empty a clip into a can just as fast as he could pull the trigger. One thing he had always been able to do was shoot. By now he was sure of the gun.

He tossed the gun onto the front seat of the car and climbed in. He started it up and drove slowly out of the pit. By the time he got back to the freeway it was starting to get dark and he was getting hungry. Once he got something to eat then it would be time to do the job.

By the time Quinn got to the home of the target it was dark. He walked silently down the black alley behind the house. Puddles glistened in the moonlight and bits of mud stuck to his shoes. He had left the car over on the next block and walked so it wouldn't be seen. He slipped between the garage and the hedge and entered the yard behind the house where he stopped to check his gun. He pulled it out of his pocket and thumbed the safety off.

The manicured lawn ran from the hedge to the back of the house. It was so neat and trim it looked like a putting green. Steps ran up from the grass and entered a laundry room that stood off the back of the house. Rhododendrons and azaleas wrapped around the rest of the house in a profuse flowerbed so thick it would take a hedge trimmer to get through. Quinn crouched in the shadows and watched. All the lights were out and there was no sign of movement. When he was sure it was safe he moved across the lawn to the laundry porch.

He climbed the stairs one at a time, stopping between each step. The old boards seemed to settle under his weight and creak with every tread he took. When he reached the top he gently rattled the knob on the back door. It was always better to be able to come through the door than to try and find a window or something. It made less noise that way. The knob turned easily in his hand. It was unlocked and the door swung open without making a sound. He quickly entered the house and closed the door.

He stood in the laundry room and listened. There was low music coming from another room. It sounded odd, like something he had heard before, yet he couldn't place it. As Quinn moved through the kitchen the music got louder.

He stepped from the kitchen into an old style parlor with a fireplace. Pictures hung from a picture rail near the ceiling, and wainscoting ran across the middle of the walls. The close pile wool carpet on the floor was dark red with a flower pattern running through it. A single lamp cast a dim light across the over-stuffed leather chair that faced the fireplace.

An old man was sitting in the chair with his eyes closed listening to the music. Quinn stood in the doorway watching him. This had to be the old guy that the lady wanted taken care of, it just had to be.

Quinn rushed into the room and quickly stuffed the barrel of the pistol into his victim's ear. The old man opened his eyes and started to sit up.

"Take it easy, Pops, or you're going to hear more music than you want to," Quinn said as he shoved him roughly back down into the chair. "Now tell me, where's the book?"

Jonathan Belial sat calmly in his chair. "Why, which book are you talking about? I have many books in this house you know."

Quinn waved the gun threateningly under his nose. "The one the old lady wants, *The Necronomicon* I think is what she called it. Now where is it?"

Jonathan Belial slowly brought his hand up from his lap and pointed at a small table in the corner. "Why, it's on the table right over there. That's where I always keep it, you know. One never knows when a volume such as that may be needed."

Quinn quickly glanced over at the table and spotted an old, large, leather-bound book sitting there. "Thanks, sucker," he said as he pulled the trigger. The gun went off twice. Both shots penetrated deeply into Jonathan Belial's right temple. He slumped forward in his chair and the music seemed to become louder.

Quinn stared at his work and watched as a trickle of blood slowly ran down Jonathan Belial's face. He still had the gun in his hand. He put it back in his pocket as he went over to the table and picked up the book. "Easiest six grand I ever made," he said to himself. He started to laugh. "Easiest six grand I ever made."

"Quinn!" A voice called out over the sound of the music as the volume instantly dropped.

Quinn turned and pulled his gun back out of his pocket. Jonathan Belial was standing next to the chair he had been sitting in. He had a handkerchief out and was dabbing at the blood that was smeared across his face.

"Quinn, or may I call you Quincy? Yes, that's it. Quincy Purcell. We have been watching you. We have been watching you for quite a while now."

"Watching me?" said Quinn. "How the hell could you have been watching me?"

"That's it exactly," said Jonathan Belial. "Hell, I mean. You know you lost your soul quite a while ago, but we felt that maybe with your small talents you could bring some more business our way. And do you know, you did that very nicely, very nicely, indeed, I must say. Though, to try and kill a demon, well, that was a very dumb mistake. If you hadn't tried that, why, there is no telling what havoc and misery you could have caused for us in the next sixty years. But still, it was just a matter of time before someone had to come and collect you. Just a matter of time."

Quinn dropped the book. It landed on the floor with a deafening thud. He raised the pistol and emptied it into Jonathan Belial's chest.

Belial just stood there as the bullets passed easily through him. They made a close group of holes in the wall behind him.

Quinn ejected the spent clip and fished the other one out of his pocket. He rammed it home and started firing.

Jonathan Belial stood there and neatly folded up his pocket-handkerchief. He gently set the blood-soaked cloth down on an end table next to his chair. "I was hoping that I would be the one chosen to come and collect you, and here I am. Now the time has come. Only it's a little earlier than we expected. Well, such is life. It's all a matter of free choice you know. All just a bunch of random connections." He pointed at Quinn. "See you in Hell."

All of a sudden Quinn felt light, almost like he had no weight at all. He tried to fire the gun again but couldn't squeeze the trigger. He looked at his hands and saw the reason. They were becoming transparent. He could see right through them! He could no longer hold onto the gun; it fell right through his hands and hit the floor. He looked down at the gun and saw that his legs had vanished. The last thing Quinn did in this world was scream! It was also the first thing he did when he entered the next.

Mrs. More opened the store the next day. She spent the whole day worrying. It hadn't been so bad in the morning but as afternoon passed into evening her worry became intense. *What if the police had caught Quinn?* she thought. Or, what if he had just taken her money and run off. How was she ever going to get the book if he had stolen her money? She felt ill. Her stomach was all tied up in knots. If only she knew what had happened, she could make her next plan.

She was sitting at her desk when the door chimed and a man entered the store. She looked up and there stood Jonathan Belial. She was terrified, but before she could say anything, he raised his hand and stopped her.

He placed a large package down on the counter. It was wrapped in plain brown paper. "Mrs. More, here is the book. It is yours." He shoved the parcel across the counter. "It seems that you have agreed to meet my price so the book is yours. It has been a pleasure doing business with you. I'll be looking forward to our next meeting." With that he turned and walked out of the store.

Mrs. More picked up the parcel. She looked at it for a while. Then she set it back down and carefully started to unwrap it.

ENDANGERED SPECIES

Jim had ordered the gun from Weller's Guns months ago. It had seemed like it had taken forever to come in, but, it finally had. He had gone down to the store in the morning to pick it up and as soon as he had gotten it back home he took it out of the box to completely inspect it.

As he looked it over, the chrome plating gleamed in the morning light that filtered into the kitchen. It was a fifty-caliber Desert Eagle, and it just happened to be the largest handgun ever made. It had been made in Israel and had gone into production just before the Desert Storm phase of the US-Iraqi war. The fifty caliber shell threw a three hundred grain load that was powerful enough to stop a bear, and that's exactly what Jim intended to do with it.

The gun was almost a foot long and unloaded, without the scope; it weighed all of three pounds. Jim assembled the three-power scope that came with it and mounted it on the shiny chrome surface of the gun. He was very careful not to scratch the finish. When he was done he checked the fit of the gun in the custom-made shoulder holster he had ordered with it. He drew the gun several times and it pulled freely from the holster every time. As a matter of fact it was perfect. Just perfect.

With the gun on he studied himself in the mirror. He finally decided that if he buttoned up his coat you couldn't even see the bulk of the gun that was hanging just below his left arm.

He looked at himself once more in the mirror and knew that the gun was well worth every cent of the twelve hundred dollars it had cost him. Once he got his bear with it though, it would more than have paid for itself.

When he was finished he took the gun into his bedroom and put it back into its case. Once that was done he slipped the case under his bed. That was where he kept all his guns. Then he went back out to the kitchen and called the gun club to make reservations for the rifle range. He set it up for the next morning. Why should he pay some gunsmith to sight in a gun when it was just a matter of setting the wind-age and the elevation? He could do that himself. All you had to do was shoot the gun a few times and see where it was hitting. Then if you took a screwdriver and made the adjustments to the sights it should be right on.

On top of that he enjoyed shooting. There was nothing like the feeling of power a large caliber handgun gave you.

After the phone call he went into the living room and turned on the TV. He sat down just as the national evening news came on, which surprised him. He didn't think it was that late. It had taken a while to put the scope together and mount it on the gun, but he hadn't thought that it would have taken that long. Yet the scope had been a tricky operation to mount and then he had also changed out the handgrips.

When the news was over he got up and went into the kitchen. He opened the fridge and grabbed a beer. He went back to the living room and flopped down in the chair and stared at the news. He took small sips from his beer as he watched. There was nothing on that really caught his interest. The TV droned on and his mind began to wander back to the events of the previous day.

He just couldn't believe his luck, that he had just happened to run into the Russian. The Russian had ended up offering him ten thousand dollars for a Grizzly Bear pelt. Jim had known that there was money to be made from bear hides, but he hadn't realized that there could be that much.

Jim considered himself a professional. He made a good living by poaching wild game and he had never even come close to being caught. In the last year he had made enough off of deer and elk to make a sizable down payment on a ten-acre piece of waterfront out at Glenoma Cove. There was an old falling down homestead on the property that he was living on now, but once he collected from this bear deal he could start fixing up the house.

He had met the Russian in the bar at Crockett's Restaurant. Ben Foremost had been the one to introduce them. Jim had just sat down at the bar when Ben appeared out of nowhere.

"Hey, Jim," he said, as he slapped Jim on the back. "How's it going?" He plopped down on the stool next to Jim spilling a little of the drink he was carrying as he landed. He set what remained of his drink down on the bar and yelled at the girl that was working the bar. "Hey, Brenda, get my buddy here a drink, will you? And make it quick. He looks like he could use one."

Brenda came over to the two of them. She carried a bar towel in one hand and discreetly wiped up the spill on the bar. "What are you having?" she asked as she finished wiping up the spot.

"Oh, let's see," said Jim, "I'll have a double shot of Jim Beam since Ben is buying."

"You want a water back for that?" she asked.

"Nope."

"OK," she said. "I'll be right back," she said as she wandered down to the other end of the bar to get his drink.

Ben called out to her as she left. "Get me another one, too, while you're at it." He picked his drink back up from the bar and drained it. Then he looked back over at Jim. "Now tell me," he said, "how've things been going with you?"

"Not too bad," answered Jim. "Actually, I've been keeping pretty busy."

Brenda came back with the drinks and set them down on the bar. Ben took a ten-dollar bill from his pocket and handed it to her. "Thanks," he said. "Keep an eye on us and when these are gone bring us two more, will you?"

Brenda scooped the money up and started back down the bar. "Sure thing, honey," she said as she went to help another customer.

"Jim, you know," said Ben, "I was just thinking about you."

"How so?" asked Jim.

"Well, with your business and all I might have found a deal for you. I got to talking to this Russian guy I met. His name is Sasha Verakov. Big guy, you know. Lives large. Well, I met him here in the bar a couple of nights ago. We got to talking and it came out in the conversation that he was really interested in acquiring a grizzly bear skin. He wants one to take back home to Moscow or someplace like that so he can have a rug made out of it. Figures his girlfriend would get a big kick out of it. And from what I could gather he's ready and willing to pay big bucks for one if he can get it." Ben picked up his drink and took a sip. "So, I told him that I just might know someone who could help him out." The ice in the glass tinkled as he set his drink back down on the bar. "Are you interested?" he asked.

"Sure, I can get him a bear if he wants one," said Jim. "The price would have to be right, though, you know. A grizzly bear, that's a big risk. Them being on the endangered species list and all. It ain't just like going out and shooting an elk. You got a way of getting a hold of this guy again?"

"He gave me his cell phone number," said Ben. "Told me that I could get a hold of him any time there."

"Good enough," said Jim. "If this works out I'll make sure you get a bunch of bear meat out of it."

"Sounds good to me," said Ben. He got up and drifted over to the pay phone in the corner of the bar. In a few minutes he was sitting back on the stool next to Jim. "It's all set," he said. "He'll be right over. His apartment is only a couple of blocks away."

Jim had finished his first drink and was well into his second by the time the Russian blew into the bar. He was the biggest man Jim had ever seen. He was huge, almost as big as the bear he wanted for himself. He was well over six feet four and had to weigh three-fifty if not more. He had sharp blue eyes and his head and face were covered in a field of thick black hair. He charged straight over to Jim. He looked at Ben then he looked back at Jim. "You are the man that can procure a bear skin for me?" he inquired.

"Yup," said Jim. "I'm the man. That is, for the right price."

"Good," said the Russian. "I am Sasha Verakov, and a pleasure it is to meet you." He stuck out a hand like a sledgehammer.

Jim took his hand and shook with him. "Jim Mayfield," he said. "Now, let's talk business."

The Russian let go of Jim's hand. He had been pumping it like a jack handle. "Good, good," he said. "A delight it is to meet a man who gets right to the heart of the matter. I have ten thousand American dollars for you, if you have for me a hide by the first of June. First of June is when I go back home. Can you do this?"

"No problem," said Jim. "I can easily have one ready to go for you by the first."

"Good," said the Russian. He reached into his coat and pulled out a massive wad of money. He started peeling off one hundred dollar bills and laying them on the bar. When he had twenty of them lying there he picked them up and handed them to Jim. "Here," he said, "is expense money. I give you the rest when you deliver the hide."

Jim took the money and shoved it into his pocket. "Partner," he said, "you've got a deal."

"Then I expect to be soon hearing from you," said the Russian. He stuffed the remainder of the wad back into his pocket. "We have drink now to seal our little bargain!" He slammed both his hands down on the bar with the force of an earthquake. "Hey, lady," he bellowed at Brenda who was down at the other end of the bar. "Bring whiskey over here for me and my new friend."

It took Jim over an hour to be able to get up and out of the bar. The Russian kept insisting on buying him drinks. Every time he would finish one the Russian would order him another. And for every one that Jim had the Russian would drink two.

He would hoist his drink and slap Jim heartily on the back and tell him how wonderful it was to be doing business with a fine young American businessman like him. By the time Jim was able to leave the bar his shoulders were starting to hurt.

He got out to the parking lot, climbed into his truck and drove straight to Weller's Gun Shop. He figured it would be a good idea to check and see if his gun had come in yet. When he got there old man Weller was working the counter and he looked up the order. He said it would be in first thing tomorrow. It was just a stroke of luck that he had ordered the Desert Eagle when he did. He had seen it in one of his gun magazines and he just knew that it was exactly what he wanted. This was a handgun big enough to hunt a grizzly bear with. When he had ordered it that was his intention, and now, all of a sudden the opportunity had come up. Some times things just worked out like that.

Well, things just kept working and when he got back to the gun store in the morning it had been there ready for pickup. And now it was his.

He went back into the bedroom and took the gun back out from under the bed. He carried it back into the living room and laid it down on the table. The chrome glistened in the light from the TV. He took a sip of his beer and noticed that it had gotten warm. He looked at the clock and realized that he had been sitting in front of the TV for most of the night. It was getting late. Where had the evening gone? He polished off his warm beer and got up. He placed the gun back into its box. It was time to go to bed. He picked up the gun box and headed for the bedroom. Tomorrow was going to be a full day.

Jim got an early start the next morning. He had reserved the shooting range for eight and he wasn't going to be late. He threw a pot of coffee on the stove and went into the bedroom. He pulled the gun case out from underneath his bed. While the coffee was perking he checked the gun over once again. When he was satisfied that everything was in order he strapped on the shoulder holster and grabbed his coat. He carried the gun case into the kitchen and set it on the table. The coffee was ready by then. He poured himself a cup and then he filled a large thermos that he kept under the kitchen sink. He was ready and it was time to go.

He went out to the truck, opened the door, and set the gun case on the seat. He threw the thermos onto the floor and got in. He started the truck and took a sip from his coffee. It was hot and burned the roof of his mouth. He threw the truck in gear and started down the driveway.

Jim's house was a quarter of a mile from the highway. The dirt driveway curved through large cedar and fir trees. Brush and undergrowth fought for any sunlight that was left. The property had been logged at least fifty years ago so the trees were ready to cut again.

The driveway was littered with potholes. In some places the ruts were so deep that you needed four-wheel drive to negotiate them. As he bumped down the road he thought about how nice it would be after he got paid for the bear to bring a bulldozer in and shape up the road. He could put it back to the way it was supposed to be.

He reached the end of the driveway and turned out onto the highway. As he turned he saw that there was an old Toyota pickup parked on the highway. It was just down from his driveway. The back of the truck was half full of bundled-up brush. As he looked he could tell that it was salal. Farther back in the woods he could see a brush picker who was working the property. Florists paid big money for a truckload of salal. It was used in flower arrangements. A good brush picker could make as much as two hundred dollars a load if he could find some place that he could get top quality cuttings. Jim's property was just such a place.

Jim stopped the truck. He opened the case and carefully took out the gun. He loaded a clip into it and then placed the gun into the shoulder holster. He made sure the safety was off and then got out of the truck.

The woods around Jim's house were posted with no trespassing signs. Jim had too much going on to have anybody snooping around his place, let alone a no-good brush-picking bum. He cupped his hands to his mouth and yelled, "Hey, you, in the woods. You're trespassing. Get the hell out of there right now, or I'm going to call the cops!"

A voice came out of the brush. "Don't worry, man. I don't want no problems. I'm coming out."

As Jim watched, a man worked his way out from the undergrowth. He looked to be in his mid to late thirties. He was dirty from head to foot and had a two-day growth of beard. Over his shoulder was a garbage sack full of salal cuttings. When he reached his truck he threw the sack in the back with the rest of the brush. "Hey, man," he said as he walked toward Jim. "What's the problem?"

"Who told you that you could pick brush back there?"

"Why, no one," said the brush picker. "It just looked like a good spot and I didn't think that anybody would mind."

Jim stood there and looked at him for a minute. "Well, it isn't a good spot," he said, "and I do mind who is out routing around in my woods. Can't you read the signs? This is my property and I don't want anybody back in these woods. Now get the hell out!"

"Well, OK, man," said the brush picker. "If that's how you want it then I'll be on my way. I'm really sorry about not asking. I just thought that this would be a good place, you know." He turned and started back toward his truck. " Maybe I could come back later," he said, "if that would be OK with you. I'll come down and…"

Jim pulled the huge gun from inside his coat and pointed it at the brush picker. "There ain't going to be a next time," he said. "Do you understand?"

The brush picker stopped dead in his tracks and stared at the gun in Jim's hand. He had lost his voice and didn't know if he could even move. He just looked at the gun. It was the biggest gun he had ever seen!

"If I see you on my property again you're dead," said Jim. "Do you understand? There ain't going to be no next time!"

The brush picker found his feet and started moving back toward his truck. "Yes," he said. His throat felt as dry as the Columbia Plateau. "You don't have to worry, I won't come back here again. You don't have to worry. I won't come back."

"Now get going," said Jim as he waved the gun at the brush picker.

The man hurried to his truck and got in. He started it up, the starter motor had to turn over several times. It ground slowly, like the battery was getting old, before it caught and started. He shifted into first gear and took off down the road for all the little truck was worth toward the town of Glen Cove. By the time he was out of Jim's sight he must have been doing at least sixty.

Jim pulled into the parking lot of the Peninsula Rifle and Revolver Club just five minutes before his scheduled range time. He would have to have to hurry if he was going to make it on time. The rifle range got so busy at times, that if you missed your schedule they gave your time away. He grabbed his gun case off the seat and rushed to the door. He threw it open and went straight to the check-in desk.

"Hi," he said to the range attendant behind the counter. "I'm Jim Mayfield." He set the gun case down on the counter. "I've got a range time for eight thirty."

The attendant opened up an appointment book and checked Jim's name. "Yup, I've got you right here." He checked Jim off in his book. "That will be seven bucks for the first hour and five bucks for every hour after that. If you run over into the next hour you pay for it in full."

Jim opened his wallet and handed over seven dollars even. "I don't think it will take me that long to sight this in," he said.

The attendant took his money. "You want a receipt for that?" he asked.

"Nope," said Jim.

The attendant looked at the case that Jim had set on the counter. "What're you going to be shooting today?" he asked.

"I just bought a new fifty-caliber Desert Eagle," said Jim as he patted the case. "And I'm hoping to get it sighted in today."

"Wow, I haven't had a chance to shoot one of those yet," said the attendant. "Let me know how it handles when you're done, will you?"

"Sure thing," said Jim.

The attendant went over to a control board and rang open range number three. The door unlocked with a click. "When you're done just press the buzzer inside the door and I'll come and let you out."

Jim picked up the case and entered the door to the range. "Thanks," he said as he closed the door.

Jim walked over to a shooting table that stood in the center of the range, away from the door and set the gun case down. He opened the case and from its foam-filled center he withdrew the gun and shells. He started assembling the gun. The range was a concrete-lined room with a steel shooting pit at the far end. It was about twelve feet wide and fifty yards long. Targets hung in rows over the shooting pit. On the bench were a pile of paper targets and a box of earplugs. A pair of shooting muffs were next to that.

When the gun was assembled he lay it on the table and opened a package of earplugs. He rolled one of the little yellow cylinders of foam rubber between his fingers until it was compressed and elongated. Once he was satisfied with it he packed it tightly into his ear. He did the same with the other earplug. Then he slipped the muffs over his head. Now he was ready to shoot.

He ran the first target out to twenty-five yards. That was a good place to start sighting the gun in. He hefted the pistol. The weight felt good and it rested surprisingly easily in his hand. He brought the scope up and aimed for the target. When the cross-hairs rested on the center of the target he gently squeezed the trigger. The gun jumped in his hand and the noise of the explosion would have been deafening if he had not been wearing earplugs. It echoed through the chamber. He ran the target back and checked where he had hit. The shot had gone just a little high and to the right. He took a screwdriver out of the gun case and adjusted the scope a little bit.

The second shot was a little to the left of center. He had over-adjusted. He took the screwdriver and moved the setting back just a hair. The third round was dead on. He fired the rest of the clip and the gun seemed to be hitting where he wanted it.

He ran the next set of targets out to the full fifty yards. Once they were there he snapped off five quick rounds. The range sounded like a Sunday morning in Gaza. If he hadn't had on the hearing protection he wouldn't have been able to hear anything for at least a month. As he squeezed off each shot he could feel the concussion hammer in his chest all the way to his feet. The concrete walls took the sound and threw it out to the next wall, which threw it back again, until finally the echo died out in a muffled flat peal. Jim's hand tingled and his wrist was becoming sore.

He ran the targets back and looked at how his shots were grouping. They were all on center. That was good enough! He removed his hearing protection and disassembled the gun putting it back into the case. He then rang the buzzer to be let out and looked at his watch. The attendant opened the door to let him out. Jim had been shooting for forty-five minutes. He had been having so much fun that it seemed like a lot less. *This gun was the most fun I have ever had*, he thought. *You could just pull the trigger and blow away an hour without knowing it!* Jim stepped out of the range.

The attendant closed and locked the door. "How'd you like the way it handled?" he asked.

"Like a dream," said Jim. "Just like a dream. It's a little bit heavy and that makes you want to drop the barrel, but once you get used to it then you could hit anything you pointed it at."

"A little bit heavy you say?"

"Yup, but once you find the balance, it's great!"

"How's the kick?" asked the attendant.

"Just like hell," said Jim. "You wouldn't want to run through a whole clip at once. Your hand would be sore for a month. Might need some kind of wrist support if you were going to shoot it a lot."

"Well, I'll have to take a try at one some time."

"Yeah, you should. It's a lot of fun! Could get expensive though. Ammunition ain't cheap. It runs a buck seventy-five a round!"

"Boy, at that price you might want to think about getting a re-loader. If you want I could check into it and see how much I could get you one for."

"That's not a bad idea," said Jim. "Let me think about it and I'll get back to you."

Jim pushed the door open and headed out to the parking lot. "See you later," he said as the door closed.

"See you."

Jim unlocked his truck and climbed, throwing the gun case on the seat. It was still early so he thought he would take a run over to the other side of Hood Canal. Maybe he could get as far as Mount Washington.

Last year the state had released some grizzly bears over there as part of a plan to restock the Olympic National Forest. It amazed him what a group of lobbyists with a lot of money could do. Hell, bears in that part of the country had been killed off at least a hundred years ago because they were dangerous animals. And now the state was being forced to turn them loose again.

The last time Jim had been up to Mount Washington he had seen plenty of bear signs. That was as good a place to start hunting for his bear as any. He might as well try to make some money.

The trip around the canal seemed like it took forever. It was going quickly until he came to Twanoh State Park. That was where a motor home pulled right out in front of him.

It did twenty-five miles an hour on the windy road that skirted Hood Canal. Jim tried to stay calm as he slowly followed the motor home down the snake-like road that followed the beach. There was no room to pass. Eighteen miles later, when the motor home pulled off at Potlatch State Park, Jim was able to put his foot into the truck and try to make up for lost time. He ran the truck up to fifty the rest of the way until he hit the turn-off at Eldon.

Eldon is a small town on the west side of Hood Canal. It is there mostly due to the extensive oyster beds that once lined the beaches. There was a small logging road just the other side of town. Once he was on it he could take it all the way to the base of Mount Washington.

He stopped in town at a Chevron station to gas up the truck. He was at less than half a tank and it really wasn't a wise idea to take off into the woods without a full tank of gas. You never knew what could happen. He pulled into the station and stopped at the pumps. He climbed out of the truck and set up for premium. Gas prices were higher than the space shuttle. It emptied his wallet just to top off the tank. He wasn't any too happy when he paid the attendant and drove off down the road. He found the logging road just as he came out of town and hung a hard left.

The dirt road followed the Hamma Hamma River all the way through to its headwaters at Jefferson Lake. A two-mile stretch of road had even been cut into the side of a sheer thousand-foot gorge that dropped into the river. Jim took the road in a cloud of loose gravel and flying dust. He blew past the Jefferson Lake campsite and finally came to the end of the road.

Old growth fir trees surrounded where Jim had parked his truck. It was national forest and had never been logged. Some of the trees were at least six feet through. They climbed up the side of the mountain until they were lost from sight. Jim shut down the truck and got out. He took the gun case and set up the pistol. There wasn't a soul around. It seemed like he had the entire forest to himself.

He started walking down a path that led toward the mountain. Just a little way up he came to an old fallen tree. It had been there forever. The bark had been gone for years and it was deep red with rot. Brush and smaller trees grew out of its top. Part way down the log it showed signs of having been recently torn up. There were deep scratch marks and rotten wood thrown everywhere. Sure sign of a bear, and from the look of it the bear must have just been there. Jim knew he was close. This was going to be quick and easy.

There was a fowl stench in the air. It floated through the woods but Jim couldn't tell where it came from. It was the worst thing he had ever smelled, like something had died. Maybe it was an old kill. *The bear should be close*, Jim thought, *real close*.

The smell seemed to be coming from the other side of the log. Jim scrambled over it to see if he could find the kill. The bear would be easy to find if he could find the kill. He landed on the other side of the log. Bear sign was everywhere! He had to be close. The whole backside of the log was torn up. Large sections of wood seemed to have been ripped right out of its heart. The brush in all directions had been broken down and trampled flat.

Jim had been right, the strange stench was a lot stronger on this side of the log. It was so strong that Jim could almost taste it. His eyes burned and watered. He moved a little way away from the log but the smell was so bad he couldn't take it any more. Even a bear wouldn't hang around. It was time to look elsewhere. He climbed back over the log and found the start of a trail. If he stayed on it he could go all the way to the top of Mount Washington.

The smell still hung in the air. It wasn't so bad on this side, but it seemed to follow him. He followed the trail and plunged into the forest. The trail would eventually put him upwind of whatever had torn up the log. He could then backtrack. He had his gun out and was ready. He hoped that the animal wasn't what had been making the odor. If it was, it was really sick and wouldn't be worth anything. In fact he would be doing it a favor by putting it out of its misery.

He had been walking for about ten minutes. The smell was still with him. He was ready all the time to shoot at the slightest sound or movement. If it was a bear it could charge him with no warning. He had to be ready. He glanced off to the side of the trail and spotted a patch of reddish brown hair. It was stuck in the brush on the side of the trail. He reached over and pulled the fur out to examine it.

It was coarse and slightly oily. It looked like bear fur but something about it just wasn't quite right. He rolled it between his fingers, feeling the texture. It definitely wasn't right. He raised it to his nose and smelled it. The odor took his breath away. That was it, this was the animal that he had been smelling and it was positively sick. This wasn't worth his time to keep tracking. He dropped the fur back onto the trail and started back for his truck. It was time to try another place that he knew about.

He opened his coat and was just going to put the gun back into its holster when he saw something move in the brush off to his left. He quickly raised the gun and fired twice. The scream that followed was nothing he had ever heard before. It was like something from another world. It pierced his ears and ran down his back all the way to his feet. No animal could make that kind of sound! He just had to see what it was he had shot. He dove into the brush to find it. It wasn't a bear!

Jim came upon the body. It was twenty-five feet off the trail in deep brush. It had died instantly. Jim's first shot had taken it in the right eye. The second shot had hit it clean in the throat. He looked at the body at his feet. It was about eight feet tall. It was covered from head to foot in the reddish brown fur that he had found on the trail and it smelled just awful.

As Jim looked at the body his eyes kept going back to the feet. They were huge. They had to be almost seventeen inches long. Jim stood and stared. He never thought in his wildest dreams that this would happen. Hell, he hadn't even believed in them until now, but now he had to. The evidence lay on the ground before his eyes. He had just killed a Sasquatch!

This was the beast that people had been looking for but could never find. Now, he had one. It could be worth millions! He had to do something and he had to do it right now! He couldn't pack the body out. It weighed too much for him to carry. By the looks of it, it had to be at least eight hundred pounds. He finally decided that it would be best to skin it and at least bring out the hide. He got out his knife and was getting ready to make the first cut when something struck him hard on the back of the head and he fell unconscious across the body in front of him.

Jim regained consciousness with a start. His eyes flew open and he sat up. That was the wrong thing to do. The back of his head felt like it was made of Jell-O. Lights flashed in front of his eyes. He was dizzy and his stomach was full of knots. He lay back against the wall and reached his hand up. There was a huge lump on the back of his head, which when he touched it, was very tender. Lights and colors danced in his eyes so he lay back down on the floor until they passed.

After a bit he started to feel a little better. The flashing in his eyes was almost gone and his stomach had started to calm down. He sat back up slowly. He was still dizzy but it wasn't as bad as it had been. He touched the spot on the back of his head again. The lump seemed like it had grown, but his hand came away clean, no blood. That was good.

There was an ache just behind his right ear. He probed it gingerly with his right index finger. Right behind his ear was a group of closely gathered stitches. He had been sewn up. Evidently he had received a cut and someone had sewn him up!

The last thing he remembered was looking at the body of the Sasquatch. Now he was in some sort of cavern. It was extremely well lit. He looked around and saw that it was enormous. It appeared that the far wall was at least a quarter mile away, maybe farther! The whole place was aglow in a harsh halogen light so bright it almost hurt his eyes. But the strangest thing was the floor. It was covered in neat rows; rows upon rows of plants. All different types and sizes, and all in pots. Every single one of them. They looked like they had been readied to be shipped somewhere.

Jim's hand groped for the holster that should have been under his arm. It was gone and so was his gun. He had a skinning knife that he always carried on his belt. It was gone too, along with his belt. He had no idea what was going on, but it was time to find out. He got up and started moving. Since he had obviously been brought in here there had to be a way out, and any direction was better then just sitting here.

He had taken a dozen steps and stopped suddenly. A soft voice echoed in the middle of his brain. "Good," it said, "you're awake." Jim turned looking for the source of the voice and then it spoke again. "I was worried that I might have hit you a fraction too hard, but now I see that the force of the blow was correct and that you are undamaged."

"What the hell was that?" said Jim.

"Don't be alarmed," said the voice calmly from inside of his head. "I have performed a minor surgery on you. As you have noticed there is a small incision behind your right ear. I was watching when you discovered it. That is where I have inserted a tiny receiver in your skull. It is so we can communicate. Do not attempt to remove it."

"So, that's what I felt behind my ear," said Jim as he reached behind his ear once more.

The voice came creeping softly into his mind. "Yes," it said. "Just a small device so we can talk. In a few days, at most, you won't even know it's there."

"A few days," said Jim. He moved away from the wall. His fists were balled and he took a defensive stance. "Who the hell are you?" he demanded. "Come out and show yourself. I want to see who you are!"

There was no answer. The cave was silent. Nothing echoed through his mind. When it was obvious that there was not going to be an answer to his demand, Jim lowered his fists and started moving again. He headed toward one of the walls that he could see in the distance.

The room was full of nothing but plants and harsh light. It took almost an hour for Jim to negotiate his way to the one wall he could see. The place was a lot bigger than he had thought it was.

When he reached the wall he gathered up several of the containers and dumped the plants randomly on the floor. He stacked the pots against the wall. This would mark his starting point. He decided that he would walk to his right until he came back to the pile of pots. That way he would at least know how big the cavern was.

All of a sudden the voice rose up inside of Jim's head. It was so quick he jumped when he heard it. "You are wasting your time," it said. "For you there is no way out!"

"We'll see about that," yelled Jim. He struck off on his trek and started searching for the way out. There was a way in so there had to be a way out. He followed the gentle contour of the wall. It was smooth and as shiny as polished glass. The wall was like an impenetrable tower that rose one hundred feet over his head. When he looked up he could not see the ceiling because it was awash in light.

He followed the wall for what seemed like miles. He was becoming tired. His head was still sore where he had been hit and the incision behind his ear was throbbing. He sat down and leaned his back against the wall. "I'll just rest for a bit," he mumbled to himself. "Just a bit." So far he hadn't found anything. Absolutely nothing but plants and wall and harsh light. He shut his eyes for just a minute, just a minute of rest. Maybe his head would stop pounding. As he closed his eyes he fell asleep. Sound asleep.

The next thing he knew he was opening his eyes. He had no idea how long he had been asleep. It could have been minutes or it could have been hours. There was no way to tell. He was still leaning against the wall in the immense plant-filled cavern. His neck was stiff and his back hurt from sleeping sitting up. The pain in his head was almost gone though, and that, he felt, was a good sign.

He started to get up when the voice in his head spoke. It was soft and pleasing. "Aha," it said. "You're awake again."

Jim finished standing up while the voice was speaking. "That's good," it said. "That's very good. I was beginning to become lonesome. It is good to see you awake."

Jim hugged himself as tightly into the wall as he could and screamed at the voice. "Who are you?"

"You need to stay calm," it said. "All this anxiety and fear that is in you is not necessary. I will not harm you. You are perfectly safe here. You should soothe yourself and eat a little something. Once you have done that I will be able to answer any of your questions."

Jim looked down at the floor and there sitting next to him was the largest bowl of fruit he had ever seen. It was just overflowing with all different kinds of fruit.

As he looked at the bowl something came over him and he started to feel a little better. This really wasn't so bad. So far nothing at all had happened except for waking up and finding himself here. There had to be a way out and if he was going to find it he had to keep his strength up. And if he was going to keep his strength up he had to eat. As a matter of fact he was feeling a little hungry, so why not eat what was offered.

He reached over to the bowl and withdrew an apple from right on top. It was large and red with a bright shiny skin that glowed with its own radiance. He brought it up to his nose and smelled it. It smelled just like you would imagine an apple would. Rich and deep. He took a small bite. The flavor of an entire Wenatchee apple orchard filled his mouth. A river of juice ran down his chin and splashed on the floor. He had never eaten an apple like this. He devoured it and reached into the bowl for another.

He started eating the second apple. He ate it more slowly than he had eaten the first. The flavor was just as delicious as the first. He savored each bite. The food seemed to help. He was no longer hungry. He eased away from the wall and started moving. Nothing happened. All he could see were rows upon rows of neatly potted plants. "Where am I?" he asked.

Instantly and softly from behind his ear the voice answered. "Why," it said, "you are in the conservatory. Where else would you be?"

Jim jumped at the sound of the voice. He looked all around and he was alone with the plants. He stepped out into one of the rows and placed his hands on his hips in a defiant stance. "All right," he said, "just what the hell is going on here?"

The voice answered at once. "As I said, you are in the conservatory. This is where we..." The voice stopped and corrected itself. "No, I can't say that any more after what happened this morning. This is where I store and sort the vegetation that I am getting readied for shipment."

"Shipment," said Jim with a puzzled tone to his voice.

"Yes," whispered the voice. "Shipment. My mate and I were sent to this outpost a hundred and twenty of your years ago. We were part of a project whose mission was to collect and save the life of this world before its intelligent inhabitants had a chance to completely destroy it.

The family, my family, became concerned at the start of what you called the industrial revolution. So far we have saved thousands upon thousands of life forms on this planet from complete and total extinction. It is our ultimate goal to some day be able to give this gift back to you. Some day when your race is older and wiser. We'll just to have to wait and see what time will bring."

Jim's mind was racing with the possibilities of his situation. He hadn't just shot a Sasquatch. He had made honest to God contact with a living, breathing alien. This could be big. Real big! All he needed was a way out. "I can't even begin to tell you how sorry I am about what happened this morning," he said to the rows and rows of plants. "I feel horrible, just horrible. It was just a dreadful accident. I thought that I was shooting at a bear. If you will just tell me the way out I'll..."

Clearly, from behind his ear the voice interrupted him. "It is understandable that you feel sorrow," it said.

Jim had to think quick before this got out of hand. He had to stay in control so the thing could tell him the way out. "Tell me," he said, "do you have a name? My name is Jim."

"Yes," said the voice. "I have a name. I am called Kasar. Kasar, of the family. Your people though have called me Sasquatch and now I will answer to that." A note of deep sadness came over the voice. "I had a mate. My mate was called Dodne," it said. "Dodne, of the family. And this morning Dodne was killed."

Jim tried to move the conversation away from the killing. "Are there others of your kind here?" he asked.

"Yes," said the voice. It was clearer and stronger. "There are several other outposts spread up and down this coast. We are few in numbers and do not have contact with the other outposts. We tend our stations in mated pairs."

A stench filled the room and two large fur covered hands rested themselves lightly on Jim's shoulders. The shock of the contact glued his feet to the floor. Fear ran down his spine in a wave. Hot breath scorched his neck. "I am Kasar, of the family. For you there is no escape. You are the murderer of my mate Dodne, of the family. Now she is gone, but you are here. We of the family do not live alone!"

MAY ALL YOUR WISHES

Greg nursed the old truck up to the back door of South's Florist Shop. He was so low on gas that the truck was running on fumes. The picking he had done today hadn't gone anywhere near as good as he thought it was going to this morning. That guy with the gun had really screwed things up. All the other places he had checked after that had either been already picked out or there was somebody else working the patch. He had only been able to get one good load of salal. Brush picking was hard work and to get enough of the right stuff for the florists could drive you nuts. He hoped that South was buying brush. If he was lucky and she wanted the load maybe he could get fifty bucks. She had done it before.

He stopped the truck in front of the service door behind the building and got out. He looked at the load in the back of the truck. It looked kind of puny. He wished he had more, but it was getting late in the season and that was all there was. He dug through the pile of brush and fluffed it up a bit so it looked like there was more there. When he had done the best he could he went over to the service door and rang the bell. A couple of minutes went by before a woman's voice came over the intercom that was hung by the bell. "Who is it?"

"Hey, Dakota," Greg yelled at the intercom box. "It's Greg. I've got a load of really nice brush out here for you."

The door slid noisily upwards on its tracks and Dakota South stepped out. She was about thirty-five years old but looked younger. She had a topknot of blond hair that shot off on one side in a ponytail, and she was wearing a red plaid shirt and blue jeans. An old pair of cowboy boots adorned her feet. "Greg," she said, "glad to see you. How you doing?"

"Not too bad," said Greg as he shuffled his feet in the dirt. He stuffed his hands in his pockets. "I've got this extra fine load of salal out here for you. It's real nice stuff and I heard that you were buying. So I figured I would give you first crack at it."

Dakota walked over to the truck and inspected the brush in the back. She pulled out a piece and inspected it for shape and color. She had seen better, but she had also seen worse. Normally she would have given somebody twenty dollars for this load, but she knew that Greg could really use the money.

She had known Greg all her life. They had gone to school together and times hadn't treated him too well. She walked around the load and poked at it. "Well, this is fine salal," she said. "If it's unloaded and all cut to the right length I could give you forty dollars for it. Not a penny more, mind you."

"Forty dollars," said Greg. "This is a fifty dollar load if I ever saw one."

Dakota played the game and poked at the load. "Well, if you would bundle it up once it was cut I could give you forty-five."

"Done," said Greg as he started to unload brush from the back of the truck and carry it into the shop.

He finished quickly and found a broom over in one of the corners of the shop. He started to sweep up the trail of sticks and twigs that had fallen from the armloads of brush. When he was done he hollered up to the front of the store, "Hey, Dakota, I got it all unloaded and cleaned up."

"I'll be with you in a minute," Dakota yelled back. She opened up the till on the cash register and took out two twenties and a five dollar bill. She put the money in her pocket, closed the register up and headed for the back of the shop. Greg was just dumping a dustpan into the trash as she came in.

She went over to the workbench and looked at the pile of brush. The salal had all been piled within easy reach of the sink and counter. The pile was almost four feet wide and three feet high. She gave it a good going over, checking out the quality of the brush. It was in excellent condition. Once it had been washed and cleaned she could get around a hundred dollars for it from the wholesaler. She would have to stay an extra couple of hours tonight to clean it and get it ready for sale in the morning.

When she was totally satisfied with the load she took the money from her pocket. "Thanks," she said as she handed it over to Greg. "That's some really nice stuff. As a matter of fact I was in some need of salal. I got an order I can fill tomorrow."

"If you would be needing some more I can bring it over tomorrow night," Greg offered as he took the money. He folded the bills and held them firmly in his hand.

"No," said Dakota. "I just have the one order. But, I'll tell you what, look me up next week and I might be able to use some more. Check with me first before you go picking though, there might be some other kind of brush I'll need instead."

"Next week," Greg said. He stuffed his hands back into the depths of his pockets. "Next week will be fine. I'll do that." He turned and slowly walked back out to his truck.

Dakota watched him as he shuffled around and a thought hit her. "Hey, Greg," she yelled. "I hear that the cafe is looking for blackberries this week. They're paying seven dollars a gallon."

Greg stopped dead in his tracks. "Seven bucks a gallon for blackberries? It's kind of late in the season for blackberries. You sure they're paying seven bucks?"

"Millie, the waitress over there was telling me that they were almost out and that the owner said that he would pay that for them if he could get them."

"Well thanks for the tip," he said. "I'll just have to check into that." He climbed into his truck and started it up.

He fingered the money in his pocket. It felt good. This was more money than he had seen in a long time, but with this he could make some more.

He knew that it was way late in the season for someone to find berries down here, but he knew of a place, way up by Staircase, where there had been one hell of a fire a while back. Berries loved to grow in places like that, where the forest had been cleared out and being up by the pass they came on later than they did down here. He went to the gas station and filled the truck. It was going to be a long drive, but he was sure it would be worth it. If the berries were there he could get seventy, maybe eighty dollars worth out of one patch.

It took twenty-five dollars to fill the truck. Greg took the twenty-dollar bill that was left and stashed it in the visor of the truck. That way he wouldn't be tempted to spend it before he found out if this berry thing was going to pan out or not. If it didn't he would still have a little something left before he had to start picking brush again. Now, with the truck taken care of he would be ready for an early start in the morning.

He left the station and headed for home. The trailer that he called home sat back off the road behind a homemade gate of one-inch pipe. He opened the gate and drove slowly down the rutted dirt road that was his driveway.

His father had bought the trailer new in 1960. It was top of the line then, but it had seen better days. It would never again grace the highway. Its time had passed. It had sat in the woods forever.

A screen door blocked the entry. The tires had been removed ages ago so now it rested two feet from the ground on concrete blocks. Moss grew in deep profusion from the roof. Several of the windows had been broken out and pieces of plywood covered over where they had been. During one of Greg's productive sprees he had attempted to build a tool shed. It hung haphazardly from one end.

Greg stopped the truck by the front door and got out. He mounted the rotten steps and pulled the screen open. It creaked loudly on its hinges as it swung. The inside of the trailer was in total disarray. Greg shoved a cardboard box out of his way and yanked open a kitchen drawer. "Where's that stinking tide book?" he asked himself. "I know I put it here somewhere." He dug through the contents of various drawers and cupboards until he finally found the book. "Here it is," he said when the errant book was found in a cabinet over the stove.

He thumbed through it until he found the right date and looked up the evening tide. The high had been at two and the low was at six. It was going to be a minus point one. He was in luck. That was a good tide. He wouldn't have to spend any of the money he had stashed in the truck. Tonight it was going to be clams for dinner! Lately it seemed to Greg that he was eating a lot of seafood. But that was OK by him, he liked it. On top of that it was easy for him to get and it was free! All he had to do was go down to the beach. He could dig a bunch of clams or pick up oysters. Sometimes he would even try his luck at catching a fish or two. It was all just there for the taking. As he walked over to the shed he thought about Ivar Haglund, the restaurateur. Ivar used to sing a song on TV about being surrounded by acres of clams. Greg had eaten enough clams to know that Ivar wasn't kidding.

He grabbed his shovel and clam bucket out of the shed and threw them into the back of the truck. He guessed that he would take a run down to Vaughn Bay. It was a lonely stretch of beach and no one would bother him there. It was only a few miles away.

It took him fifteen minutes to get to the beach. He grabbed his stuff out of the back of the truck and made his way down to the beach. He had to climb over some large boulders that supported the roadbed before he was on the beach. Once he was there he wandered around looking for the small holes in the sand that a butter clam made when it poked its neck out. It didn't take him long to find them. He had his limit dug in minutes.

It was time to get back to the truck. He tossed his shovel up to the road and started climbing over the same boulders he had traversed earlier. The bucket of clams was in one hand. He was about halfway up when he stepped on a damp patch of kelp. Instantly he lost his footing. Greg went one way; the bucket with his dinner in it went the other. He landed on his back in the hard gravel of the beach. The bucket crashed down between the boulders spilling clams everywhere.

"Shit!" was all Greg could say as he picked himself and started grubbing between the rocks for his clams. "All that work for nothing."

Some of the clams were lying on top of the rocks, but most of them had fallen down between. He scooped up all the easy ones that he could get and threw them back into the bucket. When he had gotten all of those he started hunting for the others.

There were a bunch of them he could see down in a crevasse between the rocks. He reached down and started picking them up. If he stretched he could grab one at a time and drag it back out. He had just about collected all of them that he could see when his hand brushed against what felt like a bottle. It was just at the tips of his fingers. He stretched as far as he could and was just able to grasp it. He lifted it gently out of the crack between the rocks and looked at it.

"What the hell have I got here?" he asked himself as he turned the bottle over in his hands. He had never seen a bottle that looked like this one. It was old, really old.

It was made out of some kind of black glass. He couldn't see through it. The bottom was round like one of those hand blown bottles from the late eighteenth century. The top was sealed and had been waxed over. The wax had been applied so thick that it ran down the neck of the bottle.

Greg knew that old bottles were worth money. There were a lot of bottle collectors out there. Maybe he could take it down to one of the antique shops and sell it.

He shook it gently as he put it into the bucket and a rattling sound came from within.

He climbed back up the rocks to the road. This time he was very careful about where he stepped. He got up to the road with no mishaps and put the bucket with the clams and the bottle gently in the back of the truck. He had to look around for the shovel. It had landed in a clump of bushes off to the side of the road. He retrieved it, placed it in the back of the truck with the bucket and headed back to the trailer.

Greg started up his barbecue as soon as he got back. He was going to steam open his clams. There was nothing better than fresh butter clams steamed open over a charcoal barbecue. A little melted butter to go with them and you had a styling meal.

He gently dumped the clams and the bottle out of the bucket onto the grass. He got out the garden hose and started to clean them off. By the time the coals died down the clams were clean enough to go on the grill. The bottle was another matter. It had been in the water a long time, a very long time. It was going to take some scrubbing to get it clean. Greg knew that no antique store would even consider taking it the way it was.

He laid the clams out in neat rows on the grill and closed the lid. They would be done in about five minutes, so he had a little time to work on the bottle. He picked it up from the grass and carried it inside the trailer.

He placed the bottle in the kitchen sink, turned the water on warm and started scrubbing it. He used the same scrub pad that he used to do the dishes. As he worked the scum of ages started to come off and the color of the bottle, which was a deep blue, started to shine from underneath it.

He cleaned and scrubbed the bottle all the way to the stopper. He took it out of the sink and dried it off with a hand towel. Something inside made a rattling sound. He shook the bottle gently.

Taking it into what served as a living room, he set it down on the table that was next to his chair. "Can't sell it with crap in it," he said as he sat down in the chair. He took out his pocketknife and picked up the bottle from the table. Placing it between his knees, he started to gingerly cut off the wax that surrounded the stopper. By now he had completely forgotten about his dinner.

The wax was thick and there seemed to be some kind of a stamp that had been pressed into it at one time. There wasn't much left of the stamp and he didn't want to ruin what remained. He cut around the neck of the bottle so as not to destroy any of it.

When he had cut all the wax away from the neck of the bottle he grasped the stopper with his right hand. He still held the bottle firmly with his knees. "Probably just an old hunk of cork or something," he said as he started to gently pull and turn the stopper. It was in tight, but as he worked it he could feel it starting to come loose.

"Come on out of there," he said as the stopper started to move. "That's it, come on."

The stopper came out of the bottle all at once with the force of a rocket and the sound of a large firecracker. Greg had been pulling so hard that he smashed into the back of his chair and it toppled over backwards throwing him to the floor. The bottle flew from between his knees, across the room and smashed into the far wall. It rebounded off the wall and landed in the middle of the carpet, spinning slowly. When it came to rest, a thick cloud of smoke started issuing from its mouth. The smoke filled the room instantly and Greg found himself enveloped in a lavender fog. It burned his eyes and throat.

All of a sudden a voice so loud that Greg thought his eardrums were going to burst, shook through the trailer.

"ALL PRAISE BE TO ALLAH - THE BENEFICENT KING - THE CREATOR OF ALL THE UNIVERSE - LORD OF THE THREE WORLDS - WHO SET UP THE FIRMAMENT WITHOUT PILLARS IN ITS STEAD - AND WHO STRETCHED OUT THE EARTH EVEN AS A BED. AND GRACE, PRAYER, AND BLESSINGS BE UPON OUR LORD MOHAMMED - LORD OF THE APOSTOLIC MEN, AND UPON HIS FAMILY AND COMPANIONS. PRAYER AND BLESSINGS ENDURING AND GRACE WHICH UNTO THE DAY OF DOOM SHALL REMAIN."

The lavender smoke started swirling through the air. As it moved it became thicker and as it became thicker it sank to the floor. It gathered by the bottle and started to take on form.

Greg sat helpless as he crouched and rubbed his eyes. He couldn't believe what he was seeing! The thickening smoke was taking on the shape of a man. A huge man!

He hung motionless a few feet over the living room floor as he took on form and substance. He was all of eight feet tall, and his turbaned head brushed against the tiles of the ceiling. He was dressed straight out of the Arabian Nights from his head all the way to the curled slippers that adorned his feet!

Most of the smoke had now dissipated leaving just a few wisps here and there. Greg was finally able to move and he rolled out of the over-turned chair and got up. He was still rubbing his eyes. The genie, who had just been freed from the bottle, floated in the center of the room and looked over the trailer. The ceiling appeared to grow as he slowly sank to the floor. When he landed his feet were planted wide apart and his arms were clasped firmly behind his back. He looked like a huge version of Yul Brenner straight from a performance of *The King and I*.

Greg knew that this just couldn't be happening. He had fallen asleep in his chair and this was just a bad dream. To prove it, he pinched the back of his left hand. To make sure he pinched hard enough to bruise it. "Ouch."

"Ouch?" said the genie.

Greg took a step backwards and stumbled into the fallen chair. "Who and what in God's name are you?"

"In the name of Allah I am Shahryar of the Djin!" said the genie in a booming voice. "And you little man," said the genie. "You have released me from this accursed bottle that has been my prison these many years." The genie moved his hands from behind his back and placed them on his hips. "The Sultan Zaman entrapped me in that hateful thing over two thousand years ago and I have languished within since then. Now, because of you, I am free! Once again, I am free! But first, little man, before I take my flight, I am honor bound to allow you to request three wishes. These I owe you for your small service."

Greg had read about this kind of thing in fairy tales, but he had never in his wildest dreams thought that it could ever happen. Especially to him. He stood dumbstruck beside the overturned chair.

"Hurry," said the genie. "Your time is short and I have much that I must catch up on!"

Greg was sure now that this wasn't a dream. It was all too real to be a dream. Why, he could still taste the acrid smoke that was lingering in the air. Here he was, standing in the middle of his trailer talking to a real live genie. And to top it all off, this genie had just given him three wishes! "Three wishes?" Greg asked in disbelief.

The genie brought his arms out in front of him and placed them on his hips. "Yes," he said. "That is the customary number of requests granted as a reward. Choose now! I do not have time to play your silly mortal games. I must extract my vengeance on that dog, Zaman. He shall pay for his deeds. I will make him my prisoner. This I shall do before the day is out. Now choose!"

Greg stood and stared at the genie. He scratched his chin and asked, "Could I think about this for a little bit? I mean, nothing like this has ever happened to me before and it's quite a decision to make on the spur of the moment."

"No!" thundered the genie. "Make your choice!"

Greg stood his ground and thought for a second. He knew that the genie wouldn't harm him. Why would he? Greg had let him out of the bottle. This was to be a reward! In all the stories that he had read genies always seemed to twist things around. The master made the wishes and they for some reason came out bad. This wasn't going to happen to Greg.

He knew that he needed money. He needed money badly! He just had to figure out how to wish for it so it didn't come out wrong. All he had to do was wish.

All of a sudden it was easy. Why hadn't he seen this before? This was the easiest wish in the world. Greg took a deep breath and made his wish. "I wish," he said, "for a million dollars, tax free, in small denomination bills.

Right here and right now."

"A million dollars!" said the genie. "Tax free! In small bills! Why that is a silly wish, an ignorant wish. Why, that is a wish that I would not and cannot grant!"

"What do you mean you can't grant that wish?" asked Greg in astonishment.

"Why?" said the genie. "I am giving you these wishes as a reward. I cannot possibly grant a wish that would cause you harm in any way."

"Cause me harm?" asked Greg.

"Yes," said the genie. "Cause you harm. For two thousand years I have been kept a prisoner in that bottle. For two thousand years. But that doesn't mean that I haven't kept abreast of current affairs. If for no reason you were to come into a large amount of money it would draw interest. The police would want to know how you came by it. I can tell that you are not the kind of person that usually has large sums of money lying around. Large sums in this day and age must be earned or they draw the interest of others. And for tax free, there is no such thing. The government always gets their cut, no matter what.

The third part of your wish would be the hardest though. That much money in small bills would never fit in this structure. It is physically impossible!

By the time the day is done you would be arrested and put in jail. This is the harm that would befall you. I cannot allow that to happen!

Now, make your second wish. My time moves swiftly!"

"My second wish?" asked Greg. "You said that you would give me three wishes. You haven't granted my first one yet."

The genie sat on the floor Hindu style and stared at Greg. "You may request three wishes," he said. "I did not say that I would grant them, though. Now it is time for your second. Choose!"

This time Greg had no problems; he came up with the idea for his second wish almost instantly. If he could not wish for money, then how about eternal life? There couldn't be anything harmful about that. He could live forever!

"Genie," Greg said, "I think you are trying to trick me."

"No, master, I would never attempt to trick you," said the genie as he once again floated gently off the floor. "You are capable of supplying enough of your own deception, so what am I to gain by tricking you?"

Greg moved around the fallen chair ignoring the genie's comment. "Genie," he said, "I have my second wish."

"Then request it," said the genie.

"For my second wish," said Greg, "I wish to be able to live in good health forever."

"You wish to live forever?" roared the genie.

"Yes," said Greg. "I wish to live forever. That is my second wish."

The genie started to laugh. "You wish to live forever," he said through peals of laughter. By this time he was laughing so hard that he started to bounce off the floor. He bounced like a rubber ball, ricocheting off the walls, off the ceiling. He finally landed on his feet in the center of the floor.

"You have just wasted your second wish. It was not enough for you to squander your first wish, but, now you have to do the same with your second."

Greg didn't see anything funny about his second wish. As a matter of fact he thought that it was a very good wish. "That's my second wish," said Greg again. "I wish to live forever, in good health!"

The genie stopped laughing and looked at Greg. "You wish to live forever, in good health. Why little man, nothing lives forever! Yet alone in good health," he said. "All things have their set span, a limited time on this world. The only thing that one can do is to live as best as you can and cherish every minute of your life! Why even a djin will grow old and sick and die. For, it is the word of Allah and none can change or alter it. This is a wish that is impossible to grant! Now, make your third and last wish."

"You can't grant my wish?" yelled Greg. "What kind of a scam are you running here? First you tell me that you will allow me to request three wishes, but then you won't grant any of them!" Greg stomped across the room. He was shaking his finger at the genie. "Why, I wish I had never found you!" he yelled.

"That is a wish I may grant," cried the genie. Once again the room filled with dense thick lavender smoke and from the dense fog the genie's voice rang out. "So be it!"

The smoke was so thick that Greg couldn't breathe. He was getting dizzy and the room was starting to spin. He was gasping for air and couldn't seem to get any. He fell to the floor and couldn't move. Then he heard a loud pop and everything went black.

Greg sat in the chair in his living room. He had the bottle he had found on the beach firmly grasped between his knees. By now his dinner was completely forgotten. There was something inside the bottle. He could hear it rattle as he gently worked the stopper out. You just didn't know what you would find in an old bottle, probably nothing, but you never knew. He worked the stopper back and forth until it came out of the neck of the bottle with a loud report.

He dropped the bottle as the stopper flew across the room. It banged into the opposite wall and came to rest in the middle of the room.

Greg picked up the bottle and turned it upside down. He shook it and a tightly bound wad of money fell out into his lap. The money was bound with rubber bands and Greg could tell that it had been in the bottle for a very long time. He carefully removed the rubber bands and counted out the bills. There was exactly one thousand dollars in the roll.

As Greg looked at the money he couldn't help but wonder, who would put a thousand bucks in a bottle and then throw it away. He reached over to the table and pulled a cigarette out of the pack that was lying there. He put the smoke in his mouth and lit it with a paper match. He took a drag off the cigarette. It tasted lousy! He set it down in the ashtray and looked at the money that was lying on the table.

"Free money," he said. "That's what it is. Free money. Somebody threw it away, I found it and now it's mine." He picked up the cigarette and took another drag. It still tasted bad.

An idea started floating around in his head. He set the cigarette back down and said to himself. "A thousand dollars is a lot of money. I could just up and blow it, but then where would I be. Why, no better off then I am right now. But a thousand dollars is a lot of money. If I invested it and played my cards right it could grow. Then maybe I would have a little something for a rainy day."

He picked the cigarette up and took another drag. It tasted worse than lousy. It tasted like crap! He ground it out savagely in the ashtray. "Why the hell am I smoking these things anyway?" he asked himself. "They taste awful and they're bad for my health!" he said. He wadded up the rest of the pack and threw it into the trashcan. "I guess if they don't taste good anymore it's time to quit."

He picked up the money and counted it again. Yes, there was exactly a thousand dollars there. He took the money and hid it back behind an old box of comic books in the closet. It would be safe there until Monday. He had made up his mind. He was going to take this windfall and invest it. That's what he was going to do. He had all weekend to read the papers and do some research on stocks and bonds. When Monday morning came he would go into town and see a stockbroker and invest that thousand dollars. That was what he was going to do.

THE GREEN IN THE FOREST

Dakota finished packing up the car. It was late, two in the morning, but she had wanted to get an early start. It was going to be at least a three-hour drive just to get to the ranger station. The Hoh River Rainforest Visitor Center wasn't close and she wanted to get there by dawn. If she made it that would give her all day to make the first part of the twenty-five mile hike up to the Hoh River Glacier.

She had lived in the state of Washington all her life and had never been to the rainforest. Even though it was only three hours away, this would be her first time. She was happy and excited!

She had read the books about walking into the glacier, so she knew that she could expect to do about twelve miles a day. That meant the pack in and the pack out would take her four full days. It was going to be a wonderful experience.

She had been planning this trip ever since the beginning of August, when her friend Millie and Millie's husband Ron had made the hike in. They had brought back all sorts of pictures. Pictures of the forest, trails and amazing shots of the glacier. The photos were just beautiful! After she had looked at them she had decided that she just had to see it for herself.

It was a pleasant drive all the way to the coast. There was absolutely no traffic at that time of the morning. She made good time, getting into Aberdeen in just over an hour. She stopped into a Denny's for breakfast. You shouldn't start a major hike on an empty stomach. There was a visitor center building in the Denny's parking lot. It wasn't open at this time of the morning, but there were information pamphlets in a rack outside of the door. She grabbed some on the rainforest and took them into the restaurant with her.

She sat down in a booth and started thumbing through the brochures. After a few minutes the waitress came over to her table with a coffee pot and a menu. "Coffee?" she asked.

"Yes, please," answered Dakota.

The waitress turned over one of the cups on the table and filled it with the steaming black brew that Denny's sold as coffee. "Would you care for a menu?"

"No, thank you," said Dakota. "I already know what I want."

The waitress took out her order pad. "And what will it be this morning?" she asked.

"I'll have a Grand Slam with sausage. Make the eggs over easy, and I'll have whole wheat toast with it."

"Will there be anything else?" asked the waitress.

"No, that will be it," said Dakota.

"It will be here in just a bit," said the waitress.

"Thanks," said Dakota as she picked up her cup and took a sip.

"You're very welcome," said the waitress. She took her order pad and headed off toward the kitchen.

Dakota sat in the booth sipping her coffee. She went back to the brochures she had gotten and started looking them over again. She found one that talked just about the Hoh Rainforest. She opened it up and looked it over carefully.

The Hoh is one of the only temperate type rainforests in the world. There are only two others. One is in Chile and the other is in New Zealand. This opening statement of the pamphlet caught her interest. She read further.

As she read she learned facts about the trees and the wildlife that inhabited the rainforest. She already knew that it was called a rainforest because it rained a lot. But she had no idea that it could rain as much as two hundred inches a year. "Two hundred inches a year," she said to herself. "I wonder, how many feet is that?" She figured it out in her head and was amazed when it came out to a little over sixteen feet a year. That was a lot of rain!

She finished reading the pamphlet just as her breakfast came.

The waitress set the plate down on the table and at the same time she noticed the pamphlets in front of Dakota. "Oh, are you planning on going up to the rainforest?" she asked.

"Why, yes," said Dakota. "You know, I've lived here all my life and I've never been. I'm just dying to see it!"

"You'll just love it," said the waitress. "I try to make it up there at least two, maybe three times a year. It's just gorgeous!"

Dakota asked her some questions, mainly about parking and the trail conditions. The waitress was well informed on both. They chatted for a bit more and then the waitress noticed that Dakota's coffee cup was getting low. She snatched the coffee pot from another passing waitress and refilled the cup. "Well, I have to get back to work," she said as she started to leave the table. "Have a nice trip."

"I will," said Dakota. "And thanks for all the information. I really appreciate it."

"No trouble at all," said the waitress. "You come back any time and we'll talk some more."

Dakota ate her breakfast in a hurry and left a five-dollar tip for a three dollar meal. She went up to the cash register and paid her bill. On the way out to the car she remembered that she had to top off her thermos. She had made a pot of coffee before she had left home and had already drunk about half of it on the way to Aberdeen. She picked the thermos bottle up off the front seat and headed back into the restaurant. It didn't take long. It was still dark when she got back into the car and started it up.

She drove up the coast through the towns of Copalis and Moclips. There, the road turned and headed back toward Highway 101. By the time she had gotten as far as Kalaloch the sun had just started to slowly creep over the top of Mount Olympus. She pulled the car off the road and parked on the edge of the cliff overlooking the beach. She drank a cup of coffee and watched daylight break over the Pacific Ocean.

She finished her coffee, screwed the cup back onto the thermos, and then started the car. When she turned the key the radio came on, and it was set to a country-western station. The dynamic voice of Tanya Tucker rolled out of the speakers right in the middle of her song "Fire to Fire." The song finished up just as Dakota pulled back out onto the highway. She hummed a little of "Fire to Fire" to herself as an ad for John's Used Cars in Aberdeen came on. She reached over and turned the dial until she found a news station. She was hoping to get a local weather report.

The station had just started an in-depth report on building codes and how they affect the integrity of modern structures during earthquakes. That was followed up with a sports report and finally the weather.

Dakota listened intently. Joe Markes for KVRO instant weather came on. "Today, the weather on the coast will be warm and sunny. The high will be in the low seventies with a south-southwest wind up to ten miles per hour. We can expect this pleasant pattern all the way through Thursday. That's when a front will be moving in that could give us a fifty-percent chance of rain."

Dakota had been hoping that the weather would be good, but she had packed her rain gear just in case. After all, she lived in Washington. If she got a little wet on the pack back out she could handle it.

She spotted a small sign off to the side of the road. It read "Hoh Rainforest

Visitor Center next right." She slowed the car down as she came to the turnoff.

The two-lane road that led to the visitor center ran for eighteen miles. It followed the Hoh River as it wrapped its way across the Hoh Valley. In the lower reaches, sections of identical trees were interspersed with wide-open clear cuts that were the compliments of the logging industry. Every so often an enormous blackened tree stump would loom up along the side of the road. These were the remnants of huge forest fires that had happened in the Hoh Valley in the past. To Dakota this looked just like any other logged area.

As she crossed the boundary into the federal forest the landscape immediately changed. Giant spruce and hemlock reached two hundred feet into the sky. Vine maples climbed their own branches to create a green maze. Big leaf maples wore their hanging draperies of moss just like a shroud. And the morning sun peered down through the branches to spotlight bits of the forest floor.

The road ended at the parking lot of the visitor center. When Dakota pulled in the lot was almost empty. She found a spot right next to the ranger station and parked the car. She got out and went into the visitor center to sign the hiking book. All hikers who were planning on making extensive trips into the backcountry were required to sign in. This way the rangers could keep track of people who were on extended hikes.

The inside of the visitor center was set up as an exhibit highlighting the different aspects of the forest. Dakota looked at the displays as she made her way to the reception desk. A ranger sat on a stool behind the desk filling out a report. "Good morning," said Dakota as she approached the desk.

The ranger looked up from his paperwork "And how may I help you?" he asked Dakota.

"I'd like to sign in," said Dakota.

The ranger pushed his report off to one side of the desk and replaced it with a large black book. He thumbed through the pages until he came to the last entry and slid the book across the desk to Dakota. "Just sign in here," he said. "Enter today's date, the time, and the number of days you are planning to stay in the park."

Dakota took a pen off the desk. She filled out all the information that the ranger had asked for and slid the book back across the desk. "Here you go," she said.

The ranger took the book and looked it over. "You're planning to go up to the Hoh Glacier by yourself?" he asked. "That's not a very safe thing to do, you know. It's a difficult hike and the forest is no place for someone to be alone."

"Yes, I'm planning on going up by myself," said Dakota. "I've taken many different hikes by myself and I've never run into any trouble. I'm not dumb, though, you know. I've got a can of pepper spray just in case. You know they say this stuff will stop a bear right in its tracks."

"Let's hope you don't have to prove it," said the ranger. "You might consider going in to Glacier Meadows. I've got a tour group going up there tomorrow morning and I'm sure there's room for one more. You can see the Hoh Glacier just fine from there, and that way you wouldn't be out there by yourself. As I've said, it's really not safe."

Dakota looked at the ranger and spotted his nametag. His name was Steve Donner. "Thanks for your concern, Ranger Donner," she said, "but as I told you I enjoy hiking by myself. I like the solitude."

"Well, I can't stop you from going," said the ranger. "But, I will warn you once again to be careful while you're out there. I don't really want to have to come looking for you."

"Don't worry," said Dakota. "I'm always careful."

"Sign out when you get back," said the ranger. "If you don't sign out then they will send out a search team to find you. So make sure that you sign out. If you forget and they send out a search party you will be charged for the search."

"I'll make a point of signing out," said Dakota. She left the desk and headed back out to her car go get her pack.

She got to the car and slipped the key into the lock. The tailgate came open smoothly. She reached in and pulled her pack towards the back. Once she had it resting on the tailgate she started a final inspection of her gear. She had to make sure that nothing had been forgotten. It would be awful if she got out into the forest and found out that she hadn't brought enough film or something like that.

When she was satisfied she had everything, she sat on the lip of the tailgate and slipped her arms into the straps of the heavy backpack. She adjusted the pack carefully on her shoulders and tightened all the straps. Standing up, she leaned forward into the weight of the pack. It sat heavy on her shoulders, but she knew that once she got started she would get used to it. She closed the tailgate and locked the car. Now all was ready.

The trailhead was at the other end of the parking lot. It was clearly marked with a sign right at the head of the trail that said, "ALL HIKERS CHECK IN AT THE RANGER STATION."

"I already did that," said Dakota. She set foot on the trail and plunged into the forest.

Giant sitka spruce and western hemlock made up the start of the trail. This was old growth forest. The trees towered as much as three hundred feet into the morning sky and some were at least twenty feet in circumference. Epiphytes and moss hung down from the canopy of the forest. In places they touched the ground. This gave the forest a kind of spooky jungle appearance. Dakota had traveled just under a quarter mile when she got the idea to turn around and see where she had been. There was no sign of human life anywhere. The visitor center with its parking lot was completely lost from view. The silence was almost oppressive. The only sound she could hear was the noise that her feet made as she walked the trail.

She made good time on her walk and came to Half-Way Camp at around three o-clock. The day was still warm and she was now tired from the walk. She had taken some pictures and had eaten along the way. This was as far as she was going to go today. She shook the pack off her shoulders with a sigh and sat down on the ground. Her neck hurt, her back hurt, and her legs were sore. The worst of all, though, were her feet. They just ached. She sat on the ground and massaged them for a little while.

Half-Way Camp had been set up by the forest service as a designated campsite for hikers. There was a large fire pit surrounded by stones. Several campsites were arranged around the pit. Dakota was the only hiker there. She picked out the best campsite and dug her tent out of her pack. In no time at all she had the tent set up and a small fire going in the fire pit. There was an old hand pump behind the campsites. She worked the pump and filled her coffee pot up with water. "This is it for the night," she said to herself as she set the pot on the fire.

She pawed through her pack again and found the package of freeze-dried spaghetti that would be her dinner. Once the water in the coffee pot was boiling she poured some into the spaghetti container, stirred it and in no time at all her dinner was ready. She sloshed the rest of the hot water into a cup and added some instant coffee. "Dinner is served," she said aloud as she spooned some of the spaghetti into her mouth.

She ate slowly, enjoying the taste of the food and the solitude of the forest around her. When she was done she cleaned up her mess and threw some more wood on the fire. It blazed up joyfully with the addition of new fuel. She sat next to the fire sipping coffee and planning out her next day. She would be at the glacier by noon tomorrow if she started at seven or so.

That would give her half a day and a whole evening to explore and enjoy the glacier. She took a book out of her pack and read for a little while. She was bedded down and sound asleep by eight.

Dakota was up just before dawn. She made a pot of coffee and then combed out her hair and braided it up Indian style. Two long pigtails now hung down over her shoulders. The morning was overcast and cool. It could rain any time. The taste of rain hung thick in the air. When the coffee was done she had a cup and broken camp. She was back on the trail by six.

As she walked she noticed how the forest was starting to change. She was a lot higher up than the visitor center was. The spruce, grand fir and douglas fir had given way to stands of silver fir and Alaskan cedar. The forest thinned until finally the trail broke out into a meadow. Short grass climbed up the side of the mountain like a carpet. She stood for a few minutes and thought about how it would look in the spring with all the meadow flowers in bloom. She would have to come back again just to see it.

As she increased in elevation she noticed ever more changes. The trees became fewer and shorter. Some were misshapen. This was nowhere near like the forest farther down the mountain. When you were this high a tree a hundred years old might only be three or maybe four feet tall. She finally reached the timberline where the trees stopped abruptly and tundra took over. The trail wound through the meadow right up to the base of the glacier. She could see it off in the distance. It would take her at least another hour to reach it.

It was definitely starting to get cold. She stopped, pulled her coat out of her pack and quickly put it on. She continued on and made the base of the glacier in a little under an hour. The sight was impressive. The slow moving river of ice reached up the side of the mountain. From where Dakota stood it looked like the biggest, smashed ice cream sandwich she had ever seen. Huge black rocks protruded here and there through the ice. Large boulders and stones were strewn everywhere. Water ran out of the face in a hundred little rivulets that eventually would merge to become the Hoh River. Dakota crunched across the hard-packed snow and ice marveling at this leisurely crawling beast. She went through several rolls of film.

Retracing her steps, she went back down to the trail. The glacier receded behind her as she headed back to her campsite. She had just reached the timberline when a light rain began to fall. She was glad that she had left when she did. A night in the trees was far better than a night in the open on an ice field.

Movement in the trees caught her eyes. She stopped and watched as a small herd of elk strolled out of the woods. They moved slowly across a patch of grass and back into the trees. Dakota snapped pictures the whole time.

She made camp at the tree line. It was a good place to see the sun rise over the glacier. She got up early the next morning and even though it was still misting she saw a spectacular sight. The morning light had turned the whole glacier a brilliant pink. She sat in awe as she watched the sun rise. After the sun cleared the top of the mountains the glacier turned back to muddy white and it was time to go. She broke camp and headed back down the trail.

By the time she reached Half-Way Camp it was late afternoon. The misty rain that had started earlier in the day had turned into a ceaseless drizzle and she was soaking wet. She started a fire in the fire pit just as soon as she arrived and then she set up camp. Then she went into her tent and changed into dry clothing. When she came back out it was raining harder.

By this time her fire had started to burn down. She went over to the woodpile and picked out some choice pieces. There was a rough-cut sign nailed to a tree next to the woodpile. It read, "WOOD IS SUPPLIED BY THE PARK RANGERS. DONATIONS WILL GLADLY BE ACCEPTED AT THE RANGER STATION." She walked back over to the fire and tossed in a chunk of firewood. It sizzled and hissed as the water evaporated. She set the rest of her firewood around the pit to dry out a little bit. Soon, enough pieces had dried out so that they would burn well and she added them to the flames. As the fire burned she remembered the sign by the woodpile. "Ten bucks will be a good donation," she said to herself.

She put a pan of water on the fire to boil. Once it was hot she could make dinner. Tonight it was going to be beef stroganoff. When the water got good and hot she opened up the freeze-dried package of stroganoff and poured it into the pot. She took it off the fire and set it aside for a few minutes so it could thicken and then started some more water for coffee. When it was hot she mixed herself a cup and then it was time to eat. She sat on a dry piece of wood eating her food and sipping her coffee. The flames of the fire were warm and inviting. It had been a long day and she was bone tired.

The rain quit while Dakota slowly ate her dinner. She chewed each bite carefully as she watched the fire. The fire seemed to have a kind of hypnotic effect. The flames rose gently around the logs in a leisurely dance. As she watched, pitch pockets in the wood cracked and sparked as the heat sought them out on its way to the heart of the log.

When she finished her meal she wiped out the bowl she was using with a paper towel and tossed the towel into the fire. It caught instantly and went up in a rush of flame and smoke. She put the bowl into a plastic bag that she was using to keep her garbage in. She always makes a point to take her trash out of the woods with her. To her it would be unthinkable to leave garbage somewhere in the forest. It was now dark and she was more than ready for bed.

She knocked the fire down and made a check of the perimeter. When she was satisfied that no ash or spark could settle into the woods she started to head for her tent. She pulled the flap of the tent back when from somewhere up the trail came the sound of a low moan. "Aaaaah," it seamed to be saying as it died off into the trees.

Dakota let the flap of the tent drop and listened. She had never heard an animal make that kind of sound. She reached for the can of pepper spray she wore on her belt just to make sure it was still there. It was. She wrapped her hand around the can. "I think I'll stay up for a little while longer," she said out loud to herself. She kicked the fire back together and threw on some more dry fir boughs. "That ought to do it," she said as the wood caught. It blazed up and the whole clearing was lit in a bright yellow glow. She looked all around the campsite by the light of the fire, but there was nothing there.

"It was probably just a deer or something," she said. "Nothing to worry about, go to bed." She started back to the tent when the moaning sound came again.

"Aaaaah."

Dakota jumped as the sound issued from the woods. There was something, or someone out there! She pulled the can of pepper spray from her belt and thumbed open the top. "Who's out there?" she called.

There was no answer.

She took a Mag-Lite flashlight out of the side of her pack. It was eighteen inches long and took six C-cell batteries. Not only could it throw a powerful beam of light but also it would make a good weapon. She hefted the weight of it in her hand. It felt good. She turned the lens and a white laser beam of light cut into the woods.

"Who's out there?" she yelled. "Do you need some help? Are you all right?"

The moaning had quit and once again the forest was quiet and still.

"Are you all right?" Dakota called out into the woods. "Are you hurt?

Hold on, I'm coming."

She walked up the trail in the direction that the sound had come from. She shined her flashlight in all directions as she moved up the trail. As she walked she called out, "Hold on, I'm coming."

She had gone about a hundred yards up the trail when she passed a large pile of brush. She looked at it as she went by. It hadn't been there when she had come down the trail earlier. She hadn't gone three paces past the pile when it moaned.

"I'm dying," it lamented. "Summer is gone and I'm dying!"

Dakota jumped when the pile moaned. She quickly turned and shined her light back on the pile of brush. In the beam of the flashlight the pile moved.

"Oh my God, there's someone under there!" Dakota bent down and started to remove the brush from on top of the pile. "Don't worry, I'll have you out of there in just a minute," she said.

She reached out into the pile and grabbed a large branch. When she did a wave of pure summer raced up her arm and washed over her entire body. June sang in her ears. She could smell the warm breezes that come off of the ocean in late July. The air tasted like a perfectly ripe August strawberry.

She pulled her hand back with a jerk and instantly the sensation of summer was gone. The quick movement made her lose her balance and she promptly fell over backwards. "Ouf," she grunted as she hit the ground.

The pile of brush stirred and stretched. Then, with the utmost grace it rolled over. Dakota was astonished. She had never seen anything like this. The pile of brush wasn't a pile of brush. There hadn't been a man buried under it. The pile of brush was the man! A man made of brush!

His body was constructed of vines and branches. His hair and beard were all of moss. The most startling thing, though, was his face. It was a broad oak leaf that had been contoured and sculptured. The dark green eyes stared out at her from under twiggy eyebrows. A sigh issued from his vine thick mouth. He turned his head and spoke to Dakota in a voice that was the very melody of summer.

"Thank you," he said, "but there is nothing you can do. For you see, I am dying." He sat up, threw his head up to the sky and in a voice of pure lament, cried, "Summer is ending and once again I must die!"

Dakota scooted herself back against the trunk of a large cedar tree before she found her voice. "What are you?" she asked in a quiet, trembling voice. This was more to herself than to the man.

"What am I?" he shouted as he jumped to his feet. "What am I? Do you not know me? Why, I'm the taste of morning dew on the leaves of a tree. I'm the glint of sunshine on a clear blue lake in the late afternoon. I'm the hot breeze that creeps through your bedroom in the middle of the night. Do you not know me? For, I am the very spirit of spring and the heart of summer. Some call me Jack of Green. Others call me the Leaf King for I am the Green in the Forest. I am the Green Man! I am as old as the summer and as young as the spring."

He took one step towards Dakota and she backed into the tree harder. "Do not be afraid," he said, "for when has spring ever brought any harm, or summer ever caused pain. I will not hurt you in any way."

Dakota looked at the standing figure of the Green Man and right then she decided that he looked harmless enough. Besides, she still had her hand on the can of pepper spray. So, if it turned out that he wasn't, she was going to let him have it.

"Are, are you all right?" she asked as she stood up slowly.

"I'm fine for the moment," said the Green Man. "But soon, very soon, I will die." All of a sudden he threw his head back and howled at the sky again. "I will die and winter will come!"

Dakota's arm shot out in front of her. The can of pepper spray was held firmly in her hand. "Don't you come near me," she said. "I'll spray you with this if you do!"

"Do not fear," said the Green Man. "For, I will not harm you." He turned his head and looked down the trail toward Dakota's camp. "Come, let us go and warm ourselves by your fire. The night is cold and my time is short." He turned and slowly ambled down the trail towards the camp.

Dakota stood her ground and watched him as he aimlessly wandered down the path. He staggered and bobbed from one side to the other. As she watched him, all of a sudden a thought struck her and it made her laugh. He looked just like the Scarecrow from *The Wizard of Oz*. How could anything that looked that comical ever be dangerous? There really was nothing to fear. She lowered her arm and followed the Green Man to her camp.

When she got there he was already sitting on the ground staring at the fire. "Oh, there you are," he said as she walked up to the fire. "I thought that I might have lost you in my hasty departure."

Dakota sat down on a log. She still had the can of pepper spray in her hand as she looked at the Green Man. "The coffee is hot if you want some," she said.

"Why, yes," said the Green Man, "something hot would be delightful. It would take the chill off the night. You know, I'm just chilled to the bone. Or, should I say, to the stalk?"

Dakota carefully poured a cup. "There you go," she said as she set the cup down as far away from herself as she could.

The Green Man reached ever so slowly toward the cup and picked it up. He daintily brought it to his vine lips and took a taste. His eyes sparkled and a smile crossed his broad leaf face. "Aha," he said over the steaming cup. "This is excellent. Just what I needed," he said as he set the cup down.

"Now," said Dakota, "I just have to know. What are you and where do you come from? Are you an alien from another world? I've never seen anything like you before in my life!"

The Green Man picked up his cup and took another delicate sip. "I will gladly answer any of your questions," he said, "if you really want to know. Though, I warn you that my story is a long one."

"That's all right," said Dakota. "I have nothing but time and no place to go right now. I'm ready to listen to a long story."

The Green Man turned from the fire and his full gaze fell upon Dakota. His eyes sparkled and his mouth once again broke into a broad leaf smile. "Then you shall hear of me," he said.

He spoke of the joys of spring, of rebirth and new life that comes with the change of the season. He talked of lazy, hot summer days and glorious, star-filled nights. Finally, he told of fall and death. Of the days growing shorter and the nights becoming longer.

As he spoke, Dakota could feel the changing seasons. She felt the cool rains that came in the spring splash against her face. The heat of mid-summer scorched and burned her skin. A chill crawled down her spine as a full harvest moon lit up an empty night sky and blanketed the lonely landscape in its pure light.

By the time the Green Man had finished his tale the night had grown very late. The fire had died down to just glowing embers and Dakota had lapsed into a deep sleep. She was still sitting on her makeshift chair, her head resting in the palm of her hand. Her breathing was deep and regular. Strands of hair hung down obscuring her face.

The Green Man turned back and looked at the remains of the fire. He took a deep breath and sighed. "I hope that I have not bored you or taken overly long to tell my story," he said. Dakota slept on.

He watched her in her slumber and then he carefully set down the cup he had been holding. He quietly leaned over and whispered in her ear. "You are very sweet and kind." He brushed a stray wisp of hair gently out of her face and kissed her lightly on the cheek. "Sleep well," he said, "and may your dreams be of summer."

He stood and looked into the depths of the forest. "Three seasons are but a short time," he said. "Maybe there are more out there as kind as this one. For them I think that I'll stay just a little bit longer this year. For now I am not quite as ready to die as I was." With that he turned and bounded off into the forest and was gone.

Dakota woke at dawn. The sun was beaming down through the forest canopy. Birds were singing off in the distance. It was going to be a beautiful day. Sometime during the night she had moved from her chair to the ground. She stretched and yawned. She felt great! As a matter of fact, this just may be the best she had ever felt. She had no idea why she had slept outside rather than in the tent. She must have fallen asleep while she was watching the fire. The flames could be hypnotic, you know.

She broke camp and gathered up her gear. It was time to head back to the ranger station. As she walked she thought about the extraordinary dream she had had. It was all about summer. It had pleased her immensely. She brushed her hand against her cheek and a warm glow filled her all the way to her soul.

An Indian summer started that day that was the longest ever recorded.

THE MOUNDS AT MIMA

When winter came it came with a vengeance. Two feet of snow dropped in the Hoh Rainforest overnight. The ranger station and park visitor center were covered in a deep mantle of white. The parking lot looked like the Alaskan Tundra with several car-shaped lumps bulging from beneath its frozen surface. Winter, it seemed, was trying to make up for lost time.

Ranger Steve Donner sat at his desk with a telephone glued to his ear. He was talking to the county shop supervisor down in the town of Forks. "I don't care if you've only got one working plow. I've got fifteen guests up here at the lodge and we need the road cleared before one of them with a four-wheel drive decides to blaze his own trail out and ends up in the river!"

"Calm down, Ranger Donner. We'll have the plow up there just as soon as we can."

"And when will that be?" asked Steve.

"Well, let me see," said the shop supervisor.

Steve could hear what sounded like things being moved around and the rustle of paper on the other end of the phone line.

"OK, just about an hour ago the plow was in Queets. He should be finishing up there any time and then he'll be headed out your way. If any problems come up before he gets there, I'll call you and let you know."

"Good," said Steve. "Keep me posted. These people are going to get awful antsy if it takes too much longer."

Steve hung up the phone and went into the head ranger's office. Bert Pensworth, the head ranger, was sitting at his desk going over yesterday's correspondence. Bert was a large man and on the high side of fifty. He had been head ranger at the park for the last twenty years. He slouched in his chair as he shuffled through the paperwork on his desk.

"Hey, Bert," said Steve as he came into the office. "I just finished talking to that jerk down at the county shop. He said they'll have the snow plow out here just as soon as they can."

Bert pushed a finished pile of reports off to one side of his desk. "OK," he said. "Sounds good to me." He pulled another pile of paper toward him and started looking through it. "Why don't you go out to the parking lot and take a good look around? Make sure that you put up the barricades and post the road out of the lot as closed. Let's hope that keeps them here until the plow shows up."

"Good enough," said Steve. "I'll take care of it right now." He left the office and went down the hall to his locker. He opened the locker and grabbed his heavy, wool coat. Pulling it on, he headed for the garage. By the time he opened the door and stepped out into the snow-choked parking lot he was buttoned up and bundled in.

He trudged through the snow making his way out to the garage. By now the snow was over the tops of his boots and his feet were getting wet. Off in the forest he could hear the sound of branches breaking under the heavy weight of the snow.

He made it over to the garage and unlocked the door. Each breath he took made frosty circles in the air. The thermometer that hung on the side of the building read twenty degrees. "It's flat cold," he said to himself as he opened the door. "I hope the stinking truck starts."

He went into the garage and stamped the snow off his feet. Clumps fell from his pants and boots landing on the floor and slowly melting where they lay. The garage was a little warmer than it was outside, but not much. He took off his gloves and pushed the button for the garage door opener. The door rattled open on its tracks sounding like a freight train. He climbed into the truck, started it easily and let it warm up while he hunted around the garage for the signs and barricades. He found them in a pile over in one corner of the garage buried under a pile of trail maintenance equipment. He dug them out and threw them into the back of the truck. Each one landed with an icy thud.

When the truck was loaded and warmed up he pulled out of the garage, closing the door behind him. He drove slowly across the white parking lot. The rear tires slipped and spun as they hunted for the pavement beneath the snow. He made it over to the parking lot exit and pulled the truck over. He left the engine running and the heater on full blast while he got out and posted barricades.

He set up the signs, planting each one firmly in the snow, making sure that they could be seen clearly from the parking lot. As he was setting up the last one a new Jeep Grand Cherokee rolled to a stop behind his truck.

The door of the Cherokee opened and a man got out, leaving a woman and two kids inside. "Hey, Ranger," he called as he make his way over to Steve. "What's going on?"

"I'm closing the road," Steve answered as he finished setting up the last sign.

"Closing the road?" said the man.

"Yup," said Steve. "The snow plow hasn't been here yet and the road is dangerous."

"Well, I've got four wheel drive on this baby and it can go anywhere. How about moving a couple of those barricades and letting me through? I've got to be in Seattle by this afternoon."

"I'm sorry, but the road is closed," said Steve. "Take your truck back to the lodge and have breakfast or something."

"But, I said I've got to be in Seattle."

"For right now, no one is going anywhere," said Steve. "The plow will be here some time later and then we'll reopen the road. For now, though, we are all snowed in."

"Snowed in?"

"That's right," said Steve. "Snowed in. Go back to the lodge and tell the desk clerk the road is closed. She's got a phone and you can make some calls if you need to. The road should be open later today."

The man moved back to his truck. Steve waited, watching the man as he turned his truck around and headed back to the lodge. "I hope that plow gets here soon," Steve said to himself.

He checked the barricades and signs once more, then climbed back into his truck and drove through the quarter mile of parking lot back to the lodge. He parked the truck in front of the building and got out. The blue Grand Cherokee was parked a little farther out in the lot.

The walk over to the porch was slick and covered in snow. He stepped carefully, not wanting to slip and fall. It would look really bad for a forest ranger to fall in the snow. When he reached the porch he knocked the snow off his boots and climbed the steps to the door. Linda, who was working the desk, had already swept everything off the porch. Bare wood glistened under a slight trace of wetness. He stamped his feet once more to make sure that he didn't bring any snow in with him. Linda would give him hell if he tracked any snow in on her clean floor. He opened the door and stepped into the lodge.

The lodge had been built in 1932. It was a beautiful old building done in a lot of stone and natural wood. Linda took quite a bit of pride in the building and the way she kept it. The deep red glow of old polished cedar was the first thing to catch his eye. The floors, walls and ceilings had a deep luster that only came with hours of cleaning and polishing. A huge fieldstone fireplace dominated one side of the common room. Linda's desk sat between the fireplace and a sweeping flight of stairs that lead up to the lodge's twenty rooms.

Linda had been at the lodge longer than anyone could remember, or she would admit. She was short, about five foot two, though she claimed to be five three. When Steve came into the lodge she was so happy to see him she just beamed. "Steve, I'm delighted you decided to stop in. Bert just called and said that if I see you he wants you in his office right away." The smile on her face went from ear to ear.

"Bert wants me back at the office?"

"That's what he said. Said he had something important for you to do."

"He's always got something important for me to do," said Steve.

Linda came out from behind the desk. "Before you run over there could you get a can of polish down for me? It's in the pantry on the top shelf and I just can't reach it."

"Sure." Steve grinned. He was always getting things down for Linda. He followed her around the back of the stairs. There was a pantry door built into the underside of the stairs. Linda unlocked it and turned on the light. Steve went in and fumbled around on the top shelf for the can of polish. It was way in the back and off in one corner. "This is the last can up here," he said as he handed it down to Linda.

"I know," said Linda. "I keep one can up there so when I run out before the next order comes in I still have some. I hope it comes in soon. It could be a long winter. Thanks for getting it down for me."

"No problem," said Steve. "I don't mind at all."

They came out of the pantry and Linda locked the door behind them. "You had better get over there and see what Bert wants," she said. "He sounded awfully excited."

"OK," said Steve. He headed back to the door and out into the parking lot. "I'll check back with you later to see how things are going."

"I'll be here," said Linda.

Steve got back into the truck and crept across the parking lot to the garage. "I wonder what the hell Bert wants," he said to himself as he got out of the truck. He closed up the garage door and headed back to the office. It was cold and getting colder. All he wanted to do right now was get a cup of coffee and then he would go and see what Bert wanted.

He brushed the snow off his coat and hung it back on the hook in his locker. His hands were still cold and his fingers tingled as the warmth of the locker room penetrated them. A large steaming coffee pot sat on a table off in one corner of the locker room. A metal shelf full of cups sat next to it. He dug through the cups until he found his. It was all the way to the back of the shelf. Steve filled his cup to the rim and headed into the office.

Bert still sat behind his massive metal desk. The pile of paper in front of him hadn't seemed to diminish at all since Steve had been there earlier. The left side of the desk was buried under a heap of forms and memos. That was the stuff he hadn't read yet. As he read it he would move it over to the pile on the right, which was just as impressive.

"It's flat cold out there," said Steve as he entered the office. His hands were wrapped around the hot cup of coffee. "Linda said that you wanted to see me for something."

"Yeah," said Bert. "Why don't you sit down? I've got something for you." Bert pulled a sheet of paper off the pile on the right and held it in his hand. "Last summer, you know, they put in the underground phone cable. Well, let me tell you, that's the best thing they have ever done for this old park. You know, with the old system all this snow would have taken it out and it would have been weeks before I would have gotten this." He looked at the paper and handed it over to Steve. "This fax just came in for you. It's from the Department of Natural Resources."

Steve took it and looked it over. It was a job offer for head ranger at the Mima Mounds Natural Area Preserve.

"Congratulations," said Bert. He reached out and grabbed Steve's hand in an almost bone crushing handshake and pumped his arm like a water pump. "I can't think of anyone better fitted for the job."

"Thanks, Bert," said Steve. He released Bert's hand and reread the announcement.

"I guess old Fred Cummings finally decided to retire," said Bert. "You know he's had that park ever since they opened it. That was in 1965."

"So, he's been there since day one?" asked Steve.

"Yup, that's a long time to spend in one park." Bert shoved his chair back, the casters squeaking in protest as they rolled across the floor. "You had better go and fax them back that you're going to take the job. I wouldn't let any grass grow under your feet if I were you. They want you to start next week."

"I'll do it right now," said Steve. He had gotten as far as the door when he turned around. "Bert," he said, "you know, I still have a week's worth of leave on the books and I was just wondering…"

"You've still got a week left?" asked Bert. "Well, just make sure you check out those trail heads before you start on it. I don't want anybody going up there in this snow. When that's done you can cut out of here just as soon as the road is open."

"Thanks," said Steve. He dashed out of the office and headed for the lunchroom where he wrote out his acceptance for the job. Once he was satisfied with the wording he faxed it off. He said that he would be more than happy to accept the position and that he could be ready to start at any time.

He made the security checks of the trailheads in record time. If it had been sunny and seventy degrees, instead of twenty degrees with two feet of snow, he couldn't have done the job any faster. When he was done he went back to the lodge and told Linda all about the job.

"Well, now that you're a big hot-shot, head ranger with your own park, don't forget us little people up here, will you. I expect to hear something out of you once in a while."

He told her that he would never forget the people at this park and that she should come by any time she was down and he would show her all around the Mima Mounds. He spent the rest of the day loading his things up in his truck and hanging out at the lodge waiting for the road to open.

The snowplow pulled into the parking lot at two o'clock. He was the first car in the line on the way back to the highway.

Steve spent his week off looking for an apartment in the Olympia area. He finally found one in the town of Little Rock, just outside of Olympia. It worked out really well for him as it was less than a mile from the park.

The snow that had fallen at the beginning of the week had melted and the rains had come again. It was a dark and wet Monday morning when Steve reported to the Department of Natural Resources personnel office in Olympia. His paperwork was reviewed, and he was given directions to the park, even though he told the receptionist that he already knew how to get there. He left the office and headed straight for the park.

When he arrived at the gate he turned down the gravel road that led to the ranger station. It was just a little after three when he parked the car. He got out and walked into the station to report to Frank Cummings, the park ranger. Frank was the only person there.

Frank was sixty-five years old and this was his last week with the department. His career had spanned forty years, most of it at this same park. He was six feet tall and rail thin. His gray eyes shined out at the world from a weathered and tired face that had spent a lifetime outdoors.

"You must be Frank Cummings," said Steve as he entered the office.

"That I am," said Frank. "And I take it that you are Steve Donner."

"That's me," said Steve. "It's a pleasure to meet you."

"Well, this is the park," said Frank, "what there is of it. I guess that you'll want to take a look around and make yourself at home."

The one room office had a desk and two chairs. There was an empty waste paper basket on the floor off to the right of the desk. A five-drawer file cabinet graced one wall. On the other wall hung a picture of the President of the United States. A calendar was tacked next to it. Days had been crossed off with a felt-tip marker.

"That would be great!" said Steve.

"Well, we've got the whole week to check things out. This isn't a very big a park. It's only four hundred and forty-five acres, but there are some forty-four thousand mounds out there and it will take at least a week to walk around them all.

"That's what I'm here for," said Steve. "When can we get started?"

"Right now would be good," said Frank. "I guess the best way would be for you to read up a little about us here and then tomorrow we can go out and start walking." Frank went over to the file cabinet and pulled open the top drawer, extracting a huge folder of paper. "Here's a run-down that you should look over." He handed the pile of papers over to Steve.

"Well," said Steve as he took the files, "I guess that's as good a way as any to get started." He sat down in one of the chairs and started thumbing through the history of the park.

At five o-clock Frank got up from his desk. "Well, it's time to go and close up the gate for the night."

Steve had gotten through about half of the first pile of paperwork. He set what he had left back down on the corner of the desk. Almost everything he had gone through so far had dealt with the park's billing system. It had all in all been pretty dry stuff and Steve was getting tired. "Great," he said. "I need a break anyway. Let's go."

Frank lead the way out of the office and headed for the parking lot. The only cars that were in the gravel lot were Steve's and Frank's. Frank wandered around through the lot picking up bits and pieces of trash that lay on the ground. He stuffed the trash into a huge garbage bag and threw it into the dumpster at one end of the lot. Once the lot had been picked up he went over to the steel gate and started pulling it closed. "People can be such pigs," he said. "It surprises me how many of them will just throw their trash on the ground rather than take an extra step and toss it into a can. I get at least a sack of it a night. Sometimes more, sometimes less."

Steve watched Frank snap an old Master Lock on the gate. "There, that should do it."

"Anything else we need to do?" asked Steve. He walked through the parking lot to the gate that blocked the trailhead leading out into the park. He leaned on it. It was an old gate, about six feet wide and four feet high. It just barely closed as he forced it shut. The old rusty hinges squealed as the gate moved.

"The only thing left to check out are the restrooms," said Frank. "Kids like to trash them out in the summer, but this time of year you might find somebody trying to camp out in them. You have to chase them out if they're trying to stay in there, you know."

They checked out both restrooms. The men's room was clean and hadn't been used as far as Steve could tell. Before they entered the women's Frank hollered out, "Anybody in here?" This restroom was also empty but there was a little bit of trash lying about. Frank picked it up and threw it away, locking the door as they went out. "Tomorrow I'll get you some keys," said Frank.

"Thanks."

"Sure thing," said Frank. "Tomorrow we'll start going through the park, so be here early."

"You can count on it," said Steve. "How early do you want to get started?"

"Well, I open the gate to the lot at dawn, so I guess that's going to be around six thirty. The park is open from dawn to dusk, you know. So be here at say six. That will give us a good start."

"Sounds good to me," said Steve. He started to walk toward his truck.

"Hold on a minute," Frank said as he trotted over toward Steve. "You forgot the paperwork you were going through. It's still in the office. I want you to finish reading it."

"It's just old billing stuff," said Steve. "I can go over it any time."

"Now is just as good a time as any," said Frank. They headed back to the office and Frank handed Steve the remaining piles of papers. "Go over these really well," he said. "I want you to know how the park runs and who we do business with."

"OK," said Steve as he took the pile and headed back out to his truck. "See you in the morning."

The rest of that week was filled with early morning rambles through the park. Any time he had left was spent digging through the mountainous piles of paperwork. Frank had receipts, invoices and billing information going all the way back to the opening of the park. And Frank had Steve go through it all. It was one of the longest weeks in his life. By the time he had finished going through the receipts for say, 1970, Frank would come up with the invoices for 1969.

Friday morning, before dawn, Steve met Frank out in the parking lot. Frank was standing by the gate at the trailhead, just like he had been every morning, when Steve pulled in. "Come on, kid, I've got something to show you," he said as he opened the gate and entered the park.

Steve walked through the open gate and caught up with Frank a little ways down the trail. They moved at a fast pace until they came to the observation tower. The tower was an octagon-shaped building that rose thirty feet above the mounded plain of the park. There were pamphlets and brochures about the park in a rack next to the door that Frank unlocked. When you looked inside you could see two flights of stairs that took you up to the observation deck where you could view the park.

Frank latched the door open. "That will take care of that," he said. "Come on kid, let's go." Frank started down one of the trails. After going a little ways he stopped and looked around. "This is the place," he said as he left the trail and headed out toward the center of the park.

"Hey, Frank," said Steve. "Where are we going?"

"We're going right out to the center of the park. I've got something to show you."

They ambled their way through thousands of mounds, all of them appearing to be exactly the same. A bump of grass covered earth seven feet high and thirty feet across. When Frank finally stopped there wasn't any sign of a trail. Steve felt totally lost and was glad Frank was with him. Frank turned to him and said, "You know, kid, this park has been here since 1965, and I've been the only ranger here in all that time."

"That's what I've been told," said Steve

"Well, you've been out here walking and looking things over. I've had you go through all of the paper work I could find and now I guess it's time I told you about the park."

"What's left to tell? I think I've been over every receipt there is."

Frank turned and started to climb to the top of the nearest mound. "Come on up here," he said. Steve climbed the mound and joined him.

This mound was just a little bit taller than the others in the area and climbing on the grass was slick work. When they reached the top Frank sat down and patted the grass next to him. "Sit here," he said. "I've got something to tell you."

Steve sat down where Frank had indicated. From the top of the mound you could see the entire park. The ranger station and the observation tower were a lot farther off than Steve had thought they would be.

"Take a good look around," said Frank.

Steve turned his head and looked at the park. They were surrounded by thousands of mounds as far as Steve could see. All the mounds appeared to be the same shape and size.

"Just take a look," said Frank. "That's all that's left. Four hundred and forty-five acres. Once this prairie covered twenty-two square miles! Over the years most of it has been flattened, dozed and leveled down. Now all that's left is four hundred and forty-five acres."

"Come on, Frank," said Steve, "there are lots of other mound sites. Why, I know for a fact there are sites in Oregon, California, Wyoming, Colorado, New Mexico, Oklahoma and Texas. There are even sites in Arkansas and Louisiana. It's all in the records and correspondence you had me go through."

"Sure, there are other sites," said Frank, "but none of them were ever as big as Mima."

"I didn't know that," said Steve.

"Well, now you do," said Frank. He stood up and started back down the hill toward the trail. "Come on," he said. "It's just about time to open. We'll talk some more on the way back."

They made their way down the slick hill and headed back toward the trail. Frank trudged ahead with his hands buried deep in his pants pockets. When they reached the trail that lead toward the observation tower he turned and asked, "Do you know what the word Mima means?"

"No," said Steve. "It wasn't in any of the records. I guess it's an Indian word for mound or something."

"Well, that's not it," said Frank. "It's a mystery, just like the place itself. All anybody knows is that it was an Indian word, but what it means, no one knows. Doesn't that strike you as kind of strange?"

Steve stopped. "This whole place is kind of strange now that you think about it. How do you think it got here?"

"Well, there are all kinds of theories about that," said Frank as they started walking again.

"How many?" asked Steve.

"Bunches and bunches," answered Frank. "Everything from glacial deposits to earthquakes. There is even one tall tail that says that Paul Bunyan made the mounds when he dumped huge piles of dirt out of an enormous wheelbarrow. The one that makes the most sense to me though is the one about the gophers."

"Gophers?"

"Gophers," said Frank. "Generations of gophers living in the same place for thousands of years, building on the same mounds. One scientist even thought there might have been some kind of monster race of prehistoric, pocket gopher that lived here. They could have made really big mounds you know. Could you imagine one of them? God knows, I go through a lot of rodent poison a year, but how much do you think it would take to kill one of them off?"

"How much do you go through a year?" asked Steve.

"It takes lots, I tell you, lots. Why, I go through around two hundred pounds of Dilmont Gopher Gone each month. That's the only thing I found that works. Otherwise, they would be overrunning the whole park, digging holes and eating everything in sight. That reminds me, there should be just enough Dilmont's to get through this month. You will have to order more before it runs out. If you don't, those little fellows will get out of hand and you'll have a hell of a time trying to get them back under control."

"I'll make that my first act as head ranger," said Steve.

"Good," said Frank. "Don't forget."

Frank unlocked the gate and swung it open on its hinges. "You're coming to my retirement party tonight, aren't you?"

"Wouldn't miss it for the world," said Steve.

As Frank walked through the gate and headed for his car he called back to Steve, "Well, I guess you can handle it now, so I'm going to take the rest of the day off. It's your park now, take good care of it."

"Don't worry," answered Steve, "I will."

"See you tonight then," said Frank. He got into his car and rolled down the window. "Don't forget to order some more of the Dilmont's before the end of the month or you'll run out."

"Got it all under control," said Steve.

Frank waved and drove out of the parking lot. "See you tonight," he yelled as he hit the road and headed for the town of Little Rock.

Steve's first day by himself at the park went smoothly. The only visitors were a Cub Scout troop from Lacey. Steve went out and toured the park with them. He did a pretty good job of answering all their questions. After they left everything was quiet and he spent the rest of the day alone.

At five he went out to lock up the gate. Every step he took out in the parking lot make little crackling sounds in the gravel. It sounded like the breaking of seashells. He stopped at the gate and swung it shut. It closed with a loud clang that broke the silence hanging over the park. He unlocked the heavy padlock and hooked it through the gate, snapping it shut with a secure sounding click. He started to head back through the parking lot so he could finish locking up the office and the restrooms when he thought he heard a sound. He stopped and listened. It was a very low rustling noise, like a soft wind in the trees, or maybe a very slow moving stream. He couldn't tell which direction it was coming from at first. He cupped one of his hands behind his right ear and listened. The noise seemed to be coming from inside the park.

He went back to the gate. When he touched the gate the noise stopped. He stood there for a minute and listened. The sound did not repeat itself. "Oh, well," he said to himself, "I guess it was nothing." He finished his rounds and locked up the office. On his way out to his car the rustling sound started again. A low rattle like sticks being rubbed together or the sound that dry grass makes when it's crushed under a heavy boot. He was thinking about the party so he didn't notice the sound this time.

The party was being held at the Moose Lodge in downtown Little Rock. After Steve closed up the park he went straight to his apartment to get himself ready for the party. Anyone who was anybody in the Department of Natural Resources was going to be there. Steve wanted to make a good impression. He had even bought a new suit just for the occasion. Once he was dressed he stood in front of the mirror to inspect his image.

When he was satisfied that he would present the look he was after, one of a competent and upcoming young park ranger, he left the apartment and headed out to get something to eat. He stopped at the local McDonald's and picked up a Quarter Pounder with cheese, a large fry and a cup of coffee. It was never a good idea to go to a party on an empty stomach. He knew that if he had a couple of drinks without eating something he would be on his lips. He ate slowly, making sure that he didn't drop any of the burger on his new suit. When he had finished the last sip of coffee and had stuffed the garbage into the paper sack that the burger had come in, it was time to go.

It was seven thirty by the time he found a spot to park. The lot at the lodge was full and he had to park on the street. He wasn't the first person there by a long shot, but then he wasn't the last either. He was just fashionably late, that was all. Not so early that there was no one there and not so late that it was rude. He stepped up onto the porch of the lodge and opened the door.

The place was full to the brim! There must have been a hundred people milling around the small confines of the bar. A guest book sat on a stand next to the door. Steve signed the book and looked around the room. He spotted Frank standing over by the bar. He had a drink in his hand and was talking to a distinguished looking elderly man. Steve made his way over toward them to pay his respects to Frank.

"Frank, there you are," said Steve as he came up to the two men. "Congratulations."

"Steve, glad to see you made it!" Frank turned back to the man he had been talking to. "Phil, this is Steve Donner. He's our newest head ranger down at Mima."

The elderly man stuck out his hand in greeting. "Phil Kleinschmidt," he said. "Glad to meet you."

"Same here," said Steve. They talked about the park and how Steve liked it so far. After a while Steve excused himself and wandered back over to the bar to get a drink.

The bartender stood at one end of the bar. He had a wet bar rag in his hand and was polishing a glass with it. "Hey, bartender," called Steve. "I'll have a bourbon on the rocks, if you please."

The bartender looked over at Steve. "Hold on, can't you see I'm busy here?" He set down the glass and came over towards Steve. "That's a scotch on the rocks, right?"

"No," said Steve, "bourbon."

"You said bourbon? I could have sworn you called for a scotch. Make up your mind, will you?"

"I'll have a glass of bourbon with ice," said Steve.

The bartender poured a short shot of bourbon into a glass and drowned it in crushed ice. He set the drink on the bar in front of Steve. "Let me see some ID."

Steve hadn't been carded in at least ten years. "Sure," he said as he dug into his wallet for his driver's license, handing it over to the bartender.

The bartender looked it over carefully. "This your older brother or something," he said. "It sure don't look like you."

"No," said Steve, "it's me. It's just that the picture is old."

The bartender looked it over again and then set it down in a puddle on the bar. "OK," he said, "I guess it's you. That will be two bucks for the shot."

Steve picked up his license from the bar. "Can I have something to dry this off with?" he asked.

"Why?" asked the bartender.

"It's all wet. I don't want to put it back in my wallet when it's all wet," said Steve.

The bartender set the wet bar rag down. "Here, use this," he said.

Steve sopped the rag over his license and then put it back into his wallet. He took two dollar bills out of his wallet and set them neatly into the puddle on the bar. "There you go," he said as he picked up his drink.

"What the hell do you think you're doing!" said the bartender. "I said that was two bucks for the drink."

"It's right there on the bar," said Steve.

"I don't want that soaking wet crap," said the bartender. "It will mess up my till. Let's have some dry stuff if you don't mind."

Steve took a five-dollar bill out of his wallet and handed it over to the bartender. "There you go," he said. "Is that better?"

The bartender took the five and went over to the till. He put the money in the cash register and went back to polishing glasses.

"Where's my change?" asked Steve as the bartender wiped glasses.

"It's sitting right there in front of you," said the bartender.

Steve was done with this game and he wasn't going to play any more. He picked up the soaked dollar bills and stuffed them into his pocket. "Thanks," he said as he got up and left the bar.

He took a slow tour of the lounge. The place was packed. He spotted Bert and Linda sitting at a small table over in a corner. He made his way across the floor and over to the table.

Bert saw him before he had made it halfway across the floor. He tapped Linda's hand and pointed over at Steve. "Hey, Linda, here comes Steve."

Linda looked over and waved at Steve.

Steve worked his way through the crowd, being very careful not to spill any of his drink. When he got to the table he set his it down.

"Hello, stranger," said Linda. She scooted over a little bit and tapped the bench seat. "Why don't you sit down and take a load off your feet."

Steve sat down next to Linda and said in his best John Wayne drawl,

"Why, thank you ma'am, I don't mind if I do."

Linda gave Steve a quick hug. "It's good to see you," she said.

"Great to see you guys, too," said Steve.

Bert slid Steve's drink over to him. "What do you think of the party so far?" he asked.

"Well," said Steve, "I think the party is great but you know that bartender is a real jerk."

"I suppose you gave him five bucks for a two dollar drink," said Bert.

"You hit that right on the nose," said Steve. "What's going on?"

"That's his style," said Bert. "He's tried that on everyone tonight."

"Just consider that his tip for the evening," said Linda. "Now why don't you let me scoot out for a minute so I can go and fix my make-up."

"Sure thing," said Steve.

Linda got up from the table and headed straight for the ladies room. "Back in a minute," she said as she moved out across the floor.

Steve sat back down. "Well, if I had wanted to give him a tip I would have," he said.

"Well, don't let it get you riled," said Bert. "He's just one of those poor slobs that doesn't have a soul." He took a sip of his drink. "His time is coming though. Frank told me that next week the club is going to let him go and find another bartender."

"Well," said Steve, "the sooner the better."

Bert finished his drink and waved a waitress over to the table. "You want another one?" he asked Steve.

"Sure," said Steve, "as long as it don't cost five bucks."

The waitress came over to the table. "What will it be?" she asked.

"I'll have two more of these and a Diet Pepsi," said Bert. He handed the waitress six dollars. "Keep the change."

When she left Bert turned back to Steve. "Well, what do you think of your new park?"

"It's great!" said Steve. "I don't see how Frank took care of the whole place by himself though. It's a lot for one guy to handle."

Just then Linda came back from the ladies room. "Here," said Bert as he got up. "Sit over here for a bit."

Linda slid into the booth. "What were you two guys talking about while I was gone?" she asked.

"Steve was just saying that he figured he could use some help," said Bert.

"That so?" said Linda.

"Well, the place is pretty big for just one man," said Steve.

The drinks came and the waitress set them down on the table. "Is there anything else I can get for you?" she asked.

"No thanks, that'll be fine for now," said Bert.

She walked out across the floor and started working other tables.

Bert took a sip of his drink. "Frank didn't always run that place by himself you know."

"He didn't?" said Steve. "I thought that it had always been a one-man operation."

"No," said Bert. "He had some help down there to start with. The guy's name was Glen something. Linda, what was that guy's name? You remember, don't you?"

Linda pushed her glass around the table for a second. "Um," she said. "Let me see, what was that guy's name?" She pushed her glass around some more. "I think it was Glen Nicholson. Yeah, that was it. Glen Nicholson."

"You got it!" said Bert. "I remember he was there for about two years. Am I right?"

"It was about two years," said Linda.

"What happened to him?" asked Steve. "He get laid off or something?"

"Nope," said Bert. "Nobody knows what happened to him."

Linda slowly unwrapped a straw and inserted it into her Pepsi. "He just up and disappeared one day."

"What?" said Steve.

"Yup," she said. "He just up and vanished."

"What do you mean by vanished?" asked Steve.

"Just gone," said Bert. "Here one minute and gone the next. Ask Frank about it sometime. He can tell you everything."

Bert took another sip from his drink. "Well, I'll be," he said. "Look who's here!"

"Who?" asked Steve as he turned to look over to where Bert was waving his glass.

"You see that guy over there talking to Frank?"

"Yeah," said Steve. "I was just talking to him and Frank before I came over here. Phil Kleinschmidt, I think, is who he said he was. He seemed like a nice enough guy."

"You have any idea who he is?" asked Bert.

"A friend of Frank's from what I can tell," said Steve.

"A friend of Frank's," said Linda. "Why, yes, that is Phil Kleinschmidt.

He used to be Deputy Secretary of the Department of the Interior. He retired last year."

"Wow," said Steve. "You wouldn't guess by talking to him. He just seemed like a regular guy."

Bert waved Frank and Phil over to the table. Steve slid over on the bench to make more room. Frank slipped in and Phil sat on the outside corner.

"How's retirement been treating you, Phil?" Bert asked as Phil sat down.

"Just great," he said. "I was just telling Frank all about it."

They sat at the table and talked for the next two hours, mostly about Frank's upcoming retirement, and the park system. As they talked, Steve got all the low down on the major parks in the country, what was going on in them, and when it was supposed to happen.

Linda and Bert finally decided that it was time to go. They had a long drive back to the ranger station at the Hoh and Linda wanted to get back sometime before morning. Steve and Phil walked out to the car with them.

"Don't forget to write," said Linda as she got into the car. Bert slammed the door and rolled down the window. "Stay in touch and let me know how things are going, and if you've got any questions don't be afraid to get a hold of me and ask."

"Don't worry about it," said Steve. " If anything comes up I will."

"I guess it's time I got started, too," said Phil. "It was good to meet you, Steve. I think you'll do just fine in your new job."

"Thanks," said Steve. "It was good to meet you too. " Phil shook Steve's hand and walked off into the darkness of the parking lot. Steve looked at his watch. It was only ten. He went back into the party to find Frank again.

He looked around the lounge for Frank, but there wasn't any sign of him. There was a different bartender behind the bar so he went and ordered another drink. When the bartender brought his drink Steve asked him if he knew where Frank was.

"You mean the guest of honor?" asked the bartender. "I think I saw him step outside a little while ago."

"Thanks," said Steve. He sat at the bar and finished his drink while he waited for Frank to come back in. It was getting late when he set the empty glass on the bar.

"You want another one?" asked the bartender as he picked up the empty glass.

"No, I have to get going," said Steve. "I guess I'll go out and find Frank. I think I know where he went." Steve headed out to the parking lot and looked around a little. There were still quite a few cars in the lot. Over in the far corner was a brand new motor home. Steve walked over to it and knocked on the door. "Hey, Frank, you in there?"

Frank answered from inside. "Sure am." He opened the door and Steve stepped in.

"This is quite a set-up," he said, as he looked around the motor home.

"Yup" said Frank. "Let me show you around." They wandered through the motor home. "Well, this is it," said Frank. "What do you think?"

Steve looked around and took in the whole place. "This is just great. I wish I could do something like this. When are you going to start traveling?"

"I'll be on the road first thing tomorrow morning," said Frank. "I figure if I get an early enough start I should be in Redding, California by tomorrow evening."

"Well," said Steve, "I would love to be going with you. Keep me posted. I want to hear from you at least once in a while."

"Will do," said Frank. He moved back into the kitchenette. "You want a beer or something?" he asked.

"Nah," said Steve, "but a soda would be fine if you've got one."

Frank dug through the pocket refrigerator and pulled out a Sprite. "This do?" he asked.

"Sure," said Steve as he took the can. He opened it and took a long drink. It helped to wash some of the bourbon taste from his mouth. "Hey, Frank," he said, "Bert was telling me that you had some help down at the park when you started. You think if I put in for some help they might send somebody?"

"Sure," said Frank. "I did have some help when I started out. You could probably use some too. Put in for some additional help and see what happens. It never hurts to try. What's the least they can do, tell you no?"

A dull rumble reached up through the base of the motor home. It sounded like a small jet passing deep underneath it. The motor home shook and the glass in the cabinets rattled. The shaking stopped just as abruptly as it had started.

Steve had a firm hold on the table. "What the hell was that?"

Frank sat down at the table and opened his beer. "Oh, nothing," he said. "Just a little earthquake."

"An earthquake?" said Steve.

"Just a little one," said Frank. "They happen all the time. This part of the state is pretty active, you know. They get at least one little shaker around here a year." Frank took a swig from his beer. "It's the type of ground around here, you know. It's all gravel resting on a bed of clay. You go out and talk to any of the old timers and they'll tell you that the only thing that this part of the state is good for is raising dairy cattle, gophers and earthquakes. Usually we only get little ones like this one. There hasn't been a really good one since 1965. That's when we had a six point something. Now let me tell you, that was one hell of a shake. That was right around the time that Glen disappeared."

Steve set his soda down on the table. "Bert and Linda were talking a little about that tonight. They didn't go into it much, though. Bert said that I should ask you if I wanted to know anything more."

"Well, I haven't thought about that in years," said Frank. "But, since you brought it up I guess you should know. To tell you the truth, I think it was the gophers that got him!"

"What!" exclaimed Steve.

"Yup," said Frank. "That's what I think happened. When I told my story at the inquest everyone thought I had gone nuts or something. After that I just kind of shut up about it." Frank got up from the table. He opened a cupboard and took out a pint bottle of Jim Beam. He poured a liberal splash into his beer and offered the bottle to Steve. "Here, you may want a shot of this when you hear what I have to say."

Steve took the offered bottle and dumped some into his soda.

"Well," said Frank, "Glen was sent down to help me get the park set up. Once we had the place up and running smoothly he was supposed to be transferred down to Mt. St. Helens, but we had been having a really bad problem with the pocket gophers. There were holes everywhere. I was afraid that one of the visitors was going to step into one of them and break an ankle or something. If that happened the park was going to be held liable. So Glen had been assigned to stay to help out with the gophers.

"You know, he disappeared just after that big earthquake I was telling you about. I remember now, it was a six point five. Let me tell you, that was a pretty good shake. I had never been through anything like it and I don't ever want to go through it again. It felt like the whole world was ready to cave in. I thought the station was going to collapse, but it was built to take more than that. The whole thing couldn't have lasted more than a minute, though it felt like days before it stopped shaking.

"When it was over I was kissing the floor under my desk. I don't think I have ever been so scared. I hollered for Glen. He was standing in the doorway. I mean right in the middle of the door. He said he had heard that was one of the safest places to be during an earthquake. Later, he showed me a *Life Magazine* that had a whole article about it.

"Well, we were both all right so we decided to call the main office in Olympia and tell them that we were still alive. Of course, the phone lines were all down. Nothing stable to hold up the poles, you know. So, I took the park truck and went to the police station over in Little Rock. Glen stayed to close the park down. People are really funny, you know. A thing like an earthquake and you get all sorts of them showing up just to see what happened. We didn't want anyone wandering around out in the park until we were sure it was safe to go back out there.

"By the time I got back Glen had the park shut down. He had the signs up and the parking lot blocked off. It wasn't like it is now with the gate and everything. He had gone out and stuck up barricades. I tried the phone again once I was back in the office and to my surprise it was working. It had only been down for about an hour or so. I checked in with Mildred, she was the secretary in the main office then, and reported our condition. I told her we were doing just fine, but that we still had to go out into the park and check it over for damage. Apparently we were the third place to check in and she was hoping that the phones would be up so the rest of the parks would be able to call in soon. Our orders then were to go out and make a quick check of the park and report back in.

"There was a lot of damage all over the state. The quake had been felt from Bellingham all the way down to Portland. The epicenter had been just south of the Little Rock area.

"Glen and I went out and spent the rest of the day going over the park. Nothing major had appeared to have happened. There were a few trees down, but that seemed to be about it. The only damage that we could find was a small crack in the foundation of the observation tower. It was so small it wasn't worth bothering with. You know, it's still there. The next day we were able to reopen the park. That's when the problems started to happen."

"What problems?"

"Why, the gophers, Steve. That's when the little buggers went nuts. If you think there are gophers in the park now, you should have seen it after the quake of sixty-five. During the next week they dug more holes than you would believe! There were so many holes that a number of the trails just up and collapsed into them.

"That's when we decided that it was time to start using poison. Up until then we had just been using traps and let me tell you they were full all the time but they just couldn't keep up with the little buggers. I started calling around to the different distributors trying to get the best deal on some kind of gopher poison. We didn't want to kill anything else if we could help it, just the gophers. Finally I found this outfit up in Lacey that sold me on Dilmont's Gopher Be Gone. Best stuff I've ever seen. I've been using it ever since. At the time, they told me that the stuff was new and it would take at least two weeks before I could expect delivery, so, Glen and I kept using the traps.

"By the end of the two weeks the gophers were getting smart about the traps. Glen and I would go out right after we had closed the park and set them, but the next morning, when we checked, they would be sprung. The two weeks had gone by and our shipment hadn't come in. I kept calling the distributor, and he was telling me there was a shortage at the plant, but that we could expect our order to come in at any time and that when it did he would get it to us right away.

"A couple of days after that we got a report from one of the visitors that there was a problem at the observation tower. He said that there was a huge hole in the ground on the backside and it looked like part of the tower was going to fall in. It was just about closing time so I sent Glen out to take a look. He said he wanted to set some more traps anyway so I might as well close up and that he would see me in the morning. I remember that I told him that was fine and that I would see him later. The last time I saw him he had a bunch of traps in a wheelbarrow and was heading out into the park.

"The next day I found the wheelbarrow out by the observation tower. There was fresh dirt where a hole might have been filled in but there was no sign of Glen. When he didn't call in I called his home and talked to his wife. She said that he hadn't been home and that she thought he was spending the night at the park. He had been doing that lately, trying to get a handle on the gopher problem.

"When it became apparent that he was missing the local police and the department got a search going. We must have had a hundred people out searching the park. We looked for over a month but never did find any trace of Glen. By then, my poison had come in and I had been baiting the park with it so most of the gophers were gone.

"To tell you the truth, I think what happened was he had just finished filling in the hole out behind the tower and was about to start setting traps when they got him. There must had been hundreds of them and they probably hauled him underground. That's why we never found anything. I've been poisoning the gophers out ever since and there hasn't been another incident of any kind in the park.

"That goes to show you, you have to keep poisoning to keep those little buggers under control. I think they tasted blood with Glen and if they get out of hand again there's no telling what could happen."

Steve set his drink down on the table. "So, you mean to tell me that they never did find him?"

"Nope, not a trace."

"That's quite a story," said Steve.

"Well, that's just what happened. Last I heard, Glen's wife had moved back to Texas someplace."

Steve took a quick glance at his watch. It was almost midnight. "Well, Frank," he said, "I've got to get going. Tomorrow is already here." He got up from the table and started for the door. "Well, you take care now and keep in touch."

Frank walked him over to the door. "That's just what I plan to do."

Steve opened the door and stepped out. "I'll be hearing from you."

"You can count on it," said Frank.

The party had wound down and the parking lot was almost empty by now. As Steve drove home he kept thinking about the story Frank had told him. The more he thought about it the less sense it made. Gophers just didn't attack someone. He didn't see how Frank's story could possibly be true. It had to be just a story and that was all there was to it.

A pocket gopher is a small furry rodent that is closely related to a squirrel. He spends most of his time underground and he is terribly nearsighted. A really big one is only about eighteen inches long. Sure they have huge front teeth but they are mainly used for tunneling and tearing roots and bulbs apart. It's a fact that they can cause some damage with their digging. With the holes and tunnels they burrow, farmers consider them a pest. The worst damage that Steve had ever heard of, though, was to gardens and trees. He had heard that some of the little animals had even gone as far as to actually ruin irrigation canals by their burrowing into the banks. But, all in all, pocket gophers were just too timid to be a real menace. Steve decided that Frank was just spinning him a story to justify the poisoning program that he had carried on for thirty years.

Frank was from the old school. The one that felt that a pest had to be controlled. Gophers were just natural. After all, they were just part of the environment. Right then and there Steve decided that it was time to stop the poisoning program. Let nature take its course and take care of the problem.

After all, if they did really get out of hand he could probably handle it with a shovel.

Things went smoothly at the park for the next few months. Winter had ended and the light constant rains of spring had commenced. It never really rained hard but it rained all the time. Steve had gotten a couple of letters from Frank. He was in Arizona. Steve had asked the main office several times to send him some help. The standard response, though, was always that the money for the department was too tight right now, but as soon as the new budget came in they would take it under consideration. Through the season the gophers had been very busy digging holes.

It was getting on to closing time for the park as Steve walked across the soggy grass to check the restrooms. As he passed through the parking lot he saw that there was one car left. It was a fairly new minivan, probably a Ford. He couldn't tell one from another anymore. There was still someone out wandering around in the park. It wasn't quite time to lock up so he decided that he would go back to the office and tidy up a little bit. He would lock the restrooms up a little later, just in case whoever was out in the park needed them before they left.

He went out to the gate of the parking lot and turned over the closed sign. *That should keep anyone else from showing up at the last minute*, he thought. People seemed to do that, show up at the last minute and then be ticked off when they couldn't go out into the park.

On his way back to the office he saw that he was right about the restrooms. The family from the minivan had come out of the park and was headed over that way. The man spotted Steve and called out to him. "Hey, Ranger!"

Steve stopped and answered him. "What can I do for you?"

The man walked over toward Steve at a brisk pace. "This is a really cool park you've got here," he said.

"Thanks," said Steve. "I'm glad you enjoyed it."

"Sure did. This is one of the neatest places we've ever been. All those little hills. I've never seen anything like it. What the heck are all the holes, though? I couldn't figure them out and my kids wanted to know."

"Well, to tell you the truth," said Steve, "we kind of have a gopher problem, but we're starting to get a handle on it."

"You're telling me that gophers dug all those holes?"

"Yes sir, that's what happened. They've been really busy."

"You mean they even dug that great big one out by that watchtower thing?" asked the man. "I didn't know a gopher could dig a hole that big."

"They can dig some pretty big holes," said Steve.

"Well, this one is huge," said the man. "It's big enough to dump a cow into if you wanted to. I was kind of scared to let the kids go near it."

"Thanks for letting me know," said Steve. "You said it was out by the observation tower?"

"It's right behind it," said the man. "If it gets any bigger it looks like that tower could fall right into it."

"I'll have to go out and take a look," said Steve. "Thanks for telling me about it."

"No problem," said the man. A woman called from the van and the man turned towards it. "Be there in a minute," he called back to her. "Well," he said, "we've got to be going. As I said, this is a really unusual place you've got here. We'll be back." He headed towards his van.

Steve headed over toward the restrooms to lock them up. The man waved at him as he drove out of the lot. Once the restrooms were locked Steve went out to the front of the lot and closed and locked the gate. Before he went home for the night he would have to make one more trip out into the park and have a look at this hole that the man had told him about.

He swung by the tool shed to grab a shovel. If this hole was as big as the guy said it was, he was going to have to fill it in before he went home. The shovel was sitting next to a few bags of Gopher Gone. Steve grabbed the shovel and looked at the bags of poison.

There were four, twenty-five pound sacks lying in a neat pile. Steve looked at the bag on the top of the pile. It looked just like a sack of concrete. The same type of heavy, brown paper bag sealed on both ends with a string seam. The company logo on the bag pictured a gopher walking away with a nap sack thrown over its shoulder. In bright red letters it read, "DILMONT GOPHER BE GONE." Below the picture was their guarantee. "They're gone or your money back."

Steve figured that he would have to try the poison before too long. The traps that he had set out weren't working very well. As a matter of fact, the traps weren't working at all. At first he would go out and set the traps and the next day he would check them and he would have a gopher or two. After a week or so, he would go out and check them and there wouldn't be any gophers, but the bait would be gone. Then the traps themselves started disappearing. After that pieces of the traps started reappearing. They would show up all over the park, though a lot of them were showing up near the tower. Frank had been right. You had to poison the little buggers out or they would take over.

Steve closed and locked the shed. He tossed the shovel up onto his shoulder and headed out toward the observation tower. He thought about the bags lying in the shed and he started to laugh. He had just realized that with the shovel thrown over his shoulder he looked just like one of the pictures on one of the sacks of poison.

As he walked out to the tower he looked around the park and affirmed to himself that the park was in a real mess. There were holes everywhere. It was rapidly changing from a grass-covered park to a hole farm. He was going to have to change that. He would use up the stuff in the shed, and then he was going to order some more. He was going to put the gophers in their place once and for all. Why, if one of the park inspectors showed up he would close down the park as a safety hazard. His head would be on the chopping block for letting the place get into this kind of condition.

He got out to the tower and found the hole right where the guy had told him it was, and it was enormous! Four feet across and maybe twice as deep. All sorts of dirt was mounded up around the sides, like something had dug it from underneath. It was way too big to be a gopher hole, though. A gopher would have to be the size of a German Shepherd to have dug a hole this big. It was going to take a couple of hours to fill it in. He was definitely going to be late getting out of here tonight.

Steve threw the last shovel full of dirt into the hole and patted it down. His two-hour estimate had been almost right. It had taken just a little over two hours. He stood back and inspected his work. It was a little low in the middle, but you never could get all the dirt back into a hole that had come out of it. This was good enough. At least nobody was going to fall into it now. Tomorrow he could bring out a couple of wheelbarrows full of dirt and top it off. That would finish it up just fine.

He turned to go when he heard a low rustling sound. It was just like the sound he had heard the first week that he had run the park by himself, but somehow it was a little different. It was more defined, louder, clearer. This time there was a squeaking that was the undertone of the whole sound. It seemed to be coming from over by the big mound. That was the place that Frank had led him to. Steve set the shovel down and started walking through the park toward the direction of the noise.

As he worked his way through the mounds the sound got louder, stronger, and he was right, the noise was coming from the direction of the big mound. It was so loud by the time that he got there he could feel it rising up through his feet!

He stepped out from behind one of the smaller mounds that surrounded the big mound and the sound all of a sudden just stopped. It was just like it had never been there to begin with.

Steve started looking around for the source of the noise. It had to have been coming from around here somewhere. He walked all the way around the big mound but didn't find a thing. He decided that he would have better luck locating the sound if he climbed to the top of the mound. From up on the top maybe he could see where it had been coming from. He crawled up the steep slippery sides of the mound. When he got to the very summit he found the cause of the disturbance. There was another gigantic hole, right in the middle of the mound!

It wasn't much bigger than the hole that had been over by the observation tower, but it was a whole lot deeper. Steve looked down over the vertical sides of the shaft and couldn't see the bottom. He picked up a fist-sized rock that was lying in the overburden and dropped it into the hole. It seemed like it took forever before he heard the faint sounds that it made when it impacted the bottom. He didn't know what he was going to do. It would take weeks to fill this in by hand. This was the kind of job that would take truckloads and truckloads of dirt to fill in. He would have to call this in to the main office. It was just too big for one man to handle!

He slid down the side of the mound and started back to the ranger station. What could have caused such a large hole? Were sink holes going to start opening up under the park? That would be horrible! Why, that was just the kind of thing that could get the park closed down! That's all he needed was to have his first command shut down.

As Steve was walking back to the ranger station the air became extremely still. The small noises that always went on in the park all of a sudden came to a halt. Off in the distance a single dog that was barking stopped. A flock of birds rose all at once into the darkness. Their wings, cutting through the silence, halted Steve in his tracks. He could feel that something wasn't right.

That's when the ground started to shake! The earth rolled madly and the accompanying roar was almost deafening. Steve couldn't keep his footing and was thrown to the ground. He bounced around like a leaf in a storm. It seemed to go on forever. He landed on his side and tried to dig his fingers into the tough prairie grass in an attempt to hang on to something.

The intensity of the quake increased and Steve was being thrown every which way. The ground kept leaping, and with a crack like a sonic boom the earth opened up and a long rift appeared at Steve's feet. He tried to get away from the widening chasm but the violence of the quake prevented that.

To his horror the crack continued to widen. There was nothing he could do to keep himself from falling in. Loose clumps of dirt and grass started to drift down into the crack and Steve started to slide in with them. The very rocks under his feet gave way and the next thing he knew he was rolling down the side of the cliff.

He hit the bottom and landed on something soft. The impact was accompanied by a very loud squeal. Just as suddenly as it had started, the earthquake stopped.

The something that Steve had landed on was covered in dense, soft fur! Steve got to his feet and looked at the thing he had hit. It was the biggest gopher that he had ever seen. It was so big that it could have easily made the hole over by the observation tower. It also could have dug the hole on the top of the big mound. It was the size of a German Shepherd and weighed at least one hundred and twenty pounds. And it was very dead. "I must have killed it when I landed on it," he said to himself.

Steve quit looking at the gopher and started to look around at his predicament. One side of the fissure he was in was almost sheer. The other sloped up to the top at a steep angle, but, not too steep for Steve to climb. Then he saw the remains of what had to be a tunnel. A gopher hole! It penetrated the sheer wall and ran off into the darkness. There were sounds coming from deep inside the burrow.

Steve wasted no time in climbing up the easy side of the fissure. He didn't want whatever was making those sounds to catch him in this hole. He had to get back to the ranger station and get his gun! That's what he had to do. Go and get his gun! These things had to be dangerous. If something like this got a hold of one of the visitors there was no telling what would happen. They would close down the park for sure!

Why hadn't he used the gopher poison? He should have used the gopher poison! Now he was going to have to kill them before they became a danger, because if they got out of the fissure they would become dangerous. He knew it! It was his job to protect the park.

He ran for the ranger station. The station had fared the quake well. There was no discernible damage to it. Steve unlocked the door and raced inside. He unlocked the drawer where he kept his gun, a nine-millimeter automatic, rammed a clip into the gun and raced back out into the darkness of the park. He had to protect the park!

Several minutes passed and then the sound of two shots knifed through the darkness. That's when the aftershock hit!

The search went on for over a month. Searchers combed every inch of the park and the adjacent farms. Harry, the service man at the gas station in Little Rock, said he thought he might have heard gunshots between the quakes but he couldn't tell for sure. Steve Donner had just up and vanished!

DOUBLE, DOUBLE

Carl quickly nudged the Firebird up to eighty. The car shot down the freeway leaving in its wake an afterglow of hidden horsepower. His exit was coming up and he didn't want to miss it. If he did, the next one was going to be all the way down to Fort Lewis and that was another five miles. That would be five miles out of his way.

He swung across two lanes of traffic, just barely missed a pickup, which was towing a boat behind it and caught the off-ramp with inches to spare. The truck slammed on his brakes and the horn blared. Carl just ignored him. "Stupid people," Carl said to himself. "If he had been watching he would have known that I was coming over."

Carl downshifted and came to a California stop at the light at the end of the off-ramp. Out of the corner of his eye he saw a hitchhiker standing on the side of the road. Something struck Carl about the guy standing there. Something strange, something familiar. Carl turned his head to get a good look, but it was too late. Another car had already stopped and the guy was climbing in. All he could see of the hitchhiker was the tail of his coat as he got into the other car.

Carl was almost to the bar when he realized what it was that had struck him about the guy on the side of the road. It was his coat. The guy's coat was just like the one that Carl had. He looked at his coat lying on the seat next to him. It was a custom made jacket from a small shop in L.A. The chances of someone from up here going to the same tailor that Carl had used were slim and next to none.

He grabbed the jacked from the seat and headed for the bar. He didn't have time to waste. He was going to be late if he sat here and tried to puzzle out why someone else had his coat. Once he got inside he forgot all about it.

He looked at his watch as he walked into the bar. He was right on time. Not a minute early, not a minute late. Right on time. He had been working at Follie's Restaurant and Bar for a little over a month now and he had been late almost every day. Yesterday, the owner, Dave, had collared him and told him that if he was late once more he might as well not even bother to come back. He looked at his watch again and he was right on time.

He had decided right after Dave had given him his ultimatum that he would mind his manners for at least another month. Besides, every time he had been late he had been out with Karen. She was a lot of fun but it was getting time to break off the relationship. If her husband ever found out what they were doing the shit would really hit the fan! After everything that had been happening lately that's all that he needed.

Carl had been fired from his last bartending job at the Eagles down in Little Rock. The president of the club had caught him tapping the till. Carl hadn't taken very much at a time, just a twenty here and there. When he got caught he had even offered to make it right, pay the money back. But they had fired him anyway. So, he really needed this job. At least for another month.

In another month he would have enough to quit and then he could move up to Seattle. The pickings up in a big city like Seattle would be a hell of a lot easier than they were down here.

"Cutting it pretty close, aren't you?" said Kay, the day-shift bartender, as Carl stepped behind the bar.

"And what if I am," said Carl. "I'm on my own time before the shift starts, ain't I?"

Kay came out from behind the bar. "Well, you know what the boss said and he's going to be watching you. If you want to keep working here, you had better try and be a tad bit earlier, because if you're late, you're gone."

"Sure, sure," said Carl. He put on his apron, picked up a glass from the rack and started polishing it. "As a matter of fact, Miss Be-On-Time, you should mind your own business and I'll mind mine."

Kay headed for the door. "If that's the way you want it," she said as she walked out.

"That would be just fine by me!"

Follie's was a good-sized bar, but it wasn't huge. It had four pool tables that sat out in the middle of the floor and there were several electric dartboards lining one wall. During Carl's shift the place had gotten pretty busy, but by midnight it had almost cleared out.

The clock struck twelve and there was only one customer left. He was sitting in a booth back against the far wall nursing a drink. Something about him looked familiar to Carl, but he just couldn't put his finger on it. He watched him out of the corner of his eye for a while and decided that something wasn't quite right. He didn't want any trouble and it was getting late, so he decided that now was as good a time as any to close up.

Carl didn't remember seeing the guy sitting over in the corner earlier in the evening. He couldn't even remember having served him, but with the place as busy as it had been, that wasn't unusual. He hadn't seen him come in, so Carl had no idea how long the guy had been there. As far as Carl knew, the guy could have been sitting there less than an hour or he could have been there all night. He just didn't know, but it was now time to close up.

"Hey, bud," called Carl. "Drink up. It's closing time."

The man took a sip from his drink and slid a little farther back into the shadows of the booth. "Just a minute of your time, Carl," he said as he set the glass down on the table. "We have something to talk about."

"Do I know you?" asked Carl. "I think I might have seen you somewhere before, but I don't know where."

"No," said the man. "You don't know me. You may have seen me somewhere before, though. I haven't been that careful. Which, I am glad to say, will turn out to be extremely unlucky for you. Seeing me, that is. But you don't know me."

Carl started out from behind the bar. "It's time to leave," he said. He had half of a pool cue in his hand and he smacked it into the palm of the other. "Now," he said as the pool cue came down in his hand to stress the point, "before I throw you out."

He took a step toward the table and that's when he saw the jacket. It was lying across the back of the booth. Now Carl realized where he had seen the guy. "Hey, you're the guy who was over by the freeway hitchhiking when I came in to work today."

The man receded a little farther into the shadows of the booth. "That's correct, Carl," he said.

"What are you doing here?" Carl asked. "If this has something to do with Karen you can just tell her and her old man to blow off. It's all over, you see. I'm all done with her. I ain't involved no more."

"It has nothing to do with Karen," said the man. "It has to do with you, though."

"Me?" said Carl. "What do you mean it has to do with me? You get yourself up right now and get the hell out of my bar!"

The man remained seated. "They say that it is bad luck for someone to see his own doppelganger," he said calmly from the shadows of the booth.

Carl started across the floor. The pool cue swung freely in his hand. "What the hell are you talking about? A doppelganger. Why, I ain't ever heard of any such thing." Carl stopped beside the booth. "Now get out!"

The man sat in the shadows. He slowly reached over and took another sip from his drink. "A doppelganger," he said, "is a vestige of one's own self. A being from another probability is a good way to think of it. A possible you, the person you could have been if you had only tried." The man set his drink back down on the table.

"So," said Carl. "What's that have to do with me?"

"Why, everything," said the man. "The way you are makes you a perfect target. As you would say it, easy pickings. A doppelganger could just slip right into your life and no one would ever notice. It would be a perfect exchange. Simple."

Carl brought the pool cue down hard on the table. "You get out of here right now!" he said. "And take your line of crap with you. I don't have to listen to any of this shit. Out!" Carl leaned into the booth and grabbed the man by the arm. As he pulled him out of the back of the booth he finally got a good look at the man. Carl stopped and let go of him. He took a step back and stared into the man's face. He couldn't believe what he was seeing. He was looking at himself sitting in that booth.

Carl stopped cold, his feet glued to the floor. He was just standing there staring into his own eyes. As he looked at the strange man sitting there he saw things about himself he had never even thought about. It was just like looking into your own heart.

The man sat calmly in the booth staring back at Carl. He picked up his glass from the table and finished his drink. "And now it's time," he said as he set the glass back down on the tabletop.

The door to the bar burst open. Exploding pieces of wood and metal flew everywhere, ricocheting off the walls and ceiling. What remained of the door slowly rocked back on its shattered hinges.

A huge man stood in the broken remains. His clothing was splattered all over with what looked like fresh blood. Cradled in his hands was a semiautomatic twelve-gauge shotgun. He held it like an old friend. He looked all around the bar and then his eyes fell on Carl.

"That's the last time she's ever gonna do that!" he said. He laughed a little as he raised the gun and pointed it directly at Carl's chest. "She ain't ever gonna do nothing again. That's for sure."

Carl backed up slowly until he had finally backed into the bar. He was still holding a section of the pool cue. If the chance came, he was going to try and take this guy out with it. Right now though, as a weapon, it was really puny compared to the shotgun. "Take it easy, Dreg," he said. "I think we got a major misunderstanding going on here."

The man in the booth sat quietly and watched the show that was coming down. Neither of the combatants paid any attention to him.

"No, we don't," said Dreg as he thumbed the safety on the side of the shotgun. "I think that now we understand each other perfectly. Let me tell you, Karen understands. That's for certain."

The blast hit Carl in the chest and lifted him over the bar. He lay on the floor a bleeding dying wreck. Dreg walked over to the bar and looked at his work. He reached over the bar with the barrel of the gun and nudged Carl gently with it, just to make sure he was dead. Carl made a squishy, burbling sound.

"What?" said Dreg. "You're not going to be one of them guys that's hard to kill, are you? Don't worry, I can take care of that for you right away." He placed the barrel of the gun against Carl's head and fired it off a second time.

Dreg stepped back from the bar and looked at the body lying on the floor. "Neither of you is ever gonna to do that again," he said. A smile appeared on his face as he stuck the barrel of the gun into his own mouth and pulled the trigger.

When it was all over the man in the booth got up. He went over and looked at one body and then he looked at the other. When he was satisfied that all was right he went back to what was left of Carl. He bent over the body and gently took Carl's wallet from his pocket and placed it in his own. He then removed another wallet from his coat and inserted it into Carl's pocket. He carefully searched through Carl's other pockets until he found his car keys and house keys. He then went back to his table to retrieve his glass, which he placed in the dish tray that sat next to the house phone.

He picked up the phone and called 911. It rang twice before it was answered. "911 emergency. How may I help you?"

The man was calm as he said into the phone, "This is Carl Riley. I'm working over at Follie's Bar. I need the police. You see there's been a murder."

MIRROR, MIRROR

Henry slammed on the brakes and laid into the horn at the same time. The late-model Firebird had just cut him off and then paid no attention to him as it disappeared down the off-ramp. Henry could feel the boat trailer start to sway behind his truck. He took his foot off the brake and gave the truck a little more gas. Not very much, just enough to let the truck speed back up and take the sway out of the trailer. The trailer brakes were getting tired and he was going to have to change them before too long. Things smoothed out just as soon as his speed picked back up.

As soon as he had things back under control he started yelling at the other driver. "You stupid jerk!" he shouted at the car as it vanished down the off-ramp. "What the hell do you think you're doing?" There was nothing that Henry could do but yell. The incident was over and done with and the other car was long gone. Even if he took the next off-ramp and turned around there was no way that he would ever catch up with the other car. He fumed for a little while and then he started to calm down.

Why should he let one stupid jerk wreck his trip? He was going to make a lot of money out of this shot and it just wasn't worth letting one creep ruin it. Nothing had changed. He was still heading for the boat launch down at Dupont. The truck wasn't wrecked and the boat hadn't been scratched, so what was he mad about? Life was good. If the boat had been wrecked, now that would have been another story.

The twenty-six foot Bayliner that Henry was towing was his pride and joy. It had cost him almost thirty thousand dollars, but he felt that it was worth every dime he'd spent. Everything that you could get for a boat was on board. There was radar, for seeing things in the dark or when it was foggy. A sonar unit, for finding your depth or finding fish. The neatest thing, though, was the LandSat system. With this, you could locate yourself anywhere on the planet to within fifty feet of your actual location. On top of it all, his boat could sleep six!

Henry turned off the freeway at the Dupont exit. The speed limit through the old part of town was twenty-five miles an hour. So Henry had time to look the town over as he drove through. Halfway through town on the left is the city park. It was your typical turn-of-the-century type park with a lot of grass, a big barbecue pit and a baseball diamond. Smoke rolled lazily up out of the barbecue pit as a game of slow pitch was going on. There were kids with skateboards using the sidewalks and bicycles leaned against the fence behind the baseball diamond.

Henry watched it all as he drove through and thought that it was just great. This was just the sort of place that he had been looking for all his life. Maybe, when he was done with his research out on the tide flats, he would check into this town. If his project panned out like he hoped it would, he could afford to live anyplace he wanted to.

Nisqually Flats is possibly the only natural salt flat left on the west coast. A salt flat is where a river dumps into a body of salt water creating a huge delta and marsh. All the rest of the flats have been developed over the years. The Nisqually Flats covers almost four square miles. It extends from the small town of Dupont on the north shore all the way to Dewolf Bight on the south, and from the shores of Puget Sound all the way back to Interstate Five.

Henry's plan was to spend at least a week out in the flats searching for PCBs. As far as he was able to find out this type of research had never been performed in the flats. In 1976 the Dupont Company closed down the nitroglycerin and black powder plants that they had run there. They had sold the property to the Weyerhaeuser Company. That was before anybody really knew anything about PCBs. If Henry could find any trace of toxins he would be able to show his results to the Nisqually Tribe and have them file a class action lawsuit in federal court. Once the suit was in effect he would be in fat city. He could charge big bucks for his research, not to mention what he would realize from his percentage of the lawsuit.

Henry reached the other side of town and took a left on an old gravel road that led down to the boat ramp and dock. He drove about a mile through oak and fir woodland before he reached the site of the old dock. He pulled into the parking lot just as dusk was setting in. By the time he got the boat launched it would be too late for him to get started. Henry decided that he would put the boat in and then tie up to the old dock. It would be a good place to spend the night. In the morning he could get an early start.

Launching a twenty-six foot boat by yourself, even if it is on an Easy-Load tilt trailer, isn't a simple job. To do it right, it really takes two people.

Henry had lots of practice at this, though, and eventually he had the boat in the water. It was all just part of the job. He had backed the trailer down the ramp just until water started to lap at the back bumper of the truck.

He shut down the truck, set the emergency brake and placed the transmission in park. This kept the whole operation from rolling backwards into the bay. Henry had known a guy that had let his truck slip and everything ended up in the water. It had taken a wrecker to pull the truck out and it had been a total loss. It seems that the guy had left his truck running and it had slipped into reverse. It ended up in about thirty feet of water before it had stopped rolling. Ever since Henry had heard this story he had made a point of securing his truck before he got out.

Getting out of the truck, he walked around the trailer to see how it was lined up on the ramp. Everything was sitting square in the center, right where Henry wanted it to be. He unlocked the battery-operated winch control and lowered the boat the rest of the way into the water. The trailer tipped slightly up on its axles as the boat slipped off. Once the boat was in the water the trailer was ready to be hauled out.

Henry took the painter line from the bow of the boat and tied it off to a piling that was located next to the boat launch. He unhooked the winch cable and rolled it back onto the spool. With all that done, he got back into the truck and drove it back up the ramp. He found a place to park in the empty lot, got out and locked everything up. He looked everything over once more just to see how it was and headed back down to the boat.

Marinda reclined on the very end of the dock. This was as close to the land as she dared come. The late afternoon sun warmed her as she combed her long silk-fine hair. Sunlight danced off of her tortoiseshell comb with each sweeping stroke it made through her long, lovely hair. When she was satisfied, she put the comb away and picked up her lovely, old hand mirror.

It had been a gift from a long-distant lover. A gift that she could never part with. A gift from a lover who had died a long, long, time ago. A gift from a time when magic had lived in the world.

Pearls surrounded the perfectly flawless pane of crystal that made up the lens. It was backed in the finest Irish silver that could be produced. The frame was made of the purest gold taken from a deep-water wreck off the coast of South America. It was the most beautiful hand mirror that had ever been made, a true work of art. Marinda loved her mirror and her mirror loved her in return.

She gently swished her lovely fluted tail back and forth in the water as she gazed at her perfect reflection in the mirror. What looked back at her was a vision of beauty. In the mirror, her long wavy hair shown with the mellowest shades of red and gold as it caught the fading light. The gleam off the water was captured in her eyes and showed their sea-green depth. She looked at herself and decided that she was still beautiful. This made her happy.

From the woods by the shore came a faint rumbling sound. Wafts of dust rose on the still evening air. Startled she dropped her mirror on the dock and dove into the water. The ice blue sea closed over her descending body without a ripple.

With each powerful stroke of her tail she moved farther away from the dock and closer toward the bottom. Once she reached the seabed she would be safe and free from prying eyes. The bottom came suddenly into her view. Sea pens sprouted from the mud and silt, like flowers in a mountain meadow. Their bright orange tops gently waved back and forth as she quickly swam through them.

She found a nice spot on the bottom and gently came to rest, interrupting the slumber of an old Sea Cucumber who moved slowly off. She reached out and gave him a gentle pat as he crawled away. "Silly," she said. "Where do you think you're going in such a hurry?"

She settled down onto the sea floor and removed her comb from her pocket. She started combing her beautiful hair. When she was satisfied that it was all combed out into a flowing profusion of tangle-free splendor, she reached for her mirror so she could once again gaze upon her own beauty. That was when she found that the mirror was gone!

In frenzy, she began turning over stones and long leaves of kelp in her search. She dug her fingers into the soft bottom in the hope that it had accidentally been buried there. No place was left unchecked. In despair, she was just about to give up when she remembered that she had dropped the mirror on the hard planks of the dock just before she dove into the water.

How could she have been so stupid, to have just left it lying there where it could be found by anyone? It was her mirror, her only mirror. How could she look upon herself if she lost her mirror? She had possessed her mirror for so long. Without it she would be lost. How would she be able to see her reflection if it was lost? She would once again be as she was, as she was before her long lost lover had made a present of the mirror to her. Ugly! Without a way to see herself.

She had to return to the surface and retrieve her mirror. There was no question about that. It was unthinkable to leave it just lying there on the dock. She would have to go back and get it, and if anyone else tried to claim what was hers that would be their own misfortune!

Henry shut down the engines as the boat nudged gently against the float. The tide was in and the ramp that connected the float to the dock was almost level with the dock. At low tide the float could be as much as fifteen feet below the dock. There were no other boats tied up to the float at this time. Depending on the season the place could be full, but as it was, Henry had the whole dock to himself.

He tossed the stern line out onto the float. It landed on the wet slippery deck with a watery thud. He climbed over the gunnels and made the line fast to one of the cleats on the float. He scrambled back on board and made his way forward so he could tie off the bowline. That's when he spotted something shiny up on the dock.

He stood on the bow with the bowline in his hand and just watched the gentle glow that came from the shiny thing on the dock. "What the heck is that?" he said aloud to himself. He tossed the bowline and nimbly jumped down onto the float. His curiosity had gotten the better of him and he just had to go up on the dock and see what the shiny thing was. When he landed on the dock the bow of the boat gently pivoted out and dragged the line he had just thrown into the water. It was a lucky thing that the stern was tied off or the boat would have drifted away from the float.

Henry made his way up the bobbing, weaving ramp to the dock. The evenly spaced cleats of the ramp hit the center of his boat shoes with every step. Out on the end of the dock was a brilliantly lit speck of glittering something. Henry walked out to it and stopped. He looked down at the shining thing. It was a hand mirror, but it was not like any hand mirror that Henry had ever seen. It was the most beautiful work of art that he had ever had the pleasure of seeing!

He bent down and picked up it up. The weight of it in his hand felt good. The handle rested firmly in his palm as he inspected the mirror. *How could someone have just left this here?* he thought as his eyes traced its intricate detailing. The design ran from the handle all the way up the back of the mirror. It had been cut into the gold of the casing with loving care. Mother-of-pearl had been delicately inlaid into the pattern. The lens of the mirror was surrounded with the largest and whitest pearls that Henry had ever seen. The whole mirror was beauty itself.

When Henry looked into the depths of the lens, the reflection that stared back at him seemed to have a life of its own. It was sharp and clear, just like it was looking out at him. Henry was sure that if he wanted to, he could reach right into the glass and touch it.

Just then a loud splash echoed off the end of the dock. Henry heard the noise and was distracted from the image inside the mirror. He shook his head to clear the dancing images of the inlay from his eyes and looked around. There was no one there. He grasped the mirror firmly in his hands and went back to the boat.

As he reached the boat another loud splash came from the end of the dock. Henry looked around again. There was no one there. Henry felt uneasy. Maybe the owner was coming back to look for the mirror. Maybe a thief had come to steal it from him. He looked around again as he boarded the boat. The dock was empty. When he was sure that he was alone he took his new prize down below deck and hid it carefully under a cushion in his bunk. It would be safe there for the time being.

He went back up on deck and noticed that he hadn't tied off the bowline. The bow of the boat was pointing away from the float and out toward the boat ramp. Henry retrieved the bowline from the water and made it fast to the float.

Marinda gently broke the surface of the water. She was at the exact point where she had made her mad plunge toward the depths. She watched the man-thing as he walked down the dock. He was carrying her mirror! She watched as he boarded a boat that was tied up to a float next to the dock. She could tell just by the way the man-thing moved that the mirror now possessed him. That was part of what came with having the mirror. It took a strong will for one to control the power that was contained within the mirror without having the mirror control you.

Marinda had owned the mirror for more years than she could count, and still sometimes she found herself doing its bidding instead of it doing hers.

She gently floated in the water and silently made her plans. She watched the man-thing as he tied up the boat and went inside. She knew that he had taken the mirror inside with him. He was going to hide it. She could hear the mirror as it called to her from its hidden place. She had to have it back or she would surely die! She had to reclaim it, take it back anyway she could, even if it meant touching the land.

She couldn't just climb aboard the boat the way she was. Her sleek, seal shape would prevent any climbing and quick movement when she was out of the water. So, this shape was out of the question. There was only one way that she could board the boat and move quickly and that was to change her form. She silently swam toward the beach.

As she swam she formed out her plan. She would touch the land, and as soon as she did, she would lose her beautiful shape. It would change. She would become like one of the man-things. She would lose her lovely tail and it would grow into a pair of the ugly legs that the man-things used to move around on the land. She knew that every step would be like walking on hot knives. There was always pain with a change. But for her mirror she would do anything. She would not be as she was until she had immersed herself once again in the sea. Once she changed, she would race for the boat, regain her mirror and once again plunge back into the sea. There was no other way.

When she had reached the beach, night had already fallen. Her transformation took place in the lonely darkness. She lay on the muddy sand in agony. Hot razors slashed up and down her new found legs and feet. A universe of pain throbbed through her whole body! She had never thought that anything could have hurt so much. She lay on the beach in the darkness crying. How was she ever going to reclaim her mirror now? This was all a mistake. She should crawl back into the sea where she had come from and call it quits. The mirror couldn't be worth all of this, could it?

Suddenly the magnitude of the pain eased. As it diminished, it became something that she could live with, tolerate if she had to. She knew though, that like an old friend, the pain would always be there. It would never go completely away. She rose and gingerly took a few steps. The torment of each step was immense, but she would just have to put up with it. That was going to be the only way, the only way she could get her mirror back. She took another step as the pain shot up her legs. One step at a time. That was how she was going to do it. One step at a time until she reached her goal. She slowly made her way toward the dock and as she moved the pain lessened.

Henry sat in the dark cabin of the boat thinking about the mirror. He thought about its shape. He thought about the texture and feel of the metal it was made of. He thought about its weight as he held it in his hands. He was just going to get it out when he heard a noise. It was a quiet thumping, like someone who was having trouble walking down the dock. Henry changed his mind about taking the mirror out. It wouldn't do to have someone see it. They might want it. The mirror would be safe for the time being where he had hidden it.

He came up on deck and looked down the dock. He didn't see anything. It was dark and empty. He called out, "Who's out there?" There was no answer.

As Henry listened he heard the noise again. He reached into one of the storage compartments on the back deck and pulled out a flashlight. He clicked it on and ran its beam down the length of the deck. The light permeated the darkness like a beacon. About halfway down the dock it struck its target. A woman was slowly making her way down the length of the dock toward the boat.

Henry couldn't believe it. She was the most beautiful woman that he had ever seen! And she was nude, except she wasn't. Her gorgeous long hair wrapped around her like a robe. It drug in a train behind her on the dock. Each step she took was slow and careful. Henry thought that it looked like it was causing her quite a bit of pain just to walk.

Henry jumped onto the float and headed up the ramp for the dock. He kept the beam of light on the woman all the time. "Are you OK?" he called as he headed toward her. "Do you need help?"

She didn't answer, but just kept slowly walking down the dock toward him.

Henry moved down the dock toward the woman. When he reached her she did not stop, but just kept walking as if in a daze. He gently reached out and grasped her by the shoulder. She stopped immediately but didn't say a word.

"Are you hurt?" asked Henry.

She didn't answer. She didn't move. She just stood quietly in the chill night air.

Henry took off the light windbreaker jacket he was wearing and draped it over her shoulders. "Come with me," he said. "I've got a cell phone down in the boat. We can call someone from there and get you some help."

Henry guided the woman as they started moving back toward the boat. Since the appearance of the woman he had all but forgotten about the mirror. He got her back to the boat and helped her down below. He carefully helped her to sit on one of the bunks and covered her with a blanket. "The phone is up topside," he said. "I'll just go up and get it. I won't be a minute." She didn't answer. He climbed the stairs that led up to the main deck two at a time.

Marinda sat on the bunk. Pain shot from her feet up her legs and through her lower back as she moved from the bunk. Daggers dug into her chest with every breath she took. That was all right though. She was close to the mirror. She could feel it. Despite the pain she quickly started searching the cabin for her mirror. She found it in seconds hidden in the bedding of the other bunk.

She clutched the jacket tighter around herself as she clasped the mirror to her breast. It was so good to once again be rejoined with her gift. As she sat clutching the mirror she could hear the sounds the man-thing was making as he moved around up on the deck. He would be coming back any minute. Marinda had spent much more time in this form than she wanted to. She had her mirror and now it was time to go. She cautiously got up from the bunk and carefully took the first step that lead up to the deck and back to the sea.

Henry was frantic! He had the phone in his hand and he paced the deck. Should he call 911 or not? He just didn't know what was he going to do with this woman. It was clear that she was in some kind of trouble, but what kind? If he called the cops there would be all kind of questions. The mirror suddenly snapped back into his mind! What if her trouble involved the mirror? What if she was a thief who had really come to steal it away from him? It was his now. He had found it and it was his.

Henry put the phone down. Maybe he should find out some more about this woman before he jumped into anything. He should ask her some questions and he should get some answers before he called the cops. He started back toward the cabin. He would ask her about the mirror. She had to be after the mirror. That was it. He would ask her about the mirror!

He started back toward the cabin, but before he got to the door it burst open! The woman erupted out from below deck like a storm. She was clutching the mirror in her right hand and she was moving fast. She saw Henry and put on a burst of speed as she lunged for the side of the boat. She had to reach the open sea!

All Henry saw was a flash of movement and realized that it was the woman. She was stealing his mirror! He turned and tried to tackle the passing figure, but she was too fast. He just touched her naked shoulder as she passed. She dove over the side in a graceful arch and entered the water with hardly a splash.

Henry leaned over the side of the boat as he watched the figure of the woman disappear into the deep water. He watched her as she swam deeper and deeper. When she had almost vanished from sight he thought he saw something strange happening to her. The woman seemed to be changing into a fish! Henry rubbed his eyes as he watched her legs turn into a tail and then she was gone.

He stood at the rail. He couldn't believe what he had just seen. It had to be just a trick of the water. She would have to be a mermaid or something to be able to do that and there was no such thing as a mermaid. Was there? He moved up to the bridge and turned on the big spotlight that was mounted to the side of the boat. He scoured the surface of the water for any sign of the woman. No one could hold their breath forever. She had to come back up some time.

He made several passes over the water with the light before he saw something flash. It was maybe a hundred feet off the starboard end of the dock and was definitely coming closer. It looked like it was just barely under the surface of the water. Henry just knew that it was the spotlight reflecting off the mirror. He was sure that she was still holding it in her hand. He could just feel it. He was sure it was the mirror.

He stood on the side of the boat and watched the light as it moved and flashed just under the surface. It was so beautiful. So alluring! Now it was close enough that he could just make out the shape of the mirror. It shined in the spotlight, beckoning him, calling him. He had to have it back! That was all. He just had to have it back. He had found it and it was his. What right did that woman, or mermaid, or whatever she was, have to take it from him? He had found it and it was his!

Henry dove from the side of the boat into the ice-cold water. The sea closed quietly over him.

The boat rested gently next to the float. The ropes were slack and it rocked lightly with the incoming tide. Shades of night soundlessly washed its decks as the moon and stars looked down. The spotlight threw its ghostly beam across the water until the batteries went dead.

THE LADY IN THE LAKE

Crystal Conners sat on the sidewalk and tightened the laces on her roller blades. Her friend Terry Brooks sat down beside her. He was getting tired of waiting for her.

"Come on, Chris," he said. "Will you hurry up? We're going to be late for the game, and I don't want to miss the opening pitch."

"I'm doing this just as fast as I can," said Crystal. "Besides, what's so important about an old baseball game, anyway? So what if we're a little late."

"What's so important!" said Terry as he got back up from the sidewalk. "It's just about the biggest game of the whole season, that's what's so important! If you had lived here last year you would know all about it. Last season Boeing beat Intel by just one point in the twelfth inning and that sent Boeing to the play-offs." Terry started off down the sidewalk. "Come on!"

Crystal's parents had moved from Santa Clara, California at the beginning of the summer. They had received an offer from Intel that was just too good to pass up. They had bought a three thousand square foot home in a development called North Landing. It was just outside of the town of Dupont, Washington, where Intel had opened their main plant.

"Well, I wasn't here last year," said Crystal. She finished lacing her skates and got up. "OK," she said as she started skating down the sidewalk. "Let's go."

A new Dodge Ram pickup drove slowly down the street past the two kids. It was towing the biggest boat that Crystal had ever seen on a trailer. She stopped and watched the truck as it went by.

Terry turned around and skated back to her. "What's wrong now?" he asked.

"Oh, nothing," she answered as she watched the truck. "You know, Terry," she said when the truck had turned the corner and was gone, "one day I'm going to have a boat just like that."

"Sure you are," said Terry. "Why, my dad couldn't even afford a boat like that and he practically runs the plant."

"Well, I'm going to," said Crystal. "You just wait and see."

"That's great," said Terry. "But don't expect me to hold my breath. Come on. Let's go." He skated off ahead of Crystal.

Crystal held back a little and let Terry get farther ahead. One day she was going to have a boat just like that one, she just knew it! She didn't care what Terry Brooks thought about it either.

Terry had continued skating toward the park all the while as Crystal had dallied behind and now he was halfway down the block. She put on a burst of speed and caught up with him. "Race you to the park," she said as she blew past him.

"Eat my dust!" called Terry as he easily outpaced her. He skated hard and fast. It would never do to be beaten by a girl. He was waiting for her at the bleachers when she came huffing in.

"Beat you, beat you," he catcalled when he saw her.

"Did not," said Crystal as she flopped down in the bleachers. "My skates weren't tight enough. It wasn't a fair race." She bent down and started fidgeting with one of her skates. "These laces just don't stay tight enough. They loosen up after a few minutes."

"Sure," said Terry. "I beat you by a mile!"

"I have to get new laces," said Crystal. "And next time all you'll see of me is my taillights."

They skated over to the refreshment stand and got some popcorn and a couple of Cokes. Then they went back to the bleachers, found their seats and settled in to watch the game. It was a fierce game, just as Terry had predicted. Intel took the lead early in the game, but two hours, three cokes, and four hot dogs later, they went down to defeat Boeing by a score of six to five.

After the game, Crystal and Terry headed back to Crystal's house. She had told her parents that she would back by dinnertime. Crystal was carrying her skates over her shoulder and slowly walked barefoot down the road. Terry was skating down the sidewalk beside her.

"Hey, Chris," Terry said as they came to the main gate for North Landing, "before you go home, you want to see something really cool?"

"What could you show me that was really cool?" asked Crystal as she shifted her skates to the other shoulder.

""Well," said Terry, "I don't know if anybody has taken you down to see the lake yet."

"What lake? I didn't know there was a lake anywhere around here."

"Well," said Terry, "it's not much of a lake. Actually, it's more of a pond. It's just over on the other side of the development in the woods."

"Does this pond have a name or anything like that?"

"Course it does," said Terry. "It's called Old Fort Lake."

"Old Fort Lake," said Crystal. "What kind of name is that for a pond?"

"Well, my dad said that old Fort Nisqually was originally around here someplace. That was years ago before they took it down and moved it up to Point Defiance Park in Tacoma. You know, it was one of the original Hudson Bay trading posts for this area. That was around two hundred years ago. Do you believe that? Well, I guess that the fort must have been really close so that's how the lake got the name."

"OK," said Crystal. "Let's go have a look."

They cut across to the other side of the development and headed for the woods. An old barbed wire fence ran down one side of the two-lane highway that separated the new housing development from the older farms and forest that made up the rest of the neighborhood. Nailed to the top of one of the fence posts was an old sign. It read, "NO TRESPASSING," in what use to be bright bold letters. It had been up so long that the lettering was fading and peeling. Terry and Crystal clambered between the wires of the fence and were gone like ninjas into the forest.

They ran down the trail from the road at full speed until they were sure that they could not be seen from the road, and then stopped to catch their breath. Crystal had never been here before. She looked at everything while they rested.

It was an old wood with large trees everywhere. It hadn't been logged in at least a hundred years. Most of the trees were douglas fir, but every once in a while there would be a maple or an alder. The trail cut through dense patches of brush and wild huckleberry. Ferns erupted here and there from beneath the underbrush.

"How far to this lake?" asked Crystal.

"Not far now," said Terry. "Maybe fifteen, twenty minutes at the most. We'll be there anytime."

"Let's go then," said Crystal.

"OK, sure," said Terry as he picked himself up. "Come on, it's only a little farther."

The trail rambled through the woods until it burst out onto the shore of the small lake. "You were right," said Crystal as she looked at the lake. "It does look more like a pond than a lake."

"That's the reason I don't get why the development wants to buy it," said Terry.

"The development wants to buy this?" said Crystal. She kicked a stick into the still, dark waters of the lake. "Why, this is more like a swamp than anything else."

"Yeah, it sure is," said Terry. "But, I've heard my dad talking about it and the development definitely wants to buy it. They want to dredge it out or something, you know, make it deeper. That would make it a real lake. Property values would go up. People could make a lot of money if the property values went up. The only problem with the plan, I hear, is the old guy who owns the lake. He won't sell."

Crystal stood on the shore and surveyed the pond. She tried to picture it the way that Terry had described it, but she couldn't. All she saw was a dirty swamp filled with scummy water and dead trees. A chill ran up Crystal's spine as she stood looking out at the lake. "Actually," she said, "I think the place is a little scary if you ask me."

Fallen trees lay around the edge of the pond and ran out into the lead-colored water. Moss and ferns covered everything and the ground looked like it was always wet. Mushrooms broke through the moss and looked like toes poking through a rotten bed sheet.

Terry ran off down the shoreline. He picked up a rotten stick and threw it at a lone duck that was brave enough to swim in the water. The stick struck the water and immediately sank as the duck took off in a spray of foam. "Come on," he said. "Let's go over this way. You can see Mr. Miller's house from here."

Lester Miller had owned the lake with its adjacent land for more years than he cared to remember. The driveway was a rutted track that ran for a quarter mile out to the main highway. The house sat nestled back in one of those places where sunlight never penetrates. It was always dark and damp and shadows hung over the whole place.

Lester sat in his upstairs room and peered out through the blinds. He watched the children playing on the fringes of the pond. The room had been his wife's and she had so loved the view. He smiled a little when he thought about that.

He watched the children. Children could be dangerous. There was no telling what they would do. He watched the boy and realized that he was starting to move toward the house. That was fine. Let him come as close as he wanted to. There was nothing here for him to do. Nothing here for him to see. Nothing here for him to find. He watched the girl as she started to make a slow, slick walk out onto one of the deadfall logs that lay in the lake. *This*, he thought, *could be bad*.

He let the blind fall and left the room. He slipped into his old muddy boots and pulled on a wool coat. He stopped by the door to reach for the four-ten shotgun that rested against the jamb. His fingers touched the gun, and then he drew his hand back. No, he didn't need the gun this time. If the children had been one of those pesky real estate agents from the development he would have taken the gun. He slammed the door on his way out and headed down the short path that lead to the pond.

Crystal was a little perturbed at Terry for having run off down the path without her like that. She had decided last week that she liked Terry a lot, maybe more than a lot, but she just didn't know if she especially wanted him for her boyfriend or not. And, now that he had run off like that, well, she'd really have to think about it some more.

Terry had vanished down the path into the woods. Crystal walked down the trail after him. "Hey, Terry," she called, "wait up, will you!"

She hadn't taken more than a few steps when she heard something splashing out in the lake. She turned to look out at the water. Something caught her attention. A subtle movement, just under the surface. There was nothing on the pond but the tiniest of ripples. A shimmer, the littlest dancing of light that broke the still surface tension of the pond. Almost like the wind, but there was no wind. It was coming off the end of a huge old fallen tree that lay in the lake. And all of a sudden it was starting to get cold.

She gingerly stepped out onto the log. It was a gigantic old maple that had broken from its roots during a windstorm years ago and had fallen into the pond. It was slick with slime and covered with moss. Broken branches poked up here and there like headstones in an old graveyard. Walking on it would be extremely treacherous. The tree must have extended over eighty feet out into the lake. Crystal carefully started working her way out toward the end of the tree. She had to see what it was off the end. It was as if she was being drawn out onto the log.

With each step, the log gently rocked and bobbed. Crystal had taken her time and had been careful as she had made her way out. She was now as far out as she dared to go, but that was fine. When she stopped, the disturbance moved toward her. Bubbles rose from the bottom of the lake in a slow rolling boil and the rank smell of pond bottom permeated the air. As Crystal watched she thought she could see something deep down in the lake.

She peered into the black depths trying to make out what was down there. Something appeared to be rising from the nadir regions of the pond! Bits and pieces of rotten leaves broke the surface. Mud and debris from the bottom of the pond that hadn't seen daylight in a hundred years leaped from the depths. A fetid odor accompanied the rapidly rising debris.

Crystal stood transfixed! She could not believe what was happening. The log was now vibrating in the water. She firmly grasped one of the rotten branches in her hand and hung on. As she gazed into the water she thought she could make out a figure. It was slowly starting to take shape, but it was way down deep. Down deep where it's cold. She looked harder and finely she could just barely make it out. It looked like a woman! Crystal watched as the apparition slowly started floating toward the surface. She could see strands of hair gently moving with the current. Then the head turned and Crystal could see the figure's face. She looked straight into the woman's eyes and they stared directly back at Crystal.

As Crystal watched the body ascend from the depths of the lake she heard a voice calling out to her. It was as if it came from the lake itself. "Run," it said. "Now is not the time. RUN!"

Crystal turned just as Terry came running out of the woods. He was running as fast as he could. He stopped at the end of the log just long enough to yell at Crystal. "Run, he saw me!" Then he took off up the path.

Crystal didn't know just how she got off the log but the next thing she knew she was running alongside Terry through the woods, her feet pounding the ground and her breath coming hard. She knew that she had to run. The lake had told her so. It had also told her that now was not the time, but not the time for what? If she listened, she could still hear the voice of the lake as she ran. "Run, now is not the time. Run, now is not the time." It repeated itself over and over again like a mantra.

She didn't stop running when Terry did. When they got back to the barbed wire fence, she didn't even slow down. She shot over the fence like a javelin and just kept going.

"Hey, Crystal," Terry yelled as she passed him by. He had to start running again to catch up with her. He couldn't believe it, but he just wasn't as fast as Crystal. He had never seen anyone run so fast. Even during track at school he had never seen anyone so quick! When he came to the fence he had to climb over it and by then Crystal had reached the end of the block and was still running.

Crystal reached the little park that was down the street from her house before she stopped running. It wasn't anything like the big park down at Dupont. Actually it wasn't much of a park at all, but every block in the development had one. It was just a little spot of green grass not big enough for a full-size building lot. A place for the kids to play. Every other block had a Big Toy and a sandbox but the one on her block didn't. It had a big swing, though. A big swing surrounded by lush green grass.

She collapsed onto the lawn. She just couldn't run anymore! She was exhausted and out of breath. The lake was no longer calling to her. She felt the coolness of the grass soaking up through the pores of her skin. Its heavy scent was rich in her nose. *It has to be safe here*, she thought. *It just has to be.*

Terry came huffing down the middle of the street. He was hot and sweaty. He was out of breath and his feet hurt. He plopped down on the turf next to Crystal and sat there gasping while he caught his wind. He didn't think he had ever run so hard in his life. His legs hurt, his knees hurt, his hips hurt! He knew he had never run like that. "Geez, you're fast!" he wheezed as he sat on the grass next to Crystal. "I never knew anybody who could run like that."

He sat for a couple of minutes just huffing and getting his wind back. When his chest quit hurting he turned to Crystal. "That was really close," he said. "I had no idea you could run that fast."

Crystal had been lying on the grass. She sat up and rested her weight on her elbows. "I was the fastest in my class back at my old school," she said.

"Well, thank God you're fast," said Terry. "Otherwise, we would have been caught by old man Miller."

"Who's old man Miller?" asked Crystal as she lay back down on the grass.

"He's the old guy that owns the lake," said Terry. "He's a real jerk and won't let anyone over there for nothing." Terry scooted around on the grass and got a little more comfortable. "Dan Borman, from over at the grocery store, told me that the reason Mr. Miller was that way was because he was a cold-blooded murderer."

"What!" exclaimed Crystal.

"Yup," said Terry. "He was supposed to have killed his wife. That was back in the late fifties or something. Dan said the cops came in and looked everywhere, but they never did find her body. But, he's sure that he killed her. Ever since then, old man Miller hasn't let anybody come onto his property without being asked. He put up all those no trespassing signs and stuff on the fence and Dan said that Mr. Miller wouldn't hesitate to shoot anybody he caught there."

"I hope he didn't see the lady out there then," said Crystal.

"What lady?" asked Terry.

"Why, the lady I saw out in the lake," replied Crystal.

"There was a lady in the lake?" asked Terry. "Well, he must not have seen her or otherwise we would have heard his gun going off, I can tell you that."

"I hope you're right," said Crystal. "I would hate to see her get hurt, she seemed like such a nice lady."

All of a sudden Crystal seemed removed. She got very quiet and kept staring off into the distance, back towards the lake and the woods. Terry noticed the change. "Crystal," he asked, "are you all right?"

"Yes," she said after a few seconds. "I guess I'm still just a little bit scared." She stood up and looked at her watch. "Gosh, it's getting late," she said. "I've got to be heading home." She started out toward the street. "My mom gets really mad if I'm late for dinner, you know, and I'm really tired." She waved to Terry who was still sitting on the grass. "See you tomorrow," she called as she ran off down the street.

Crystal unlocked the back door and stepped into the kitchen. The lights were out and the room was dark. "Hey, Mom, I'm home," she called out as she closed the door. There was no answer from any of the other rooms in the house. She called once more. "Hey, Mom." Then she noticed the light blinking on the answering machine.

She went over to the phone and pushed the button. The blinking light went out and the message started to play. "Honey, Daddy and I have to work late, so we won't be home for dinner. Fix yourself something. I'll call you later. Love you, bye."

Crystal let the message rewind. She had been so worried all the way home about the lecture that her mother was going to give her for being late. Now she wasn't going to have to listen to it, what a relief!

She didn't know why but all of a sudden she was really tired. She felt like she hadn't slept in months. Her body ached and she just wanted to go to bed. She wondered if she was starting to come down with a cold or something. She went over to the fridge and opened the freezer compartment. Icy breath rolled out from inside in a cooling fog. It hung in the air like smoke. Little tendrils of cold seemed to reach out and touch her. They wrapped around her head and a cooling mist started to form.

She reached inside and picked out a package of Hot Pockets. Vapor swirled around the box as she pulled it out. The box was intensely cold, almost like dry ice. It made the tips of her fingers so numb when she touched the package. She set it quickly down on the counter. The freezer door appeared to pause for a second before it swung closed on its hinges. The kitchen vibrated with the impact of its closing.

Crystal took out one of the Hot Pockets and set it in the microwave for a minute. While the sandwich was cooking she got out a plate and napkin. When it was done she placed it on the plate and ate it at the kitchen table. It was hot but didn't seem to have any taste.

When she was done she was more tired than she had been just a few minutes before. She set the plate in the sink. She was so tired! She had never been this tired. She could barely keep her eyes open. She kept hearing someone in the kitchen telling her to go to bed. She thought maybe it was her mother, but her mother wasn't home. Whoever it was, was telling her to go to bed and get some sleep. She would need sleep because now was not the time. That's what the lady who was not her mother kept telling her.

Crystal could see her now. She was standing at the bottom of the stairs. Crystal stopped at the bottom of the stairs and the lady gave her a quick peck on the cheek and told her goodnight. Crystal climbed the stairs. Each step was heavy and she felt like she was moving through a pool of lead. When she reached the top of the stairs she turned to look back down at the lady. She was still standing there. Just standing there and watching.

Crystal slowly walked down the hall toward her bedroom. She felt like she was already asleep and this was all a dream. She kept repeating what the lady had said. "Sleep, go to bed now. Later, later the time will be right and we will do what must be done." She climbed into bed without taking any of her clothes off. She was asleep before her head touched the pillow.

It was a little after ten when the car pulled into the driveway. Crystal's mother reached into the center console and found the garage remote door opener. She pressed the button and the door grumbled into life. Crystal's father pulled the car into the garage and shut the motor off. As they got out Crystal's mother pressed another button on the wall and the garage door closed behind them as they went into the house.

"I hope Chris found enough to eat," her mother said as she hung up her coat.

Crystal's father walked into the kitchen and saw the remains of her meal. "I'm sure she didn't have any problem," he said.

It was a mild evening, but the house seemed cold inside. Crystal's mother went down the hall and looked at the thermostat. The temperature in the house was only fifty degrees. The thermostat was set at seventy and the furnace was running full blast. She tapped it a couple of times and then turned it up. "Honey," she called, "there's something wrong with the heat."

Crystal's father came down the hall and looked at the thermostat. "It seems to be working now," he said. "I guess I'll have to call someone in the morning to come and have a look at it."

Crystal's mother stood over by the bottom of the stairs. "Did you see Chris when you came in?"

"No," answered Crystal's father. "She must have gone to bed early."

"I'll check on her while I'm upstairs then," she said as she started to climb the stairs.

She opened the door to Crystal's room. Cold air rolled out. It felt like it was colder in Crystal's room than it was in the rest of the house. She left the door open as she went down the hall to the linen closet and took out a quilt. It was an old thick down quilt that her mother had given to her. The patterns in the patchwork were worn and faded. She went back into Crystal's room and spread the quilt out over her sleeping daughter. Crystal didn't stir as her mother adjusted the quilt and closed the door.

At three in the morning the house was dark and still. A bracing cold was everywhere, filling the air. In the kitchen, condensation formed on the counter tops and ceiling. Drops of ice-cold water ran down the front of the stove. The carpets throughout the house were crisp with frost. Crystal's bedroom door was frozen shut. Icicles coated the frame in a maze of shapes and sizes. A thin sheet of ice crept out from underneath the door and crept down the hall like a glacier. The cold hung in the air. Crystal's parents slept soundly under their electric blanket. It was turned up to high. The furnace still roared on full, but they were so deeply asleep that they didn't notice.

Crystal stirred in her sleep, and then opened her eyes. She was not awake, yet she was not asleep, either. She was somewhere in between. A land of its own. The lady had come to her and spent time with her in her dreams. She got up and moved toward the window. The lady had told her that now was the time. Her breath made little clouds of ice in the air. She placed her hands on the frozen sash and the window seemed to open of its own accord. A cloud of frost rolled out of the house and into the night air.

Crystal carefully walked across the slick roof and climbed down a fir tree that grew next to the garage. Once she was on the ground she started toward the lake. She had to go back to the lake.

All was quiet as she hurried through the development. She wasn't heard.

She wasn't seen. She crossed the road that divided the development from the woods. A lone car appeared and caught her in the beam of its headlights as she clambered over the fence. Before the driver could even slow down she had vanished deep into the woods.

It was late and Lester couldn't sleep, which was nothing new. Sleep was not a friend to him. Whenever he slept, his dreams were filled with thoughts of her, so he tried to sleep as little as possible. He had done this for years. He could do it for years more if he had to.

He closed his eyes and fell into a light sleep. Instantly, he could see her. She was dancing lightly across the floor in the old attic bedroom of the house. She danced with so much style, so much grace. Suddenly she stopped and turned to laugh at him. That had happened many years ago. Lester turned restlessly in his sleep.

"What do you think of this, Lester?" she jeered as she once more took a slow flowing turn in the middle of the floor. "Dan Borman seemed to like it quite a bit when I showed it to him."

In a fury Lester flew across the room. With both hands he seized her around the neck. "Dan Borman!" he screamed as he slammed her against the wall. "You'll be the death of me! What would people say if they saw you hanging around with Dan Borman?" He threw her to the floor.

She hit hard and Lester thought he heard a bone crunch. He knelt down beside her and tried to help her sit up. Tears streamed from her eyes. As he reached out his hand to wipe them away she spit in his face. Her voice was deep with venom. "The death of you. What would people say? I could care less, you son of a…"

Quicker than he knew Lester had wrapped his hands back around her pretty throat and cut off the horrible last word she was about to speak. He wasn't going to listen to her anymore. He just wasn't going to! She clawed and kicked but the steady pressure exerted by his strong hands was unmerciful. It was over almost as soon as it had started.

Now that it was over he was calm. He was no longer mad. Everything became clear. He could see just what needed to be done. He bundled the body up in an old blanket and dragged it out to the small lake that was behind the house. That would be a good place to dispose of her. He added some heavy rocks to the blanket for weight. That way it wouldn't float. He walked out on a freshly fallen tree that jetted out into the lake. When he thought he had gone out far enough he slipped his bundle into the dark water and went back to the house. That night, sleep eluded him as it had been eluding him every night since.

No one had questioned his story that she had just up and left him one night. They didn't even try to find out where she had gone. As time passed, Lester became more secure with her disappearance, but his nights were always long.

He opened his eyes and sat up. There would be no sleep for him this night. He got up and was going to go back downstairs when he thought he heard a noise. Something was out by the pond. He peered out the window and in the dim light of the crescent moon he saw a girl by the water's edge. The sound of someone lightly dancing on a hardwood floor wafted through the room.

He watched the girl. It was the same girl that he had chased off earlier that day. What was she doing back again? He raced downstairs. He would fix her, snooping around here in the middle of the night. What did she think she was doing? He would fix her good! He'd make sure of that. When he was done she wouldn't be in any kind of shape to be snooping around again. He slammed the door on his way out of the house and plunged into the night.

Crystal emerged from the woods and stood by the edge of the lake. The water gently lapped over the bracken that lined the shore. Moonlight glistened off its deep, dark surface. A chilled breeze followed her. Ice crystals danced in her hair.

For just a moment Crystal didn't know where she was. Then she remembered. She was at the lake. The pond that Terry had taken her to earlier in the day. This was the place where she had seen the lady, the strange, sad lady. Now she understood why she was here. This was the place that the lady had wanted her to come. She had told her so in her room. Right here!

Crystal stood for a minute and thought. Why had the lady wanted her to come here, though? There was something that the lady needed. That was it, but what did she need?

Cold surrounded her. Fog drifted across the lake and through the woods. It touched Crystal's face and a chill ran down her back. That's when she remembered what the lady wanted. She wanted help! She needed help, and only Crystal could provide it. That was it, that's what the lady wanted. And the time was now! She stood on the edge of the pond and felt the cold like a hand on her shoulder. She could just see the house through the trees on the other side.

As she watched the water a phantom glow started to form out in the lake. It was almost at the same place out along the fallen log where she had been earlier, but it was starting to move in. A pale, green disk shape started to spread across the water. It looked almost like spilled paint. Deep and rich.

Crystal stepped out onto the log and started making her way out toward the spot. It was almost like the stain was calling to her. She didn't know how a spot on the water could call to her, but if she listened really closely she could hear it. It kept calling, almost like a chant. "The time is now. He is coming. I will be the end of him. The time is now. He is coming. He is coming. The time is now!"

She stood at the place on the log now, staring at the tinted water. She watched it move and grow. That's when Lester Miller came charging out of the woods. She was in a land of her own and didn't hear him as he broke from the woods. All of her attention was focused on the light dancing in the water.

The light wasn't exactly in the same place that it had been earlier in the day. It was closer to the shore. As she looked down she could almost see the bottom of the lake. The soft glow shimmered just about four feet down. In its glow she could make out bracken that protruded from the mud beneath. She stood and stared into the shadowy pond and the water slowly started to move.

At first, infinitesimal trails of mud and slime stirred and swirled in the depths. As she watched, the trails became stronger and larger. Soon, the entire bottom of the lake was a seething mass of mire and muck. Her attention was now totally fixed. She couldn't have looked away if she had wanted to. And right now she didn't want to. She was fascinated by the patterns that the mud was making in the water. As she watched, she realized that something was being uncovered. Something that had been buried in the muck. Something that had been buried in the muck for many years. Something that she should not know, something she should not see.

From the bottom of the lake she could hear the lady. Her voice echoed inside Crystal's head. The lady's voice was loud and clear. Crystal heard it as clearly as if she had been standing right next to her. It was almost screaming from the depths. Her words popped like bubbles on the water. "THE TIME IS NOW. YOU WILL BE MY REVENGE!"

Lester crashed out of the woods and stumbled through the mud on the shore of the lake. He stopped and stood for a second and then he realized that this was the place. The same place where he had slipped her under the water. The place where he had left her forever.

He took in everything at once in the faint moonlight. The old, fallen oak tree was still there and there was the girl standing out on it. She was staring at something in the water and was standing at the exact spot where it had happened.

He had felt safe for all these years with his wife buried deeply under the water. Now he had his doubts. He had never meant for her to be found. Ever! And now, this girl had come snooping around. She shouldn't be here. This was his property and all of it was posted with no trespassing signs. She shouldn't be here!

He had no use for the real estate agents or the damn people from the development bothering him. He didn't want all the strangers and the kids that kept hanging around and coming on his land. He wanted to be left in private. He lived in seclusion and didn't need all these people dangling off his doorstep. His secrets were his and he meant to keep them that way!

Lester started moving toward the girl. It was plain the girl had no right to be out there. He would fix her, that's what he would do. He had done it once and he could do it again. "I'll kill you," he said to himself as he stepped out onto the log. "I'll put your body down in the lake next to hers. They'll never find you, just like they have never found her." He slowed his pace and moved carefully on the slick log. "What's the disappearance of one more girl anyway? Girls disappear all the time."

Crystal didn't hear him as he moved down the log. She was so immersed in what was going on in the water that she didn't realize that he was there at all. She just stood and stared into the depths of the pond.

Lester finally got out to where the girl was. He thought it funny that she hadn't tried to escape. She hadn't moved at all. The log was treacherous and extremely slick out where they were. He slipped as he make a grab for the girl and instead of clutching her by her long fine hair as he had planned, he planted his palm square in the center of her back.

The instant that Lester hit her, the lady quit talking and Crystal snapped out of the trance she was in. She screamed and instinctively threw her arms out in front of her as she fell, trying to catch herself, but she pitched head first into the dark, dirty water of the pond. It wasn't as deep as it looked and she sank to the bottom quickly. Her right arm plunged into the soft slime that made up the bottom and sank all the way to her elbow before her decent stopped.

That's when her fingers came in contact with an object. She had no idea what it was, but, it was something hard and she grasped it. Her fingers dropped neatly into two holes that broke the smooth surface of the object. All of a sudden the voice of the lady returned sharp and clear. She roared through

Crystal's head. "Now, now, now is the time! You can help me, I can help you. Now! Strike quickly!"

Lester thrust his arm down into the water and grabbed his prey by the ankle. All the old rage came welling up inside him, all the old rage that he had kept so carefully under control. "I'm going to kill you," he shrieked as he dragged Crystal from the water.

Crystal screamed as she broke the surface and swung the heavy thing she was clutching in her hand at her assailant. She swung it just as quick and just as hard as she could! It hit Lester on the left side of his head, shattering on impact.

Lester dropped the girl back into the water and reached his hand up to the side of his neck. It came away red and sticky. He could feel a warm river of blood pulsing from the wound as it ran down his shirt. The girl had been completely forgotten as a crimson river flowed from Lester and stained the water beneath him. All of a sudden he was so tired. He had never been so tired in all his life. He slumped on the log to rest. It would be so nice to just go to sleep.

As he closed his eyes he heard her voice, the voice of the lady in the lake. "You always said I would be the death of you."

Crystal stood on the shore looking out at the pond. She didn't know how she had gotten there or where she was. She didn't know what to do. She saw the body draped over the log out in the lake and then she remembered. She started screaming.

Lester lay draped over the log. One arm floated lazily beside him in a dark growing pool of arterial blood. Broken and discolored shards of bone were scattered around. A sharp, shattered piece of human jawbone stuck out of a massive wound in Lester's neck.

THE GHOST LIGHTS

The old man stood out in sharp relief in the headlights of the speeding car. Rain shimmered on the road as it pelted the pavement. Horizontal rain is what the locals called it. The driver of the car could see that the man was soaking wet. He could almost hear the squishing sound that his shoes would make with every step. He blew past him at almost one hundred miles an hour. The fine spray that was flung by the tires mixed with the downpour to further saturate the miserable pedestrian.

The red glow of brake lights illuminated the damp night as the tires screeched on new found pavement. The man looked up from his wet misery as the car straddled the middle of the road and slid to a stop. The interior light came on and the passenger door flew open. In the dim light from the inside of the car he could see the driver staring at him.

The old man made a half-hearted attempt to run for the open, inviting safety of the car. When he got there he threw himself into the seat and slammed the door. Water gushed from his clothing, drenching the seat and the carpet. The heater came on high and the doors locked as the car took off down the road.

He settled into the comfort of the plush leather seat. It seemed to conform to his body as he diligently watched out the rear window of the car. The spot, where he had been picked up, dwindled into nothing before he turned around. He was a small man, about five foot seven, and he couldn't have weighed more than one hundred and twenty pounds. His hairline was receding into a widow's peak. The thick glasses that he wore perched on the end of his nose were surrounded by heavy black plastic frames.

He nervously wiped his right hand on his shirt. When he was sure it was dry he offered it to the driver. "Thanks for stopping back there," he said. "It's raining like the proverbial cow you always hear about. My name's Emmett Watson. What's yours?"

The driver sat rigidly behind the wheel and stared straight ahead at the road. He didn't make a move to accept Emmett's proffered hand. To do so would mean that he would have to remove his hands from the wheel and it had taken him forever to get them locked in at the ideal driving position of ten and two. "Woody," he said and once again his full attention was focused firmly back on the road.

"Well, Woody," said Emmett, "let me tell you once again that I sure do appreciate your stopping like that."

Woody chanced a glance over at Emmett. "It was nothing," he said. The car swerved a little to the right and Woody's concentration automatically jumped back to the highway.

"Nothing!" said Emmett. "Why, you just saved my life, you know!"

"Saved your life?" said Woody. "How could I have saved your life?" His hands locked tighter onto the steering wheel and he refused to let his eyes waver from the road as he waited for an explanation.

Emmett sat quietly for a minute. He had to gather his thoughts before he started. "Well," he said, "before I start my story could you answer just a couple of questions for me? Like, where the hell are we and what day is it?"

Woody didn't look up from the road. "Index," he said. "We're just the other side of Index heading east on Highway Two. We'll be coming up to Steven's Pass soon. And as for the day, I think it's the twenty-second. Yeah, that's it, the twenty-second."

Emmett's mouth fell open and he took a deep, sharp breath. "The twenty-second," he said. "The twenty-second of what month?"

"February," answered Woody.

"How can that be?" asked Emmett. "Why, just yesterday it was the eighteenth of October. The eighteenth of October, I tell you. And I'm not crazy. The only way that could happen is if I was traveling at the speed of light. Just like in the science fiction books. You know, about time and how it changes at the speed of light. So, if it's February twenty-second it has to be true!"

Emmett hunkered a little farther down in the seat as the car sped into the darkness. He stared through a lion-shaped crack in the windshield that he hadn't noticed before. The night surrounded the car. "Five months," he said. "I've been gone five whole months. And I did it in one night. I tell you; yesterday I was down in Olympia. That's where I saw the thing that grabbed Mrs. Simms.

"It was getting on late. The lodge closed the bar down at two, so I left and was on my way home. I don't know why I even bother to belong to that lodge anymore. It's all the way down to Little Rock, which is clear on the other side of Olympia. I haven't lived down there for years. I live way north of there now, up near Lacey. So, going down to the lodge is one hell of a drive.

"I was driving by North Landing. That's one of them new up-scale housing developments by the little town of Dupont. Lots of computer types living there. Years ago there used to be a Nitro plant out that way, but now it's all houses.

"Well, I'm driving along when all of a sudden this little girl comes running across the road. Just right out of the darkness across the road and into the woods. She was running fast like something was chasing her. I can tell you I stopped the truck right then and there! I ain't the kind to be letting some little girl be alone and scared in the dark.

"I got out of the car and looked around, but didn't see anyone. If she was being chased I must have frightened them off. I hollered out to the woods that everything was all right and that I could give her a ride, but she didn't answer me. She had vanished into the woods.

"So, finally, I got back into the truck and drove down to the convenience store that's on the other side of the development. I went in and old Dan Borman was on that night so I told him about the girl. Him and I go way back, but we've never really been friends. He thinks I drink too much. And sometimes maybe I do, but let me tell you, I don't lie. I might tell a story once in a while, but I never lie.

"You may not believe this, but he tried to give me the brush off! He said that I was drunk and that there was no girl. That I was just telling him this tale to try and get him to sell me a beer. I mean I may have had a forty-ounce Mickey's in my hand that I wanted to buy but that wasn't the reason I was there. He told me that it was too late and the state would shut him down even if he sold me just one.

"Finally, I convinced him that I wasn't there for the beer and that there really was a girl so he called the cops. After that, I headed out the door, got back into the car and started for home. Once I was out on the road I looked down on the seat and there was that bottle of beer. I must have forgotten about it and packed it out of the store in all the excitement. I'll have to go back and pay Dan for it one of these days. I figure that'll be OK. He won't mind too much.

"When I got home it turns out that it was the only thing in the whole place to drink. Speaking of something to drink…" The glove box popped open and a silver, pint flask fell out. Emmett reached for it like a dying man.

"Why, thank you!" he said as he unscrewed the cap and took a long pull.

"That's mighty kind of you. Talking is dry work and I was getting real thirsty. Why, I guess that it's been five months since I've had a drop! That's a long time to go without a drink."

He passed the flask over to the driver. Woody's eyes flashed away from the road for a split second and the car swerved the slightest bit. Woody's eyes snapped back to the road. "No," he said. "I'm driving right now and I can't."

"Well, suit yourself," said Emmett. He screwed the cap back on and placed the flask back in the glove box. "That really hit the spot," he said. He resettled into the depths of the seat and resumed his story.

"Well," he said, "as I was saying, I just pulled into my driveway and that's when I saw the ghost light."

"A ghost light," said the driver. "What's a ghost light? I've heard of spirit lights and such, but I don't think I've ever heard of a ghost light." The car veered slightly to the left and Woody's attention was instantly back on the road. He straightened the car out quickly

"A ghost light," said Emmett. "You've never heard of a ghost light? Why it's just one of those bright lights that people say they see in the sky. Usually they're yellow. The one I saw was. Some people say they've seen red and green ones, though. I spent most of my life hoping to see one of them. My grandmother used to tell me about how when she was a girl she would see them all the time. That was when they lived out on the farm. I've been looking for one ever since I was a kid and this is the first one I've ever seen.

"I was standing in the kitchen when I caught a glimpse of it. I knew right off the bat that it was a ghost light. I've never seen anything that bright, so I turned and looked. There it was, hanging low over the tops of the trees. And sure enough it was the brightest color yellow I think I've ever seen. It was so bright that I would say you could have read by it if you had wanted to. The TV news will tell you that when somebody sees something like that it's usually Venus. But, let me tell you that if Venus had been out that night it would have been put to shame by that light.

"I set what was left of my beer down on the counter and went outside to have a better look. I sat on the porch and watched it for a while and that's when it started kind of pulsing. You know, it would get brighter and then it would get darker. Brighter and darker. All of a sudden a hum started coming out of the ground. It sounded just like a beehive, only muffled like it was inside a wall or something. The volume got louder every time that the light got brighter.

"And all of a sudden it was gone! I don't mean that it was really gone, though. I mean that the light dropped from the sky so fast that you couldn't see it move. One second it was there and the next it wasn't. After it dropped, the whole sky lit up! It was just for a second, but, let me tell you, everything seemed to take on a brightness of its own. Then the hum stopped.

"I saw at once that the light had dropped right over Old Lady Simms's place. Old Lady Simms has got to be at least a hundred and ten years old. I remember her from when I was a kid and she was old then. Her place is about a quarter mile down the valley from mine, so that makes her my closest neighbor. Everything else around there is either part of Fort Lewis or timberland.

"Well, let me tell you, I couldn't let something like that go on without my seeing what was happening. So, I started off through the woods toward Old Lady Simms's house. I don't know why I didn't take the car instead of hoofing it across the field and down through the woods, but it was a lucky thing that I didn't. If I hadn't been walking they probably would have heard me coming.

"I was coming through the woods and as I said there was this light coming from Old Lady Simms's place. I tell you it radiated up into the sky just like a searchlight. It had to be one of the brightest lights I've ever seen. It was brighter than the light put out by an electric arc. You know the kind, like when somebody is welding and the rod puts out that intense light. Why, that light is so bright it would burn your eyes if you were to look at it too long, and the one that was coming from Old Lady Simms's was brighter.

"It would start out a deep green, almost a forest green. Can you imagine that, a forest green light? Well, it would start out that deep green and then as it pulsed it would work its way all the way up the spectrum and end up bright red. Then the whole damn thing would stop for a second and start all over again. This went on the whole time I was in the woods. It must have been the by the grace of God that it went out just as I came to the end of the trail. If I had been out in the open with that much light they would have seen me.

"Old Lady Simms's place is surrounded on three sides by deep woods, and the trail from my place runs down the hill and almost comes out in her backyard. Out in front of the house is a huge field. It's at least five acres. That's where the cow lived before she disappeared. That happened one night last year. It was really funny about that cow, you know. Old Lady Simms was real partial to her and we looked everywhere for it. Never did find it, though.

"Old Man Simms, when he was alive, at one time had big plans for that field. He was going to plant it up as a Christmas tree farm and make his fortune. He never did, though. From what I understand, he died before he could do it and Old Lady Simms just let the place go to weed after that. She never did anything to it. Just kind of let it all go natural-like, and just let that cow wander around out there.

"Well, I looked over at the house and every light in the place was on. It was lit up just like a holiday. The back door was wide open and creaking noisily on its hinges. I knew that Old Lady Simms would never leave all her lights on, let alone go away with the door wide open like that. So, something wasn't right. But, let me tell you I ain't dumb. I wasn't about to go busting in to see what was wrong! That's a really good way for a person to get himself hurt or something. You know, sticking your nose right in the middle of somebody else's business. You hear about it all the time. Some hero up and jumps right into things. Next thing you know he's scared some little old lady so bad that she accidentally shoots him in the middle of his left ear with her .357 magnum.

"I wasn't about to let something like that happen to me, so I turned around and started back to my place. I figured this was a good job for the cops. That's when I heard this noise coming from the other side of the house.

"It was one of them kind of noises that when you hear it you just have to look to see what the hell was making it. So, I real quiet like snuck around to the other side of the house to see what it was. Well, now I ain't asking you to believe this. I mean if somebody told me a story like this I wouldn't believe it. But I ain't lying! This is the honest truth. Sitting out there in the middle of that unmowed field was one of those damned flying saucers you keep hearing about!"

Emmett reached for the glove box and pulled out the flask. "I sure could use another swig off this if you don't mind."

"Help yourself," said Woody. "I can't drink it."

Emmett unscrewed the cap and took one more long drink from the flask. He screwed the cap back on and placed the flask back in the glove box. "Thanks," he said. "Storytelling is thirsty work." He eased back into the seat once again. Lights danced through the multicolored crack in the windshield. "Yup, it was one of them flying saucers," he said. "It was sitting right out in the middle of that field. For a minute I thought it was one of those amusement park rides like they have out at the fair every year. But let me tell you it was no amusement.

"I would say it was maybe sixty feet across and about twelve feet high. It bulged up in the middle and narrowed out to nothing on the edges. It kept flickering, though it was nowhere near as bright as it had been when I had come out of the woods. It sat right out in the middle of the field, well away from the house. You know, I'll bet you it left one of them crop circle things in the grass. There were no windows on the outside of it that I could see, but there was a big door. It opened from the bottom of the thing and extended all the way to the ground. I looked real hard but I couldn't see anything past the bright light that blocked the door.

"As I looked at the ship all of a sudden I noticed some movement going on out in the grass. As I said, Old Lady Simms never mowed that field and since the cow had vanished the grass had grown really tall. It must have been waving back and forth so much that it caught my attention. I looked at what was causing the movement and out there were these aliens! They were making their way back toward the ship. And let me tell you, it must have been a piece of work for them. Those skinny little guys were just a huffing and a puffing.

"You ever heard of what the UFO people have been calling a Gray? Well, that's what I figured they were. I mean, if I had to call them anything I would call them a Gray. They fit the description you hear perfectly. Gray skin, big black eyes, skinny and short. And they were out in the field working themselves to death because they were packing Mrs. Simms back to their ship!

"Let me tell you a little about Mrs. Simms. I already said she was old. She likes to tell everybody she's sixty, but she's got to be at least eighty-five, possibly ninety. It's been a long time since Mrs. Simms has seen sixty. She's five feet four and weighs around one hundred and eighty pounds. So that makes her short and kind of compact. She would have been a really difficult load to carry, especially if you were only four feet tall and weighed in at sixty pounds.

"The aliens had by now reached their ship and were starting up the ramp. This really got my dander up. What did they think they were doing, hauling Mrs. Simms off like a sack of potatoes? I couldn't let them get away with that! After all, she is my neighbor and neighbors have got to watch out for each other, you know. Before I knew what I was doing I had crept out from behind the house and started working my way down into the field. Turns out it was a lot easier than you would have thought it would have been. You would think that these aliens would have some kind of security when they did this sort of stuff, but there was absolutely nothing. I could have just walked right on down there. As it was, though, I took my time, so by the time I got there they already had Mrs. Simms loaded into the ship.

"I picked up a small tree limb on the way down to the ship. It was just lying there and I figured it would make a good club if I needed one. It was a piece of Madrona. You know how hard a chunk of wood a dry piece of Madrona can be. I probably could have bashed my way into that saucer with it if I had to.

"So, picture this. Here I am, standing just outside of a space ship with a tree limb in my hand. That's when I started to think about what I was doing! I mean, I've got no idea what to do next. That's when things got a little bit scary and I realized that I had made the wrong move. I should have gone and gotten the authorities. That's what I should have done.

"I was just about to go back up to the house when I heard this muffled noise coming from inside of the spacecraft. I just knew that it had to be Mrs. Simms making that noise. And let me tell you, I got mad! I don't think I've ever been that mad before! What right do these aliens have coming here and abducting people anyway? What makes them think they can just go around sticking pieces of metal in someone's body and messing around with their memories, or do any of that other stuff, you know, that you see on the TV shows about them. Just what gives them the right?

"Well, I just got so mad that I couldn't help myself and before you know it I was charging up that ramp. Let me tell you, General Custer would have been proud of the way I blundered head long into the heart of that ship. I was screaming at the top of my lungs and just waving that stick around in the air for all it was worth. I was bound and determined that I was going to bust an alien head or two!

"The next thing you know my damned feet get tangled up and down I go flat on my face. This is it, I thought! They're going to get me before I even have a chance to do anything. But nothing happened. Nobody came running to see what had happened. It was just like the place was empty

"I got up from the floor clutching my piece of wood just as tight as I could. I couldn't believe what I was seeing. I told you that the ship was about sixty feet across outside. Well, it was a whole lot bigger inside than it was out! I don't mean it looked bigger, I mean it was bigger. A whole hell of a lot bigger! How something can be bigger on the inside than it is on the outside I don't know, but this thing was just huge. It must have covered at least an acre or possibly two.

"Looking around, I knew that I would never find Old Lady Simms in that immense place. I guess, though, one of them aliens must have got a little bit clumsy and happened to drop something. The noise seemed to echo off the walls like a shot and right off I could tell where it was coming from. I headed in that direction and sure enough, after a little while, I caught up with them.

"I came around a corner and they had Old Lady Simms on a sort of cart. They were just rolling her into a room off the side of the corridor. There was no door on this room. As a matter of fact, there were no doors on any of the rooms I'd passed. I crept up to the opening and peeked inside. It looked like they were preparing her for something. I had never seen anything like it before, though. She was suspended about three feet off the floor on a beam of lime-green light. There was no table under her or anything. She just floated in the air. The Grays moved around her and dipped in and out of the light. They moved just like a bunch of puppets.

"I watched for a minute or two until I figured out just what they were doing. You wouldn't believe it! I wouldn't have believed it if I hadn't seen it with my own eyes. They were cutting her up! You could tell though that they weren't just cutting her up for the sake of cutting her up. There was defiantly a reason, a method in what they were doing. It was more like a planned and orchestrated dissection.

"You could tell that every cut was made with exact precision, like it was plotted out beforehand. Everything was real clean. There was no blood or anything, no mess at all, and it didn't appear like Mrs. Simms even knew it was going on. She just sort of kept floating there in her shroud of green light.

"I watched as they removed one of her fingers. It was the little finger of her left hand. They took it off and then held it up to another source of light. It looked like they were inspecting it or something. Then the strangest thing happened. They put her finger back on!

"They didn't sew it or anything like that. They just put it back onto her hand like it had never been taken off. Then they just started hacking her up, inspecting parts, and then putting her back together. All the king's horses and all the king's men couldn't have done to Humpty Dumpty what the Grays were doing to Old Lady Simms.

"I couldn't take it! It just wasn't right for them to be doing that. I took a firm grip on my stick and stepped into the room. That's when everything turned red. The whole room had changed from the green that it had been, to red! The Grays were still standing over Mrs. Simms. They didn't pay any attention to me or the change of lighting. They just kept on doing to the poor old lady what they had been doing.

"I took a practice swing with my branch just as hard as I could. I could feel the muscles in my shoulders. The branch cut through the air just fine. I swung it again and it made a satisfying whooshing sound, the kind of sound that would make your hair stand on end. Let me tell you that if that branch had been a baseball bat it couldn't have made a better sound.

"I stopped just inside the door and took a stance. I figured that the little buggers now knew that I was there and they would attack. I was ready to bash some heads, but you know, they didn't pay the slightest attention to me. They acted like I wasn't there. They just kept on cutting up Mrs. Simms and putting her back together again.

"Well, after seeing something like that I just couldn't take anymore. I hoisted my branch over my shoulder and strode smack toward the center of the room. I was going to teach them a real good lesson if it was the last thing I ever did.

"That's when it hit me. I waltzed right into that scarlet light and it hit me real hard. I mean I ain't ever felt so tired in my life! I just wanted to lie down right then and there and go to sleep. I kept trying to fight off the drowsiness, but I just couldn't. I remember dropping my stick and sitting down on the floor. I couldn't keep my eyes open. The last thing I remember is laying down on that ever-so-soft floor, being bathed in a warm red light and just going to sleep.

"I woke up on the side of the road in the pouring down rain and I was soaked to the bone. I don't have the slightest idea how long I lay in that ditch, but it must have been a while for me to get so wet. I got up to the road and started walking, and that's when I saw the lights from your car."

Emmett leaned forward and shifted around in his seat. For some reason, it just wasn't as comfortable as it had been when he first got into the car. And the longer they drove the more uncomfortable it got. His back was starting to hurt and his neck was getting sore. He transferred his weight again and looked out the window. He kept staring at the broken spot in the windshield. "Well, that's my story," he said. "I told you that you wouldn't believe it. I mean, if it hadn't happened to me I wouldn't have believed it."

"I believe every word of it," said Woody. "Every single word of it."

The car slowed and started to pull off to the side of the road and Emmett could see the lights of a lone service station. The rain had picked up and now was coming down hard. The car pulled in underneath the service station awning.

Emmett fumbled with the door handle for a second. "Well," he said as he finally opened the door. "This looks like as good a place as any for me to be getting out." He climbed out of the car and stood by the open door. "I guess I can call a friend of mine from here and he can come and get me. Thanks for the ride," he said. "I hope I can repay you the favor someday."

He closed the door and then stood looking at the car. A moment later he reopened the door and stuck his head back inside. "You know," he said, "the whole time I've been in this car, something has struck me as kind of odd. And now that I'm out I realize what it is." He paused for a moment and scratched the stubble on his chin. "It's that crack in the windshield," he said. "That's what it is." He looked at the outside of the crack and ran one of his fingers over the flawed glass.

"I been looking out of that crack the whole time I've been in this car and I'll be damned if it don't look just like a tattoo. A tattoo of a lion. You know one of them really fancy ones that they do up in lots of colors. Maybe you should get it fixed."

He straightened up and stepped back from the car. The door seemed to close all by itself. The window rolled down and the driver called out as the car vanished into the night. "I've tried, but the car likes it that way."

Water leaked into Emmett's shoes as he tramped across the sodden pavement to the door of the service station. He fumbled with the latch on the door and at last it came open. "Hey," he called to the man behind the counter, "you got a phone around here?"

The man pointed to a pay phone over in a darkened corner of the room.

"Thanks," said Emmett. He trudged over to the counter and fumbled around in his pockets. Ultimately, he came out with an old battered billfold. He dug through its inner compartments and retrieved a single battered and bruised dollar bill. He set the bill gingerly on the counter. "Can I get some change for the phone?"

The bill disappeared like magic and four shiny quarters appeared in its place.

"Thanks again," said Emmett as he picked up the change from the counter.

The attendant watched the old man as he meandered toward the phone. There was something wrong with the old guy, but he just couldn't tell what. It took the old man a long time to get the phone to work and to place his call. He seemed to be having some kind of trouble with his hands. He finally hung up the phone and headed for the door. He had some more trouble with the door before he got it open.

The attendant watched him leave. As the door closed, the old man placed one of his hands on the glass and gave it a shove. That was when the attendant finally saw what was wrong with his hands. He had never seen anything like it before. The old man's hands…they were backwards. His thumbs faced out. The old man's hands were backwards.